MYSTERY IN THE CHANNEL

1931: The *Chichester* is making a routine journey
across the English Channel on a pleasant afternoon
in June, when the steamer's crew spot a small yacht
bobbing aimlessly in the water. Upon boarding the
vessel, they discover two male corpses. Both must
have been shot, but there is no sign of either the
murderer or the pistol. Inspector French is put on
the case, and soon establishes the identity of the
dead men: Moxon and Deeping, the top dogs at one
of the largest financial houses in the UK. What's
more, the firm is on the brink of collapse. One and
a half million pounds has gone missing, along with
Moxon and Deeping, who seem to have been
fleeing the country with their ill-gotten gains. So
who killed them, and how?

Mystery in the Channel

Freeman Wills Crofts

ISIS
LARGE
PRINT

First published in Great Britain 1931
by
W. Collins Sons & Co.

First Isis Edition
published 2017
by arrangement with
The British Library

A catalogue record for this book is available
from the British Library.

ISBN 978–1–78541–303–2 (hb)
ISBN 978–1–78541–309–4 (pb)

Published by
F. A. Thorpe (Publishing)
Anstey, Leicestershire

Set by Words & Graphics Ltd.
Anstey, Leicestershire
Printed and bound in Great Britain by
T. J. International Ltd., Padstow, Cornwall

This book is printed on acid-free paper

Contents

Introduction

Mystery in the Channel is a classic crime novel with a strikingly modern sub-text. The story begins with a shocking discovery. The captain of the Newhaven to Dieppe steamer spots a small pleasure yacht lying motionless in the water, and on closer inspection, sees a body lying on the deck. When members of his crew go aboard the yacht, they find not one male corpse but two. Both men have been shot, but there is no sign of either the murderer or the pistol.

The dead men, it quickly emerges, were called Moxon and Deeping, and they were chairman and vice-chairman respectively of the firm of Moxon General Securities, one of the largest financial houses in the country. Inspector Joseph French of Scotland Yard is called in, reporting directly to the Assistant Commissioner, Sir Mortimer Ellison. French soon discovers that Moxon's is on the brink of collapse. One and a half million pounds have gone missing, and so has one of the partners in the business. Moxon and Deeping seem to have been fleeing the country with their ill-gotten gains, but who killed them, and how? French faces one of the toughest challenges of his

1

career, and in a dramatic climax, risks his life in a desperate attempt to ensure that justice is done.

Mystery in the Channel was originally published in 1931, at a calamitous time for the world economy. Moxon's was a well-established and reputable firm, but had struggled "as a result of the generally depressed conditions . . . Then before they could get right there came the Wall Street crash and after it the Hatry crash". A number of the firm's partners were, Ellison says bitterly, "Figureheads . . . At least, that's the excuse now. Knew nothing about what was going on. It's a lovely system! They were got in because they had handles to their names, to create public confidence. Public confidence!" His sympathies lie with "all the innocent people who are going to suffer through these dirty scoundrels".

Freeman Wills Crofts had a closer understanding of business life than many crime writers of his or any other generation, and several of his mysteries unfold against a corporate background. He was a natural conservative, but it is plain from his novels that he shared Ellison's scorn for the unacceptable face of capitalism. Time and again (even in this book's penultimate paragraph), he shows empathy with 'the thousands of unfortunate people who had entrusted their money to the firm, and of whom many are irretrievably ruined'. Nor does Crofts overlook the consequences for luckless members of the Moxon's workforce: "The failure was for them an overwhelming blow. Not only were their cherished beliefs thus rudely shattered, but the same cataclysm took from them their means of support." It is thought-provoking to compare

Crofts' observations with analysis of the global financial crisis more than three-quarters of a century later. His critique of the figureheads in Moxon's might equally be applied to some nonexecutive directors of financial institutions in the early years of the twenty-first century.

Detective stories written during "the Golden Age of Murder" between the two world wars have long been stereotyped (especially by people who have not bothered to read much of the best work of the period) as dry, intellectual puzzles which paid little or no heed to the real world. The truth is rather different, and is more complicated and interesting. Crofts' work is a case in point. As a writer, he seldom indulged in literary flourishes, and this helps to explain why his books have often been dismissed as "humdrum". Yet he had deeply held spiritual convictions, which are evident in several of the novels he wrote during that fascinating but fearful decade, the Thirties, most directly in another mystery republished as a British Library Crime Classic, *Antidote to Venom*.

Trains and boats and planes keep passing by in many of Crofts' books, and *Mystery in the Channel* contains a good deal of information about sailing (some of it rather technical) that is crucial to the plot. By profession, Crofts was an engineer, and his practical turn of mind proved invaluable when it came to creating ingenious murder mysteries — and describing how patient detective work could solve them. In this book, he sets out his credo: "Detection is very much like any other constructive work. The solution of every difficulty becomes the premise of a further problem.

Such work advances by the overcoming of a never-ending series of difficulties, each of which is raised by the preceding success."

Freeman Wills Crofts (1879–1957) was an Irishman who, at the age of fifty, retired from a career in the railways and moved to Surrey to write full-time. By then, he had become one of the most highly regarded detective novelists, and for the rest of his life, he continued to design complex mysteries to test the wits of the affable but extremely persistent Inspector French.

In person, Crofts was reserved but kindly, and nobody seems to have had a bad word to say about him. Even Dorothy L. Sayers, an often acerbic critic, and a writer who aspired to literary heights in a way that Crofts did not, called him "one of the most honest craftsmen in existence. He leaves no flats unjoined." A modest and unassuming man, Crofts no doubt regarded that as high praise. Writing about Inspector French, he once admitted, "He's not very brilliant. In fact, many people call him dull." But criminals underestimate French at their peril. And Freeman Wills Crofts was a capable crime writer who has himself been under-estimated for too long.

MARTIN EDWARDS
www.martinedwardsbooks.com

SELECT BIBLIOGRAPHY:
Freeman Wills Crofts and Golden Age detective fiction

Melvyn Barnes, "Freeman Wills Crofts", in *St James Guide to Crime and Mystery Writers* (1996)

J. Barzun and W. H. Taylor, *A Catalogue of Crime* (1971)

John Cooper and B. A. Pike, *Artists in Crime* (1995)

John Cooper and B. A. Pike, *Detective Fiction: The Collector's Guide* (2nd edn, 1994)

Martin Edwards, *The Golden Age of Murder* (2015)

Curtis Evans, *Masters of the "Humdrum" Mystery: Cecil John Charles Street, Freeman Wills Crofts, Alfred Walter Stewart and the British Detective Novel, 1920–61* (2012)

H. R. F. Keating, *Murder Must Appetize* (1975)

H.M. Klein, "Freeman Wills Crofts", in *Dictionary of Literary Biography, Volume 77: British Mystery Writers 1920–39* (1989)

Erik Routley, *The Puritan Pleasures of the Detective Story: From Sherlock Holmes to Van der Valk* (1972)

CHAPTER
ONE

Death on the High Seas

The captain lowered his six — diameter prism binoculars.

"Not moving, is she, Mr. Hands?"

"Doesn't seem to be, sir," said the second officer, who was also the officer in charge.

The steamer was the Southern Railway Company's *Chichester* and she was half-way to France on her usual day trip from Newhaven to Dieppe. A fine boat she was, the Company's newest for that route, and she was doing her steady three and twenty knots with scarcely a quiver to indicate the enormous power that was being unleashed in the cavernous holds far down below her decks.

It was a pleasant afternoon towards the end of June. The sea was like the proverbial glass, well burnished, and with a broad track of dazzling sparkles where the sun caught the tiny wavelets. A slight haze filled the air, not enough to be called a fog, but enough to blot out the horizon and everything above two or three miles distant. Hot it was; indeed, but for the breeze caused by the steamer's motion, it would have been grilling. It was just the day for luxuriating with closed eyes in a deck chair, and the rows of recumbent figures which covered every scrap of clear space on the decks showed that the passengers fully realised the fact.

There was quite a crowd on board. It was well into the holiday season and besides the ordinary passengers the members of more than one conducted tour were making the crossing. The labels on their suit-cases sorted them into sheep and goats. Here was a party on the way to spend a Week in Lovely Lucerne, there a group bound for the castles of the Loire, while still others were contenting themselves with a long week-end in Paris.

The object which had attracted the attention of the ship's officers was a small pleasure yacht which lay right ahead. As she was heading across their bows, they thought at first she would have pulled clear of their track long before they came up. But a few seconds' inspection showed that she was lying motionless. A shift of helm to pass behind her stern was therefore necessary, and the second officer crossed to the wheel-house and called sharply, "Starb'rd two degrees!" to the quartermaster at the wheel. As he returned, the captain again lowered his glasses.

"A fifty-foot petrol launch, British built, I should say," he observed. "Can't see her flag. Can you?"

"No, sir," the second officer answered, gazing in his turn. "Nor can I see any one on deck."

"Navigating from the wheel-house," the captain rejoined, "if that hump forward is a wheel-house and not merely sidelight screens."

"A wheel-house, I fancy, sir. But I can't see any one in it."

"Scarcely close enough yet."

With this the second officer dutifully agreed. There was silence for a moment and then Mr. Hands went on, "She must be broken down, sir, surely. Else why should she lie there?"

"Not asking for help at all events," Captain Hewitt replied. He paused, searching the yacht with his glasses. "That is a wheel-house," he went on. "I can see the wheel. There's no one there."

"Too high and mighty to keep a look out, I suppose," the second officer said disgustedly. "And then they're surprised if anything goes wrong. Of course if it does, it's the other fellow's fault."

The captain did not reply. He was still fixedly examining the tiny vessel, which they were now rapidly approaching. She was obviously a pleasure yacht, well kept, from the brilliant flashes which leaped from her brasswork and the dazzling white of her paint. Every moment she grew in size, while objects aboard took on form and definition. Her deserted decks could now be seen with the naked eye. Soon they would be up with her.

Suddenly the captain's regard grew more intense.

"What do you make of that dark thing near the companion?" he asked sharply.

Mr. Hands also stared intently.

"Uncommonly like a man, sir. By Jove, yes, it is a man! Lying in a heap on the deck. Good God, sir! He must be either ill or dead!"

"It doesn't look too well." Captain Hewitt glanced down at his passengers. "Pity to wake up all these sleeping beauties," he went on, "but I'm afraid there's no help for it. Give her a call, Mr. Hands."

An ear-splitting roar went out from the foghorn. As a breeze ruffles the surface of a cornfield, so a little movement passed over the deck as the occupants of the chairs opened their eyes, sat up, glanced round, muttered imprecations, and once more resigned themselves to sleep.

But the blast awakened no answer from the yacht.

"There doesn't seem to be any one else on board," the captain went on. "It looks like something badly wrong. I don't like the way that figure is lying bunched up in a heap. And what's that dark mark beside it? Seems very like blood to me. Give them another call, Mr. Hands."

Two more raucous blasts roared out, reawakening the deck chair enthusiasts and even sending some of the more energetic to the rail in search of the cause of so unwonted an outrage.

Still there was no response from the yacht. The man on the deck made no movement nor did any one else appear. The shining brass wheel could now be plainly seen in its tiny wheel-house, deserted.

"It's blood, that mark is, as sure as we're alive," said Hands. "A pretty bad wound to have bled like that."

The yacht was now close by. The powerful glasses reduced the distance to a few yards.

"Yes, it's blood right enough," the captain agreed after another look. "Damn it, we'll have to stop. Chap may not be dead, and in any case we can't leave that outfit bobbing around to put a hole in somebody's bows. Ring down, Mr. Hands."

While the second officer rang his engines to "Stop!" and then a few seconds later to "Full Speed Astern!" the captain turned to the able seaman in attendance.

"Tell Mr. Mackintosh I want him here at once. And get the chief steward to find out if there's a doctor on board and send him here also."

For a moment all was ordered confusion. Whistles resounded, bells rang, figures hurried to and fro. A slight continuous tremor ran through the ship as if overwhelming activities were in progress below. From the safety valve pipes on the funnels came an appalling roar of escaping steam. Quickly men approached one of the starboard lifeboats, politely moved the passengers back, and uncoiled ropes and knocked out wedges. The canvas boat cover vanished with incredible speed, the chocks fell aside, and the patent davits moved forwards. In a few seconds the boat, already manned, was swinging motionless over the sea.

By this time the passengers were awake to a man, or rather to a woman, and were pressing to the rail to see the fun. A little buzz of talk had broken out. Jokes were cracked, while those behind pushed forward, clamouring for information from those in front. Glasses and cameras were brought out and hopes of a thrill were expressed. Then as the yacht with its sinister burden floated into view, voices were hushed and all stood silent, overawed by the presence of tragedy.

There was indeed something dramatic in the situation which stirred the imagination of even the most prosaic. The little yacht, with its fine lines and finish, its white deck and gleaming brasswork, its fresh paint and brightly coloured club flag, looked what it so obviously was, a rich man's toy, a craft given over to pleasure. On such the tragic and the sordid were out of place. Yet now they reigned supreme. The space which should fittingly have resounded with the laughs of pretty women and the voices of immaculately clad men, was empty, empty save for that hunched figure and that sinister stain with its hideous suggestion.

Such thoughts, however, were far from the minds of the ship's officers. With ordered haste they carried on. Discreet inquiries among the men in the smoking-room had found a doctor, and he had been hurried to the bridge. The third officer, Mr. Mackintosh, had just preceded him.

"Dr. Oates?" the captain was saying. "Very good of you to help us. Mr. Mackintosh, I want you to board that yacht and see what's the matter. If the man is alive, send him across with the doctor. If not, let him stay. If there's no one else there keep a couple of men and work her to Newhaven. Take a megaphone and let me know how things are and, if necessary, I'll send you help from Dieppe. And for the Lord's sake look sharp. We're late already."

In a few moments the boat had been lowered to the water, the falls cast off, and Mr. Mackintosh and his party were slowly rising and falling beside the *Chichester's* towering side. "Give way, lads," invited

Mackintosh, and the *Chichester* with its rows of staring faces began to fall slowly back.

"Not often a cross-Channel boat halts in mid-career like this," Dr. Oates essayed, when they were fairly under way.

"I only mind it happening once before," Mackintosh admitted. "That was when we sighted the *Josephine*. You didna see about her in the papers? She was a tr-r-ramp, an eight-hundred-ton coaster, from Grimsby to Havre with oils and paints. My wor-rd, she was a sight! We saw the smoke of her ten miles off, going up like a volcano."

"Burnt out?"

"Burnt out? Aye, I think she was burnt out. I never saw, before nor since, flames rising like yon. You'd ha' thought they were a mile high. The paint, you know."

"Any one lost?"

"No. They were in the boats and we picked them up. Say, doctor, that's a tidy enough yacht. The *Nymph*, Folkestone," he read. "What do you make her? A bit under fifty feet, I'd say. A good sea boat, but old-fashioned. She's twenty years old, if she's a day. Nowadays they give them higher bows and lower sterns. Eight to ten knots, I reckon. Likely a new motor; she'd be built for steam."

"Strong, but not comely, she looks to me."

Mackintosh nodded. "I reckon you're no so far wrong, though, mind you, she's well finished. Now, doctor, we'll see what we shall see." The yacht swung up alongside. "Easy on there. Easy does it."

A man bow and stern grappled with boathooks and in a moment the two craft lay together, rising and falling easily on the swell. Mackintosh stood up, unhooked the gangway section of the yacht's rail, and swung himself aboard. Dr. Oates followed more circumspectly.

A moment's glance showed that the deck really was deserted save for the sinister figure near the companion. Closer inspection only confirmed the previous impression of the taste and wealth which had gone to the furnishing of the little vessel. The deck was broken only by the wheel-house, two skylights, two masts, and the companion, leaving an extraordinarily large promenading area for the size of the boat. The wheel-house was well forward, about eight feet from the bows. Then came a skylight, the saloon from its size, then the companion, and lastly a smaller skylight, apparently a cabin. Round the deck was a railing of polished teak on dazzlingly white supports, from which hung four lifebuoys, bearing the words, "M. Y. *Nymph*, Folkestone," in neat black letters. The deck was holy-stoned to the palest sand colour, and everything that could be polished glittered like gold.

But it was not on these things that the gaze of the two men lingered. There were more evidences of tragedy than they had realised. At the step at their feet was a little pool of blood, and from it, running across the deck to the prone figure lay a trail of drops, as if the man, desperately wounded at the side of the yacht, had yet halted there for a moment and then staggered forward to where he had fallen. Quickly the newcomers noted the marks, then hurried forward to the body, for something in the attitude told them that they had come too late to be of service.

It was that of a tall man of spare build. He was dressed, not in yachting clothes, but in a dark gray lounge suit of expensive looking cloth, as far as they could see, well cut. On his feet were dark gray silk socks and neat black shoes. His thin left hand, like the claw of some great bird, was stretched out, hooked, as if attempting to grasp at the deck. He was lying hunched up on his face with his right arm underneath him. His hat had disappeared. His head was bald, surrounded by a fringe of thin gray hair, and the gold hook of a pair of spectacles showed round his ear. He was wearing a double collar, but except that he was clean shaven, his face could not be seen. Spreading out from his head was that ominous stain of dark red.

The doctor knelt beside him.

"I wouldna touch him unless you canna help," Mackintosh advised.

"I want to lift the head." Dr. Oates did so and drew in his breath sharply. "Shot," he said as he gently lowered it again. "Quite dead. I can do nothing."

"Shot, is he? Bless us all! Is it long since, doctor?"

"Quite a short time. There's no appreciable cooling. Probably within an hour or so."

"Is that a fact? Tell me, can you see the right hand? Is there a gun in it?"

The doctor shook his head. "I can't see and I'll not move him. It'll be a job for the police. You're going to take him back to Newhaven?"

"I reckon I'll have to. Well, let's have a look below and then you can get back aboard."

He plunged down the companion steps and instantly gave a cry. "Good God, doctor, hell's been loose here!" Oates followed and the two men stood staring blankly.

The companion led into a good-sized cabin about ten feet long and occupying the whole width of the yacht. Along the right side was a folding table, spread with some portion of a meal and with a seat-locker behind it. A seat-locker also stretched along the left side, while directly opposite was another door and an electric fireplace. On the walls were bookshelves, a clock, an aneroid and some rolled up charts in a rack. The place was brilliantly lit by the reflection of the sun from the waves and ceiling.

Here again, however, it was not to these details that the men's attention was directed. In the middle of the floor, as if having risen from the meal, lay another man. This time there was no doubt of his condition. He lay sprawled on his face, but his forehead could be seen, and on that forehead was the deadly round hole where a bullet had entered. He seemed a younger man than the other, of medium height and rather stout build. His hair was plentiful, and though naturally dark, it was now graying. He also was dressed in town rather than yachting clothes, a dark brown tweed lounge suit, brown shoes and a wing collar, all very neat and expensive. Both arms were thrown out as if in an attempt to ward off some attack. This time there was but little blood.

Mackintosh swore, then pulled himself together.

16

"You canna do anything, doctor?"

Oates briefly examined the body.

"Nothing. It was instantaneous. And quite recent, like the other."

The vision of Captain Hewitt, impatient on the bridge of the *Chichester*, was evidently in the third officer's mind, for he hurried Oates on.

"We'll have a run through the rest of her and then you can get away."

A door aft from the cabin led to a small two-berth cabin in the stern. Forward of the saloon were a tiny pantry-kitchen, a lavatory and bathroom, the motor-room beneath the wheel-house, and right up in the bows, a store with two bunks. The two men spent no time looking round. Simply they made sure that no other person, alive or dead, remained on board. But even in that short survey they could not help being impressed not only with the luxurious appointments, but also with the extraordinarily clean and efficient way in which everything was kept.

Though they had not lost a moment, they were not quick enough for the captain of the *Chichester*. Scarcely had they completed their survey when a couple of stentorian blasts came rolling across the sea. Mackintosh smothered an imprecation.

"For the love of Mike, doctor," he cried, "look alive. We mustna keep the old man waiting." He leaped to the deck. "Smith and Wilcox," he shouted, "lay aboard here at once. Snelgrove take charge and get away back to the ship. Hold a sec, the doctor's going. Right, doctor?

You'll tell the old man? Away you go, then! Put your backs into it, lads!"

The lads put their backs into it and the water frothed from the boat's stern. Mackintosh turned to his two helpers.

"Get below, you two," he said sharply, disregarding the wondering looks they bent on the dead man. "Start up that engine and find out how much petrol there is. Look alive now. I want it done before that boat gets picked up."

He leaned on the tiny engine-room hatch, watching the efforts of his men below. Smith, he knew, had been a motor mechanic before he started sailoring. His presence in the boat had been a piece of luck which the third officer had not been slow to take advantage of. Now almost caressingly the man's hands passed over the machine, turning taps, making adjustments, moving levers. Then he gave a sharp tug and with a hesitating little cough the motor gave a jerky rotation and then settled down into a merry chuffing. Another minute and Smith called up that there was plenty of petrol in the tank.

"Enough to get us forty miles?"

"Twice that, sir."

The men in the boat were just grabbing at the swinging falls as Mackintosh stood up and raised his megaphone.

"Am staying to work her to Newhaven," he roared. "I dinna require any help."

The captain waved his arm. As the boat rose dripping from the water the *Chichester* began to move.

18

Quickly she regained speed, and soon her rails with their rows of white faces vanished and she became a rapidly diminishing smudge in the thick air.

The need for immediate action over, Mackintosh called his crew together.

"Stop that engine of yours, Smith, till we get this body covered. Any flags in the locker?"

They searched the little vessel, at last finding the flags beneath the cabin seat. From the bundle they extracted a blue ensign — the only large flag there was — while they lowered their voices with rough reverence for the cabin's other occupant. On reaching the deck Mackintosh shut the companion door.

"We'll no need to go down there again," he declared. "Get some weights, Wilcox, to keep this ensign down. Here, Smith, help me spread it."

Carefully the prone figure was covered and spare parts from the engine-room laid along the edges of the flag. It was the only way in which they could pay their tribute to the dead. Mackintosh automatically recording the hour, ten minutes to two o'clock, turned away to consider the situation.

It was a police affair, this that he had got mixed up in, and the police would expect evidence. He was the first man on the scene and they would want to know what he had found. Was there anything that he should do or note, he wondered, before setting off to Newhaven?

That the affair was either murder or suicide was obvious. Mackintosh was inclined to the murder theory, as in his hurried glance over the saloon he had seen no weapon. Though in a way it was not his business, he felt it was a point which he would like to settle. Breaking through his own regulation, he climbed once more down the companion steps and entered the saloon. No, there was no weapon. There was no place in which it could have fallen and lain hid. The affair was therefore murder.

Then he saw that he was wrong. This conclusion did not follow. The thing might have been a suicide pact. If there was a weapon in the hand of the man on the deck, he might well have shot first his companion and then himself.

"Job for the police; let them worry it out," thought Mackintosh, looking carefully round.

At once he noticed something that he had missed on his first inspection. The dead man wore a wrist watch, and the glass was cracked, evidently from striking the floor. The watch had stopped at 12.33.

If this were the hour of the tragedy, it worked in well enough with what the doctor had said. Mackintosh wondered if he could get any other corroboration.

He moved to the engine-room and felt the cylinder jacketing.

"How long do you reckon she was stopped?" he asked the expert, Smith.

Smith said he had felt her all over when he came down first, before he had started her up, and he would guess that she had been stopped about an hour. Mackintosh nodded.

"I want you to mark everything," he said. "Petrol-paraffin set, isn't she? Well, mark the level of the petrol and the paraffin. Also there is lubricating oil. Mark it too. Let's see you do it. We may both have to swear that it's right."

The record was carefully made. There was nothing else, so far as Mackintosh could see, of immediate importance. He turned back to the men.

"It's two o'clock," he observed. "We'd best get away for Newhaven. Start her up again, Smith, and let's see what she'll do."

Wilcox was installed helmsman at the little brass wheel, while Mackintosh stood watching the water slip slowly past. As he had imagined, the speed was low; less than ten knots, he reckoned. They should get in about six.

The air had cleared somewhat, but it was still thick enough to require a constant look out. When they had got under way they were alone on the sea, but almost at once a tiny craft had crept into view from the nor'-nor'-east, coming up on the *Nymph's* starboard beam. Mackintosh had a look at it with a pair of glasses which he found in the wheel-house. It was still too far away to see its details, but he thought it was a small petrol launch. It was heading straight for the *Nymph*, and from the little specks of white at its stern, seemed to be coming at a fair speed. No fear, he thought, of a collision with that, as he slowly filled his pipe, an unwonted luxury while on duty.

Though Mackintosh was no chicken and had seen War service, he felt a trifle overwhelmed by the horror of this tragedy with which he had been brought so closely in contact. Up to the present he had had no time to think about it, but now that there was nothing more to be done than this mechanical job of keeping a look out, his mind naturally became filled with it. Who were these men and how had they come to meet so terrible a fate? Was there a revolver in the hidden right hand of the figure on deck, and had he murdered the other and then committed suicide? If so, where was the crew, for both the deceased were evidently landsmen? Or had both been murdered by some third party, who in some way had left the yacht?

The third officer had no leanings towards detective work, though his natural curiosity tempted him to make a further detailed examination of the deceased, in the hope of finding an answer to some at least of his questions. But he refrained from doing so.

The little he knew about police methods made him quite certain that his duty was to touch nothing and even to keep away from the actual position of the bodies, lest his movements might obliterate some trace left by the murderer.

"A shoemaker shouldna leave his last," he said to himself with the common sense of the hard-headed practical man. "My job is to get this outfit to Newhaven, and no to make a story about how the damage happened."

But in spite of this laudable conclusion, he was to have more to think of than navigation before he reached port.

CHAPTER
TWO

Mackintosh Receives a Visitor

In spite of Mackintosh's horse sense, he found he could no more refrain from speculations as to the cause of the tragedy than he could keep his heart from beating. Slowly he paced up and down the unstained portion of the deck, drawing ruminatively at his pipe, and by force of habit casting a mechanical glance round the horizon at every turn.

He was more intrigued by the disappearance of the crew, if there had been a crew, than by any other feature of the affair. Such a yacht might well have carried a couple of hands, one to steer and look after the motors — there was a complete set of controls from the wheel-house to the motor — the other a cook-steward, who would also clean up and do odd jobs. At the same time, the boat was small enough to be run by the owner and his friends, should their tastes lie in that direction. There was really nothing to show what had obtained. The fact that neither of the bunks in the store appeared to have been occupied suggested that no crew had been carried. On the other hand, the deceased men did not look like sailors, at least if one was to judge by their clothes.

Their clothes indeed were rather a puzzle. Mackintosh had never seen the occupants of a small pleasure yacht so garbed, at all events, certainly not on a yacht in mid-Channel. There must have been something quite unusual about the trip from the very start. These men were dressed neither for yachting nor travelling. They looked, indeed, as if they had stepped aboard from some formal business conference in London. Surely, therefore, they must have been passengers, and unintentional passengers at that?

Mackintosh was proceeding to follow up this idea when another and more personal side of the affair struck him. He was, he believed, about to find himself famous. This case, no matter who the dead men were, would arouse enormous interest. The mere circumstance of a pleasure yacht being found floating alone in the middle of the English Channel and bearing such a terrible freight, was in itself dramatic. The story would have an instant appeal. Editors would push it for all it was worth. Mackintosh saw his name in heavily leaded type on the principal page of the leading dailies. And there was a certain young lady who would see it too.

As he chewed the cud of this entrancing idea, he noticed that the motor launch, which had been making a beeline for the *Nymph*, had swung round towards the west and was now heading as if to pass across the yacht's bows. It occurred to Mackintosh that their paths were now converging and that in a couple of miles they should be close together. Idly he once more picked up the high-powered binoculars and focused them on her. She was a small motor launch with a deck cabin stretching from the bows for about two-thirds of the way aft. She was running about the same speed as the *Nymph* or a little faster. Mackintosh could see only one man aboard her, standing at the tiny wheel in her well.

While he was watching, the man picked up something, evidently glasses, and gazed through them at the *Nymph*. Immediately, probably as he saw that he was being observed, he dropped the wheel and began gesticulating and waving a small flag.

It was obvious that he wanted to speak to the *Nymph*, and Mackintosh, thinking that for once he was not running to schedule, gave the order to stop. It would only take fifteen minutes to see what was wanted, and another fifteen minutes delay in reaching Newhaven would make but little difference.

He signalled what he was doing, and as the *Nymph* lost way, the launch again shifted her course to head straight for her. Smith, learning that his motor would not be required for a few minutes, came on deck and in low tones discussed the situation with Wilcox in the wheel-house. Mackintosh paced slowly to and fro, still glancing automatically round the misty horizon, but save for the rapidly approaching launch, they were alone on the sea.

The launch was steering to slightly behind their stern, but as she came close her helm went over and she bore round, coming at last to rest parallel to the *Nymph* and some thirty feet from her. Mackintosh now saw that she was built like a small-sized navy launch, some two or three and twenty feet long, with of course the cabin added. A great model they were, these navy launches, with their double diagonal sheeting, their square sterns, their deep draught and their propeller shafts inclined to one side so as to leave the sternpost uncut. No fliers of course, no more than was this small sister, but they were a fine job, roomy and steady and safe in any sea. Money apparently had not been considered in her construction. She seemed quite as well found as the *Nymph*, and her spotless paint and shining brasswork showed that she also received the best of attention.

So far only one man had appeared, and Mackintosh now saw that he was of medium height and build, thin and dark as to face and intelligent as to expression. A rather large nose and a strong chin showed distinction of character and determination. An able and efficient man, thought Mackintosh, who prided himself on the rapidity of his character reading.

"Yacht *Nymph*," the man shouted. "Is Mr. Moxon aboard?" and in his voice and manner Mackintosh recognised a puzzled bewilderment.

It was a simple question, but Mackintosh couldn't answer it.

"There's been an accident aboard here," he called back. "I'm third officer of the Southern Company's *Chichester* and I'm in charge. May I ask your name and what you want?"

"My name's Nolan, though I don't suppose that's any help to you," the stranger called. "And I'm wanting to see Mr. Moxon, my partner in business, if he's there."

26

"Best come aboard, Mr. Nolan. Come alongside and make fast."

"Right you are." The newcomer backed his launch, then came forward again, bringing up skilfully against the *Nymph*. Mackintosh held out a fender, while Smith and Wilcox made fast the bow and stern ropes which Nolan threw over. Side by side the two little vessels rolled placidly on the short swell. Nolan climbed energetically aboard.

"Holy saints!" he cried as his eyes fell on the bloodstains and ran along them to the blue ensign. "What's been happening here?"

"Something pretty like murder, I'm thinking, Mr. Nolan. Better come and have a look."

Nolan stared at him, a great wonder in his eyes.

"What's that you're saying? Murder? You're not serious?"

"Look for yourself."

At a sign from Mackintosh the two men raised the ensign. An oath burst from Nolan's lips as he stood gazing down at the still figure.

"Holy saints!" he cried again. "Deeping!" He stared helplessly, then swung round on Mackintosh. "Deeping dead! And you're telling me he was murdered! Good God! Surely not!"

"I'm feared it doesna look like an accident."

"But this is terrible altogether. Poor old Deeping!"

"You knew him then?"

"Knew him? Of course I knew him. Sure wasn't he another of my partners in the business? I was talking to him only last night, and he was as well then as I was myself." He paused, shook his head, then went on in tones of growing amazement, "And he never said a word about going out in the yacht! Never a blessed word! That was in the middle of last night and he never so much as mentioned the subject. I can't understand it at all."

At another sign the flag was replaced and Mackintosh pointed to the companion.

"That's not the whole of it, Mr. Nolan. There's more trouble below. Come down and have a look."

When Nolan saw the second body his emotions nearly overcame him. The sight of the man he had called Deeping had awakened horror and surprise, but not such horror and surprise as he now exhibited. Moreover to these feelings was added another, an evident sense of personal loss. The man he recognised at once. It was that Moxon for whom he had first asked. Moxon, he said, was his partner and friend. He had talked with him also on the previous evening. Both he and Deeping were then well and strong and obviously looking forward to many years of life. And now their lives, such as they had made of them, were over and done with. Both dead! Nolan could scarcely realise it.

But besides the horror and the shock, the man's amazement at the tragic happening seemed only to increase. "Why," he declared, "this beats me altogether! Only last night, practically this morning, Moxon told me he couldn't make this trip! In fact, it was he asked me to make it for him: that's why I'm here."

Mackintosh was silent. All this seemed only to add to the mystery. He would have liked to have questioned Nolan, but his thoughts returned to his own position and responsibilities. He realised that they were wasting time.

"You'll find there's a reason for it all right," he said with a rough attempt at sympathy. "But, Mr. Nolan, we can't stay here all afternoon. I'm putting into Newhaven and I must get her going. Come up on deck. We can talk there."

Nolan nodded, and with another shrinking glance at the tragic figure on the floor, he followed the third officer.

"We'll go ahead with our motor in the meantime. That launch of yours will be all right where she is."

Again Nolan nodded absently, his mind evidently too full of the tragedy to be interested in anything else. Smith and Wilcox took up their respective stations and the *Nymph* was restarted. The other two men fell to pacing the deck, while Mackintosh recounted the sighting of the yacht and the discovery of the tragedy aboard.

"They were a pair of the best," said Nolan when the story came to an end, "right good fellows as you would wish to meet. Moxon has been a good friend to me and an old one, too. For the matter of that, so has Deeping, though I haven't known him so long. And now they're gone, and gone in this terrible way. My God, but it's awful to think about!"

"You havena any theory of what might have happened?" Mackintosh put in.

"Theory?" Nolan made a helpless gesture. "No more than the babe unborn! The thing's the most extraordinary mystery. I tell you I saw them late last night, indeed early this morning, and there wasn't a word out of either of them about going on the *Nymph*. Moxon said definitely he wasn't going. He had intended to, but he'd had bad news and changed his mind. What could have brought them here I can no more imagine than you can."

"You say Mr. Moxon had asked you to go instead of him? Where was that to? You dinna feel disposed to give particulars?"

"Certainly, I'll tell you. There's no secret about it at all. These two were partners with me in Moxon's General Securities. You've heard of it, of course; one of the biggest financial houses in the country. Moxon acted as chairman, Deeping as vice-chairman, and I was one of the supervising executives."

"What did you deal in?" Mackintosh asked with an air of shrewdness.

"Money," Nolan returned. "Investments and loans and so on."

"In London?"

"In London, in Threadneedle Street. Well, there was a French financier, by name of Pasteur, that Moxon was wanting to meet. There had been negotiations going on between them for some time, and now Moxon was wanting a personal interview. This Pasteur was staying with friends at Fécamp. He was by way of being a yachtsman; fond of the sea anyway. Moxon thought he'd bring the *Nymph* across with him and take

Pasteur out. It was business he had in mind, for he thought Pasteur would be pleased with the trip and would be easier to come to terms with."

"Pr-ractical psychology," Mackintosh suggested.

Nolan grunted. "Sure it was only business. Anyway, that's what he did. He was to dine with Pasteur this evening and they were to go for their sail to-morrow. Well, that was all right, but there was a difficulty in the way. There was a dinner in London last night. It was a big financial affair and every one that was any one had to be there. He and Deeping and myself were there, as well as a couple more of our partners. Well, you can see that it didn't leave much time for Moxon to get the *Nymph* over to Fécamp and dine with Pasteur at eight o'clock this evening."

Mackintosh admitted it would be pretty tight running.

"The way he intended to do it was this: He had brought his car to Hallam's, where the dinner was, and he meant to leave immediately the dinner was over and run down to Folkestone, where the *Nymph* was lying, sleep on board, and start first thing this morning. I suppose, as a matter of fact, that's what he did. But he told me he wasn't going to, and that's one of the things that make this whole business so queer."

"He didna give a reason?"

"He did. Just after the dinner was over, when we were all getting ready to go home, he came up with a face as long as a horse's and said he'd just had a phone call from his sister in Buxton. He told me his brother-in-law had been knocked down and killed on his way home from the theatre, and said he'd have to go to Buxton to look after things. So he said he couldn't go to France and he asked me to go instead. He said I knew the whole business, and more than that, I was the only other that had a launch and could take Pasteur out. 'Besides,' he said, 'you'll have Raymond with you.'

"This Raymond was another of the partners. I knew he had been going with Moxon, so it was right that he should come with me. He was a young man, the youngest of us, and he was going, partly because he was a good chap socially and would be useful for entertaining Pasteur, but also because he could write shorthand and type, and could so do confidential clerk if they got anywhere with their negotiations. Moxon didn't want to take a stenographer for fear it would look as if he was trying to rush Pasteur. I asked Moxon how we would get word to Raymond, for he seemed to have gone home. Moxon said Raymond had not gone home, that he had gone to get Moxon's car, and that he, Moxon, would fix things up with him. He said he would arrange for him to be at my rooms at whatever time I appointed, and I could take him down in my car to Dover, where my launch was lying. We settled that I would leave at four-thirty, so as to get away on the launch by seven-thirty. I thought I'd have to start by seven-thirty if I was to be in Fécamp in time to dine with the Frenchman."

"What does she do?" Mackintosh inquired.

"Close on ten knots."

"Aye, you ought to have got in about five or six o'clock."

"Before that, I thought, but I wanted to allow a margin. Well, I hadn't more than got home when Deeping rang up; that's the poor chap —" Nolan made a gesture towards the ensign. "The last time I heard his voice! Well, he told me he had just seen Raymond and he had said he wanted his own car at Dover on our return, so he would go down by himself and meet me there in the morning. So that was all right.

"I should have explained that Moxon had given me the file of papers about the business. He seemed very grateful and all that about my going. But what could I do but agree?"

"What else?" Mackintosh agreed laconically. Then a professional point striking him, he added: "How did you get your launch ready in time?"

"When I got home to my flat at St. James's I rang up the night porter at the Lord Warden at Dover, where I always stay, and asked if he'd send word at once to my caretaker that I'd want the launch to be ready for me to start at seven-thirty in the morning. You see, I was afraid of getting stuck by the tide. I keep the launch lying up in the Granville Basin, and if she wasn't got out before the tide fell, the gates would be shut and I couldn't get her till the next tide."

"Aye, that's a fact. I know the place well."

"I told my own man what I wanted, and he set the alarm for four. While I was dressing and getting out the car he made me a bit of breakfast. I got away shortly after half-past four and went straight down to Dover. I was there by quarter past seven. The hotel porter had sent the message and the caretaker had got it in time.

The launch was lying outside the gates alongside the Crosswall Quay, all ready to start."

"A bit of luck, getting her out in time."

Nolan smiled grimly.

"Maybe it was, and maybe it wasn't," he returned. "If he hadn't got her out I wouldn't have been here now."

Mackintosh agreed shortly.

"Then occurred the first hitch," continued Nolan. "There was no sign of Raymond. At half-past seven he hadn't turned up. I waited and waited, but there was no sign of him, then I thought if I stayed any longer I'd be late at Fécamp. So at eight I put out alone. It was a confounded nuisance, but I couldn't help it."

"As it turned out, it didna matter," Mackintosh remarked dryly. "So then you came on here?"

"I did, and you can guess my surprise when I saw the *Nymph*. First I saw a small boat heading across my bows; then I thought it wasn't unlike the *Nymph*; but I never for a moment believed it was she. But when I came closer and saw the curve of that wheel-house I knew it must be. Moxon got that altered and I don't suppose there's another afloat just like it. I couldn't make out what she was doing there." He shook his head sadly. "But nothing I could have thought of would have been the equal of what has happened."

For a few moments they paced in silence, then Nolan went on.

"It'll be a bad thing for poor Mrs. Moxon. It'll just about kill her when she hears about it, and she ill herself. And Mrs. Deeping too and the family.

Deeping'll be missed. He had a boy just about through college. One blessing, they were both well off, those two. There'll be no poverty to be met."

Mackintosh agreed that this was an important alleviation, though his thoughts remained with the abstract problem rather than with its human effects. "Tell me," he went on, recurring to his earlier difficulty, "they surely werena alone, these two on the *Nymph?*"

"I couldn't tell you. Sure I know no more about it than you do yourself. But there wouldn't be any crew. Moxon, though he doesn't look like it in all those City clothes, was as good a seaman as ever put out of an English port. He never took any help. He had a man to look after the yacht in port and keep her clean and all that, but never anybody at sea."

Mackintosh felt that the whole business was beyond him. It had been bad at first, but the coming of this Nolan had made it, if anything, more puzzling. Then he saw that an explanation for at least part of it was forthcoming.

"I'll tell you what's happened," he suggested. "After Moxon had asked you to go to France he went home, and when he got there he found another phone from Buxton that there had been a mistake and his brother-in-law wasna hurt at all. He would then think, 'Here I've sent Mr. Nolan away to France for no reason,' and he would send you a message that he would go himself after all. Well, if by some mistake you didna get the message, there would be the whole thing. Would you no think so?"

Nolan was evidently impressed. He thought indeed that this might well be the truth. But, of course, it did not explain the tragedy.

"No, it doesna explain everything," Mackintosh admitted in a voice which suggested that Nolan was hard to please, he, Mackintosh, having really done extraordinarily well. But he saw that it certainly didn't explain the men's death. However, thank goodness it was none of his business. He was a sailor, not a blinking policeman. He looked round at the sea.

"Well, I dinna know how it'll be explained," he concluded, as if dismissing the subject of the tragedy, "but I do know that as far as this trip's concerned we're no making much of it. She's no tug, this *Nymph*. I'm thinking you'd be better back in your launch, Mr. Nolan, cast off and keeping us company under your own power. You're coming to Newhaven, I suppose?"

"I am so. Sure what else could I do? Faith, I believe you're right, Mr. Mackintosh. It'll double our speed."

The manœuvre was carried out and at half-past six that evening both vessels passed slowly in behind the breakwater at Newhaven.

CHAPTER
THREE

Enter the Law

A little group of men were awaiting them as they steered to the gangway indicated by the harbour authorities. There were Sergeant Heath and two men of the Sussex County Constabulary, the harbour-master and a couple of his myrmidons, as well as, in the background, a number of the curious who had sensed a thrill as the vulture senses carrion. They stood watching as Mackintosh brought the *Nymph* slowly alongside, seemingly hypnotised by the stains on the white deck and the terribly suggestive shape beneath the ensign. When the yacht was moored Nolan laid the launch alongside her, dropping in a fender and attaching her with bow and stern ropes, as had already been done in mid-Channel. Mackintosh was a well-known figure in Newhaven and was recognised by all, but questioning glances were levelled at Nolan and the launch.

"We had a message from Captain Hewitt," the harbour-master called down when the berthing was complete, "so we were expecting you, Mr. Mackintosh. But who is this you've got along with you?"

"Mr. Nolan," Mackintosh shouted up. "Gentleman who knew the deceased. He came up in his launch just after the *Chichester* had gone on."

"That's all right," returned the harbour-master, and conferred with Sergeant Heath.

"I'd be obliged if both you gentlemen would stay where you are for the present," the latter called. He had some further discussion with the harbour-master, who nodded and walked off. Then the sergeant climbed somewhat ponderously down the gangway ladder, followed by his two constables.

Sergeant Heath was a pleasant-spoken man who did his duty quietly and efficiently and was a general favourite in the neighbourhood. He greeted Mackintosh as an old friend, gave Nolan a civil good evening, and then turned to survey the traces of the tragedy.

"A bad business, this," he said, following with his eyes the track across the deck. "I've been talking to Captain Hewitt and that doctor on the phone, so I know something about it. Have you made any further discoveries, Mr. Mackintosh?"

"No," said Mackintosh, "only what Mr. Nolan here told me. As I said, he knew the deceased."

"So. We'll go into that later. Meanwhile let's see what's to be seen. Let's have the flag up, Mr. Mackintosh."

Once again the still, gray-clad figure was revealed with the sinister pool beside the head. The men ranged themselves round and stood looking down.

"He hasn't been moved?"

"No, sergeant, only when the doctor lifted his head."

"The doctor said he was shot. You've not found a gun?"

"No, but we havna yet seen the right hand."

The sergeant nodded.

"We'll not move him now. Let's see the other body."

They trooped down to the cabin. Heath stopped on reaching the bottom of the stairs, Mackintosh looking over his shoulder. The two constables, after peering and craning for some moments, gave it up as a bad job and returned to the deck.

"I see," the sergeant said presently. "We'll leave everything undisturbed in the meantime. Now, Mr. Mackintosh, I'd like a statement from you and Mr. Nolan. Just short ones; you can give fuller details later."

They returned to the deck and Mackintosh gave him a rapid account of the sighting and salvage of the *Nymph* and the arrival of Nolan.

He had scarcely finished when there was a diversion. A middle-aged man in plus fours, well set-up and with a military bearing, appeared at the edge of the gangway, and climbing nimbly down the ladder, stepped on board. The sergeant swung round, then saluted.

"Evening, sergeant. Evening, men," said the newcomer pleasantly. "So the yacht has turned up? I thought I'd look in on my way home to find out."

"Just come in a few minutes ago, sir. I was beginning to make my examination."

"Good, good. And these gentlemen?"

"This is Mr. Mackintosh." The sergeant made a half-bow. "He's the officer from the Dieppe boat who went aboard the yacht and worked her in. The other

39

gentleman, I understand, is a Mr. Nolan, who turned up later in his launch. I've not had his statement yet." He turned to the others. "Gentlemen, this is Major Turnbull, our chief constable."

The major courteously acknowledged the introduction.

"I don't want to interfere with what you're doing, sergeant," he went on, "but while I'm here I'd like to see what's to be seen. A terrible business; terrible! These are the first marks?" He pointed to the trail of blood. As he spoke he moved along it to the companion, then rapidly examined the further grim evidences of the tragedy.

"Dear, dear! A terrible affair! Those two poor fellows," he murmured in a sort of running commentary. "Terrible! Nothing has been touched as yet, I suppose?"

"No, sir, except for the doctor," and the sergeant repeated what Mackintosh had told him.

"Dear, dear! Very sad; very sad indeed. Have you had a statement yet from Mr. Mackintosh?"

"Yes, sir."

"On paper?"

"No, sir. Just a short verbal statement so as I might get the hang of the affair."

"Quite right; quite right. Well, suppose we ask Mr. Mackintosh to repeat it for my benefit? I think we might as well get it down on paper at the same time. Either of these men write shorthand?"

"Both do, sir."

"Good, good. Then let's sit down. The constable can write on his knee. Hard lines, Mr. Mackintosh, to ask you to go over it all again, but I'm sure you won't mind obliging me. By the way, Mr. Nolan, won't you come aboard and join us? We shall also want to hear what you have to tell us."

Along the rail there were seats, to which the party moved. Mackintosh had noticed some deck chairs in the store, and for these he sent his men. As the chief constable pointed out, they were here as comfortable as in the sergeant's office and almost as private. The tide was out and they were too far below the level of the inquisitive on the gangway for anything that was said to be overheard. They also had the advantage that they remained on the scene of the tragedy and could make examinations as and when these became necessary.

"By the way, sergeant," Turnbull went on, "I wish you'd send your other man for a photographer. Then let him go on and ask Dr. Nelson to step down. I think we must see if there's anything in that poor fellow's right hand. Now, Mr. Mackintosh?"

For the second time Mackintosh told his story, giving it this time in fuller detail.

"That makes things clear so far," Major Turnbull approved. "We have already had telegraphic reports from the captain and doctor, so I think we can picture the thing pretty clearly, eh, sergeant? Got all that down, constable?"

"Yes, sir."

"Good, good. We'll get it transcribed and then we shall ask you to sign it. An amazing business, amazing! But most cases look like that at first. Now, Mr. Nolan, perhaps you would tell us what you know? Your full name, please, and address?"

"John Patrick Nolan, 506 St. Mary's Mansions, St. James's."

"And your business?"

"A partner in Moxon's General Securities."

The chief constable looked up sharply, as if about to make some remark. But he evidently thought better of it and merely resumed his questions.

"I understood Mr. Mackintosh to say that you knew the deceased?"

"I did. They were two of my partners; Mr. Moxon, the chairman, and Mr. Deeping, the vice-chairman."

The chief constable whistled softly, but made no other comment. For a moment he seemed lost in thought, then he went on: "I think, Mr. Nolan, I must ask you to tell me your story in your own way. I don't want a fully detailed statement; that can wait. Give me just a rough idea of things, so that I may settle our line of action. This may not be a matter for the Sussex police at all."

Nolan hesitated as if to collect his thoughts, while he nervously lit a cigarette. The scene would have struck an onlooker as highly unconventional, if not actually incongruous. The peaceful summer's evening, the warm atmosphere, still slightly hazy, the somnolent shipping of the little port, the quiet wharf across the river, the gangway with its spidery, seaweed-clad piles, the soft murmur of the tiny ripples, and the yacht, so evidently a rich man's toy, all were far removed from tragedy and the grim realities of the law. The little knot

42

of inquisitives had melted away, and save for the muffled clanking of a distant crane, loading cargo on the night boat to France, there was neither sight nor sound of human activity.

"If it's only a rough idea you want, I can give it to you in a couple of words," Nolan said at last, and he went on to repeat the story he had told to Mackintosh. He explained about the French financier, Pasteur, with whom Moxon had been in negotiation, and about the meetings for that evening and the next day in which these negotiations were to culminate. He told of the dinner in London on the previous night, of Moxon's request to him to make the journey to France in his place, and of the means he had adopted to get away from Dover in time.

"That's all very clearly put, Mr. Nolan," the chief constable commented; "very clearly put. I think we all understand. Now I expect you're tired and want to get away, but I'd be glad if you'd stay till we've settled our procedure. We'll have to wait for the doctor and photographer before disturbing the bodies. I'm anxious to see about that gun. Look if there's any sign of either, will you, sergeant?"

As he spoke a small man bearing a big camera appeared at the edge of the gangway and began gingerly descending the ladder. Hesitatingly he turned to the sergeant, but Major Turnbull got up and greeted him.

"Just ready for you," he said cheerily. "Now come here and I'll show you what we want."

First the trail across the deck was photographed from different points of view, Major Turnbull having first

43

placed a two-foot rule on the deck beside it. Then once again the blue ensign was removed and a number of views were taken of the grim, grayclad figure. The photographer then went below, while Sergeant Heath drew in chalk on the deck the outline of the body. This was repeated in the cabin.

By the time these operations were completed there was another interruption. A hail came from the gangway and a rotund little man began with much puffing and blowing to climb down to the yacht.

"Good-evening, every one," he beamed as he bustled on board. "Evening, sergeant. How are you, major? Serious affair this. That you, Mr. Mackintosh? You're the hero of this unhappy occasion, eh? Bless my soul, major, it's not often tragedy comes to Newhaven. Two men killed, is it?"

"Two men, doctor. Both reported to be shot dead, though we've made no detailed examination as yet."

"Huh. Soon find that out. Can't remove the traces of a bullet. That's something beyond even the cleverest murderer, eh, major?"

"We don't know yet if it is murder."

"Shouldn't be hard to find that out, surely? What about the weapon?"

"That's just it, doctor. What we want to know at this present stage is really only whether or not there's a weapon on board." They had approached the figure on the deck. "You see, the right hand is covered. We want to know if this man fired the shots."

"Bless my soul," Dr. Nelson cried again, staring at the still figure. "And where's the other?"

They went once again to the cabin.

"No doubt about that, eh, major? Shot through the head! Instantaneous? Oh, yes, quite. A biggish gun, possibly a service revolver, though it's too soon to be certain of that. Nothing in either hand. Well, major, you don't want me to look for a gun here? Job for your people, isn't it?"

"Of course, of course, Dr. Nelson. It's the deck case that we were doubtful of."

"Yes, well I'll soon tell you that. Here, men," and he beckoned to the constables.

Under the doctor's directions the body was reverently turned over on its back. At once the injury to the head became visible. In this case also there could be no doubt as to the suddenness with which death had occurred. But what interested the police even more was the fact that though the right hand was clenched, it was empty. Nor was there any sign of a pistol.

"Then it's murder!" The chief constable made the exclamation, then for some moments the little group remained silent. On Dr. Nelson's face there gradually grew a puzzled expression. Turnbull noticed it and presently asked the cause.

"Why, it's this," the little man returned. "That wound on the head would cause instantaneous death. As you know yourself, major, a dead body doesn't bleed; at least, not much. Now there's a fair amount of blood round here; more than ever came from that wound. There must be another wound somewhere, though I don't see it."

Turnbull slowly nodded.

"Very true, doctor; very true. I hadn't thought of that. You suggest then that the man was wounded first, but not killed; that he lay bleeding for some time, and that then there was this second shot in the head which finished him off?"

"Looks like it. Must make a proper examination before I can say."

"I don't think we need mind that for the present. We'll get the bodies moved to the mortuary and any further examination necessary can be made there. Will you arrange it, sergeant? Very much obliged to you, doctor, for coming down."

Dr. Nelson took a somewhat voluble farewell. He was followed by the photographer, after the latter had received instructions to work all night if necessary, but to have the prints ready for nine o'clock next morning. It was then the third officer's turn.

"Well, Mr. Mackintosh, I'm sure you've had enough of it. You can get away any time you like. I'm sure we're all very much obliged to you. Of course you'll be wanted at the inquest."

Mackintosh immediately vanished and the major turned with a smile to Nolan.

"What did you think of doing, Mr. Nolan?" he asked politely.

"London," the other answered. "I must be getting back as soon as possible. Now that these two poor fellows are gone, I believe I'm the senior partner, and I'd like to be at the office in the morning. To tell the truth, it'll not be easy to follow such a pair."

Once again the major glanced curiously at the speaker, but all he said was: "Well, you can't do much by rail. You've missed the 8.5 and there's only a slow train to-night which doesn't get to Town till about one in the morning. But it happens that I have to go to London almost at once and I should be very pleased to offer you a seat."

"Very good of you, major. Thanks, I'll take it."

"Well, we'll go to the hotel for a snack. I'm afraid there'll scarcely be time for a proper dinner. We should be in Town by eleven-thirty or twelve. That do?"

"Suit me first rate, thank you. But there are a couple of things that I must settle before we leave. First, I must wire to M. Pasteur at Fécamp, that no one from our firm can go over. Second, there are three keys to the strong-room in the Securities building, any two of which will open it. One was held by Moxon, one by Deeping and one by myself. To-morrow we'll be wanting the strong-room opened so we'll need those keys."

"Right, right. I'll tell the sergeant to get them while we're at supper. Also if you draft out your message to Fécamp, the sergeant will send it."

"Thanks. Another thing. What about my launch? Can you people look after her, or shall I make an arrangement about her with the harbour-master?"

"We can do it for you for the present," Turnbull replied. "You'll have to come down here for the inquest in any case, and perhaps then you could make your own arrangements."

"Then I'll just get my papers."

He dived into the launch's cabin, returning immediately with a despatch case. "The business with Pasteur," he explained. "I'd better take the papers with me. No objection, I suppose?"

"Of course not, Mr. Nolan."

Nolan produced a small bunch of keys.

"Then here are the keys of the launch, and perhaps the sergeant would lock her up before leaving?"

Turnbull said he would see to it, then excusing himself, drew the sergeant out of earshot.

"I've been thinking this matter over, sergeant, and I've come to the conclusion that we'd be very foolish to take anything to do with it. It's not a local crime. It didn't take place within thirty miles of us and all the people concerned are Londoners. It's a job for the Yard and I'm going up now to see them about it. I'm sorry, sergeant, to seem to take away your opportunity," the major prided himself on his tact, "but if you think of it you'll see that all your inquiries would have to be made in London. You understand, don't you?"

The sergeant, the weight of a great trouble rolled from off his shoulders, saluted delightedly.

"Now to-night," went on Turnbull, "will you get the bodies of those two poor fellows up to the mortuary, then seal the cabin door and put a couple of men on to see that neither the *Nymph* nor the launch is interfered with. Have the photographs in the morning and be ready to give the Yard officer any help he may require. And another thing, sergeant. I wish you'd get those two statements typed out now and bring them to the hotel, together with the keys from the dead men's pockets. I'll see some one at the Yard to-night and I'd like to have these things with me."

Again the sergeant saluted as the major led his guest to the waiting car.

CHAPTER
FOUR

Scotland Yard

"I've just told the sergeant," major turnbull said to Nolan as he drew up at the London and Paris Hotel, "that I've decided to hand this affair over to Scotland Yard. That's why I'm going up to Town; it's really to the Yard. Now, Mr. Nolan, they're sure to want to see you to get details at first hand. It's rather a lot to ask you after all you've been through to-day, but it really would be very helpful if you'd come there with me."

Nolan agreed readily. "I'm at your service, major," he declared. "Anyway I expect I've no option in the matter."

"Oh, yes, you have," Turnbull answered. "I've no power to compel you to do anything you don't want to. Now, while I'm telephoning to them, perhaps you'd order supper?"

If Nolan had overheard the ensuing conversation he might not have taken his association with the police so complaisantly. Turnbull began by asking to be put through to the Assistant Commissioner, of whom he was a personal friend. Sir Mortimer Ellison was at dinner at his home, but he came at once to the instrument. He refused to listen to the chief constable's apologies for introducing business at such a time, and heard his story of the tragedy with evident interest. "You know, Ellison," Turnbull went on, "this afternoon I heard some dashed nasty rumours about that very firm. A man on the links told me. Some friend on the Stock Exchange had telephoned advising him if he had any money in it for heaven's sake to get it out while it was there to get. The friend thought a crash was coming. And then on the top of that, this business here! It looks badly, Ellison. Had you heard anything about a crash?"

Sir Mortimer was not communicative, but he admitted that he had heard the rumours. He would himself return to the Yard, so as to be there on the major's arrival, when they would have an immediate conference.

"Thanks, Ellison. Very good of you, I'm sure. There's just one other point. I think your people should keep in touch with this man Nolan. In the light of this rumour the whole thing looks fishy. I'll explain what I mean when I see you. He has promised to call with me at the Yard on the understanding that he won't be kept more than a few minutes, but I suggest that he should be shadowed from there. In fact, I asked him to come with me with that in view."

At supper Turnbull proved himself a pleasant and entertaining host. His great enthusiasm, it appeared, was golf, and as Nolan was a player, they were soon deep in a conversation intelligible only to the expert. A common hobby being one of the most direct routes to intimacy, the meal was not over before Turnbull found himself considering Nolan no longer as a possible defaulting partner in a shaky firm, but as a fellow sportsman, an amateur of the royal and ancient and utterly honourable game.

Supper over, they got quickly under way. Major Turnbull was a fast driver and the needle of his speedometer crept continuously up and down between the thirty and the fifty marks. It was still daylight as they skirted the valley of the Ouse and ran through the old town of Lewes with its steep and narrow exit, but dusk fell quickly and by the time they reached Ashdown Forest it was dark. A slack came as they passed through East Grinstead, then they had a good run to Purley, after which slow speeds again ruled. At five minutes before midnight they reached the Yard. A constable met them, and saluting, led them to the Assistant Commissioner's room.

It was a comparatively small office, furnished plainly, but in good taste. In the middle stood a flat-topped desk bearing a blotting-pad with extra wide memo slips at the sides, a stand with various kinds of notepaper, a date calendar, a telephone, a writing lamp, a small carved ebony block with seven white labelled bell pushes, and three empty letter trays. Behind the desk, dreamily smoking a cigarette, sat Sir Mortimer Ellison, a slim, rather elegant looking man with tired eyes. A couple of easy chairs, not too easy, stood in front of the desk. There was a steel vertical filing cabinet in one corner and between the two high windows a safe, while the whole of the opposite wall was covered with glass-fronted bookcases. Standing with his back to the empty fireplace, was a stoutish man of rather below middle height, with keen dark blue eyes and a leisurely, comfortable air.

Sir Mortimer rose to his feet as his visitors appeared.

"Ah, Turnbull. Glad to see you," he said cordially, advancing with outstretched hand. "A long time since we met, I'm afraid. D'you remember that round we had at Portrush, just, what is it, nine years ago? Jolly fine, wasn't it? And this is Mr. Nolan? How are you, Mr. Nolan? Sorry we meet under such distressing circumstances." He swung round. "This is Inspector French, gentlemen, who will be taking charge of the case. Sit down, won't you?" He took out a box of cigarettes and passed it round.

They settled themselves, Turnbull and Nolan in the arm-chairs and French with a note-book at the end of his superior's desk.

"I'm afraid this is a very sad affair for you, Mr. Nolan," Sir Mortimer went on. "Major Turnbull mentioned in his telephone call that you were able to identify the deceased gentlemen; that they were two of your co-partners in Moxon's General Securities?"

"They were, Sir Mortimer," Nolan nodded.

"Well I expect you want to get away as soon as possible, so I shall not waste any time in preliminaries." He turned to the major. "Perhaps, Turnbull, you'd let us have the facts you've learned so far?"

The major took some papers from his pocket and handed them over.

"There," he said, "are the statements of Captain Hewitt of the *Chichester*; of Dr. Oates, a passenger who went with Third Officer Mackintosh to the *Nymph*; of Mackintosh himself, and of Mr. Nolan here. I think you should read these first. They will really give you all the information that we've got up to the present."

The Assistant Commissioner glanced at the documents, then passed them back.

"Read them out to us like a good fellow," he begged. "Then Inspector French will hear them also."

Major Turnbull read them aloud, continuing:

"To these statements I may add that the two bodies have been photographed, and after a short examination by our local police doctor, have been removed to the mortuary at Newhaven. The doctor provisionally reports that both men were shot dead by what looked like, though he was not sure of it, a service revolver. Neither was grasping a weapon, nor did a search, admittedly somewhat casual, reveal a weapon anywhere on board. I don't think there can be the slightest doubt that it's murder."

"No. That part of it seems clear enough."

"It then seemed to me," went on Turnbull, "that the case was really one for you. I don't know if your jurisdiction extends out on to the high seas, but I'm quite certain that ours doesn't. As I said to Mr. Nolan, there's nothing connecting Newhaven with the tragedy except the mere accidental fact that Mackintosh brought the yacht in there. So I suggest that it's you for it."

"I think you're probably right," Sir Mortimer agreed, "but you must, of course, make the usual official application for help."

54

Turnbull shook his head decisively.

"No, Ellison, that's not it at all," he declared. "We don't want your help. We want to hand the thing over to you and be quit of it altogether. That's one reason I came up to Town."

Sir Mortimer smiled.

"I see your point," he admitted. "However, we needn't expose these skeleton-in-the-cupboard wrangles to outsiders. Let us finish with Mr. Nolan, so that he may get away. I should like, Mr. Nolan, to ask you a question or two before you go."

For a time the Assistant Commissioner skirted round the subject, asking about matters of detail which, it must be admitted, none of his hearers thought particularly important. While doing so he had been shooting little appraising glances at Nolan, much as had Turnbull earlier in the evening. The same thought was evidently in his mind as had been in the chief constable's, and at last he turned to that phase of the subject.

"My next question, Mr. Nolan, is unfortunately rather an unhappy one, and I want to make it clear to you that you needn't answer it unless you like. You are, of course, aware of the unfortunate rumours about your firm which are in circulation. Now, my question is: Are these rumours well-founded, and if so, can you trace any connection between them and the death of your friends?"

Nolan's face, which at the opening of these remarks had registered a mild dismay, now showed absolute bewilderment.

"Rumours?" he repeated. "I've heard no rumours. Please explain, Sir Mortimer."

The Assistant Commissioner observed him closely.

"Do you really mean to tell me, Mr. Nolan, that you, a partner, have not heard what's being said about Moxon's General Securities?"

"Never a word!" Nolan declared emphatically. "I haven't the least idea what you're talking about."

Sir Mortimer nodded.

"I can well understand that you might be the last person to hear them," he said easily. "In that case I'm afraid it becomes my unpleasant duty to inform you of them." He hesitated, as if doubtful of the best words in which to do so, then went on: "All to-day there have been persistent rumours that all was not well with your firm; in fact, not to put too fine a point on it, it is said that an immediate crash is inevitable."

Nolan stared as if stupefied, then he shook his head emphatically.

"In all my life," he declared with energy, "I never heard anything to equal that! Holy saints! An immediate crash!" He swore with comfortable assurance. "I'd like to get hold of the man that started that tale!"

"Then it's not true?"

"True? I should think it's not true. It's an absolute lie from beginning to end. That's what it is; an absolute lie! There's no sounder corporation in the entire country than Moxon's General Securities."

"You're quite certain, Mr. Nolan? I've heard the rumours on very good authority."

56

"Of course I'm quite certain." The man spoke almost angrily. Then he paused as if a sudden idea had struck him, and though he repeated, "Absolutely certain," it was with less conviction.

Sir Mortimer sat watching him in silence. It was evident that something had occurred to the man which was gradually robbing him of his assurance. Presently uneasiness appeared on his face. It grew slowly more acute until it became actual dismay. He moved restlessly in his chair.

"What exactly have you heard?" he said at last in changed tones.

"Simply what I've told you," Sir Mortimer replied. "No details. Three separate people — friends of mine in the City — rang me up to-day to know if I had any money in Moxon's General Securities, as if so they advised me to get it out without a moment's delay. They said it was believed the concern was unsound and would crash within a day or two. I heard the same rumour from different people in my club at lunch time. Why, the major tells me he heard it at Newhaven."

"A stockbroker gave a friend of mine the same warning," Turnbull declared. "I couldn't make up my mind whether to speak to you about it or not, Mr. Nolan. I didn't want to put what might be an embarrassing question."

Nolan seemed scarcely to hear him. The shadow of a great fear appeared to have taken hold of him. He sat gazing vacantly into the distance, while the colour slowly ebbed from his cheeks.

"My God!" he said at last in a tremulous voice, and then again, "My God!"

The Assistant Commissioner sat for some moments unobtrusively watching the changes of expression on the man's face. In the silence the atmosphere of the room grew gradually more tense. At last Sir Mortimer spoke.

"Something has occurred to you to make you fear the truth of this story. Do you care to tell us what it is?"

"I don't know anything to prove it," Nolan returned, but he looked acutely unhappy.

"You don't *know* anything, no doubt, but you fear something. I better tell you what's in my mind, Mr. Nolan, because I want some help. Here is this rumoured failure on the one hand: no business directly of ours. On the other hand there is the unexpected — eh — journey of the two principal partners, followed by their tragic death. Now I think it's not too much to suggest that there may be a connection between these unhappy events, and if so, the possible failure at once becomes our business. You follow me, Mr. Nolan?"

The man seemed dazed, but he nodded.

"Very well," Sir Mortimer resumed, "if you can see your way to tell me what's in your mind, it might be a help, remembering, of course, that you are not bound to do so unless you like."

It was not, however, till after a good deal of persuasion that Nolan consented to lay bare his mind.

"I'm upset about this, Sir Mortimer," he began. "It's not because I've any real ground for believing the rumour. It's because, if there should be anything in it, I feel personally guilty as to the way I carried out my own duties. I'll explain what I mean.

"As I was telling you, Moxon was chairman and Deeping vice-chairman of the concern. These two dealt with policy. Of course decisions were theoretically taken by the whole of the partners, but none of the rest of us knew anything like as much about the business as those two, and what they said went. I'm not saying this to try to shirk responsibility. I know well enough that if trouble is coming, I'm going to be in it, and I hope I'll take my medicine without grousing. I'm simply telling you the fact that these two controlled our operations and that I wasn't up in what they were doing, as I admit I should have been."

"Very fairly put, Mr. Nolan," Sir Mortimer commented. "I think we all understand." He looked at the others, who nodded.

"The staff was supervised by another partner, Raymond, and myself. We acted as executives. Our job was really to see that the decisions of Moxon and Deeping were carried out. That's why I'm beginning to be afraid that if there's anything wrong, I mightn't have known about it."

"Yes, I understand your position," Sir Mortimer repeated. "But was there anything to make you doubt that all was well?"

Again Nolan hesitated, and again it was with obvious unwillingness that he spoke.

The most significant point seemed to be that on the following day — or rather that day, for it was now past midnight — a large amount, nearly a million and a half, was due for settlement by the firm. Nolan was now senior partner, and as such would be responsible for this settlement. The realisation of cash to provide for it had been entirely in the hands of the deceased, and Nolan didn't know what had been done about it. Owing to his ignorance of these details, he was extremely uneasy as to how he would fulfil his new duties.

All this was not exactly an answer to Sir Mortimer's question, but the answer could be read between the lines. It was evident that Nolan feared that funds to meet the approaching settlement might not prove available. The responsibility of dealing with the situation would then devolve upon him, and he was unprepared to meet it.

This uneasiness and doubt was considerably increased by the fact that the only two really confidential officials were both absent. Esdale, the chief accountant, had gone to Paris on the firm's business, while Knowles, the chief clerk, was on sick leave. There was no one left, in fact, thoroughly conversant with the firm's position. To this, of course, was added the fact of Raymond's failure to turn up at Dover. Though obviously there might be nothing sinister in this, it could not fail to add to Nolan's perturbation. The other partners were mere figureheads.

Questioned further, Nolan admitted that for some time both Moxon and Deeping had been looking extremely worried. Also that on different occasions when he had suddenly entered the room of either of them, he had found them in conversations which they had immediately broken off. Though it had not occurred to him at the time, he now thought that there might have been something afoot between them which they were keeping to themselves.

It had, of course, never occurred to him to couple such an attitude with a doubt as to the firm's position, but in the light of the Assistant Commissioner's statement, it added to his worry.

Though there was little that was actually tangible in these suspicions, there was enough to make a very strong impression on his hearers. When Nolan had finished there was not one of the four men present but believed that Moxon's General Securities was in danger, and that the death of its two most prominent representatives was in some way connected with its position.

It was now getting on towards one o'clock and Sir Mortimer became apologetic about having kept his visitor so late. "There's no reason, is there, why we should trespass any longer on Mr. Nolan's time?" he said. "What do you say, French?"

"If Mr. Nolan will tell me where I can find him when I want him, that's all I require at present, sir."

Nolan made a gesture of despair.

"Goodness only knows, Inspector," he returned. "It's maybe thrown to the lions I'll be before this time to-morrow. You have my home address in my statement and I'm sure you know the Securities building in Threadneedle Street. I expect to be in one or other continuously. If I want to go away any place I'll ring you up and let you know. That do?"

"That'll do, sir, thank you. What about your despatch case?"

Nolan smiled wearily.

"Well, what about it? Do you want to look through it?"

"If you have no objection, sir."

"You can keep it and go through it at your leisure."

"Thank you, sir. Then, that's all we want now. Shall I show Mr. Nolan out?"

"Do, French, and then come back here. Goodnight, Mr. Nolan, and I needn't say that I earnestly hope your fears will prove without foundation."

"We're having him shadowed as you suggested," Sir Mortimer went on after the door had closed. "What is it exactly that you feared?"

Turnbull felt in his pocket.

"Give me another of those cigarettes, will you? I've left mine behind. What I thought — Thanks, I have a lighter. What I thought was that our friend was in the same mind as the other two; that the three of them saw trouble coming and were journeying to a happier shore while the fates smiled on travelling."

"Independently?"

"I don't know, but I imagined not. I thought Nolan might perhaps be following the others up in that launch of his and that the three would join forces and vanish in the wilds of France."

"You didn't suspect Nolan of the murder?"

This seemed a new idea to Turnbull.

"Of the murder? No. I don't see how he could be guilty of that. But I thought if he was mixed up in the other he might try another get-away to-night."

"I agree, Turnbull. There certainly is the possibility. Come in! Look here, French," he went on as the inspector entered, "Major Turnbull has been putting up an interesting possibility. He suggests that these three partners smelled bankruptcy in the air and were going while the going was good; that Nolan was following the other two, intending to join forces. What they'd have done then doesn't appear, possibly sunk the *Nymph* and gone ashore in the launch at night at some deserted point on the French coast. But, of course, when Nolan came up with the yacht and found Mackintosh and those sailors on board, he couldn't carry on. In fact, he could only do what he actually did. That's why the major wanted him shadowed; lest he'd try another break-away to-night."

"He'll not make it if he does," French answered grimly.

"But how does that theory strike you?" the Assistant Commissioner persisted.

French hesitated. "I'd rather think it over a bit first, sir," he said. "The major didn't suspect him of murder?"

Sir Mortimer smiled in mock triumph.

"My very words, Inspector! Great minds! But we're both wrong. You didn't, major?"

"When Sir Mortimer put that up I told him I didn't see how the man could be guilty of murder. However, it's for you to say, both of you."

"It shouldn't be a big job to find out," French considered. "The evidence is that the two men had been dead for about an hour when they were found; say the crime took place about half-past twelve. Very well: what time did Nolan leave Dover? It should be easy to check that up. Would it then have been possible for him to reach the yacht in time? If so, the question lies open, but if not, he's cleared."

"True, Inspector, very true," Turnbull agreed. "That should be conclusive. And there's another thing that I think shouldn't be overlooked. When I saw that line of bloodmarks from the gangway entrance to the companion I thought that Deeping had been wounded near the gangway and had staggered forward, to collapse at the companion and there bleed to death. So far as I know, every one else made the same assumption. Now our doctor down at Newhaven pointed out a difficulty in that theory. The wound in Deeping's head must have killed him instantaneously. Therefore, not only could he not have crawled across the deck, but he would not have bled to any extent when he fell."

Both his hearers were listening intently. French made no secret of his interest and the Assistant Commissioner leant back in his chair with half-closed eyes, a trick that to the initiated showed close attention.

"To meet the difficulty the doctor suggested that the man must have been wounded twice, first a non-fatal injury which bled, and secondly, the head injury which killed him. But the doctor could only find one wound. Admittedly he was unable to make a thorough examination, but it seems impossible that a wound which would produce all that bleeding could be overlooked."

"Quite, I should say."

"Very well. If so, it follows that those bloodmarks must have been made by a third person."

"Bravo, Sherlock!" murmured Sir Mortimer.

Turnbull grinned. "I thought you'd scarcely see it for yourself, Watson," he retorted, "so I'm telling you. What I was going to say when you interrupted me was, Who could that third person have been? Now, it's inconceivable to me that there could have been any one there except the murderer and the murdered. Therefore this third person must have been the murderer. That is to say, the murderer must have been wounded. You see what I'm coming to? Is there a wound on Nolan?"

"Bravo, Sherlock!" Sir Mortimer repeated. "Quite good, all that, I think, French? Make a note to think up some reason for having Nolan examined by a doctor."

French added the item to his already growing list. This conversation was going to help him. Usually he had to do all the preliminary thinking himself. There was never much to show for it, but this first detailed consideration invariably meant a good deal of concentrated work. He had to get the various incidents clearly fixed in his mind, to note their relations one to another, to separate between what was essential and what was accidental, to make a list of possible clues and decide how he should work them. This point, for instance, about a possible wound on the murderer, might be very valuable. No doubt he would have thought of it for himself in time, but to have it presented to him in this way meant that he was just that much further on.

"There's another thing," Sir Mortimer went on slowly, looking up with a slight narrowing of the eyes. "I am wondering whether in all this excitement any money has disappeared?"

French nodded approvingly.

"That's what I've been wondering too, sir. All these missing partners and officials see this trouble coming

65

and know they're going to get roasted for it. So they do a bunk. Well, a man can't do that sort of a bunk without money."

"Exactly my idea, French. I shouldn't be surprised to hear that there had lately been a good deal of realising in Moxon's General Securities. Nor should I be astonished to learn that the cash in hand there at the moment is surprisingly low."

"It's not only the cost of the actual flight," French went on, warming to his subject. "If they had got away, these three would have had to start life again. A bad thing at such an age! Much better to have an assured income."

"Another note, French. Find out first thing whether our friends have gone with full or empty hands. And if with full — ?"

"And if with full," French repeated with a wry smile, "find the cash, I suppose?"

"In one," Sir Mortimer returned approvingly. "I can see you're going to have something to keep you busy for a day or two."

French shrugged. "All in the day's work." Then after a pause; "Is there anything else you would suggest, sir, that I should see to? Or you, sir?" He turned to the major.

"Why, French, I think we'll leave that to you. In excellent hands, you know, as I'm sure you'll agree. Besides, no use in keeping a dog, etcetera, is there, Turnbull? No, French, seriously I think there's nothing more. You go ahead on the lines we've been discussing. I'm sure Major Turnbull's men will give you all the help they can. You start right in."

"Very good, sir. I'll go down to Newhaven in the morning and have a look round. I think I'd better take a representative of both Moxon's and Deeping's families. We must have independent identifications." He looked at the clock. "I'll ring them up now."

"I don't know, French, that you shouldn't go round and see them. You have their addresses in Nolan's statement."

French rose. "Right, sir, I'll go at once." He was moving to the door, but Turnbull stopped him.

"A moment, Inspector. If it would be any help to you I can take you down in the early morning. My car's here and it will hold five comfortably. I'll simply go to some hotel nearby for a few hours. Any good to you?"

French was grateful. It would certainly be a convenience. After discussion it was decided that if French could get representatives of the two families, the party would meet at the Yard at six-thirty.

French began by sending instructions to Sergeant Carter to be on duty at six-thirty in the morning. Then he rang up the late partners' houses. In each case he had a deal of difficulty in getting through. To each he merely said that he had some very serious news to impart and that he was going round immediately. Then phoning for a police car, he set off.

First he called at Moxon's house in Hampstead. Mrs. Moxon had gone to bed, but in a surprisingly short time she appeared, terribly shocked and anxious.

"Bad news about my husband?" she said without further greeting. "Tell me, please, at once."

It was a job French hated. An intimate acquaintance with human misery had not blunted his feelings, and he found it a real effort to tell this poor woman that her husband was dead. Of other possible sorrows he said nothing. These would come soon enough.

Mrs. Moxon seemed quite stunned. French rang, and having learned from the butler that no other member of the family was at home, he sent for her maid. Then he told her about the journey to Newhaven. She declared at once that she would accompany him.

"If I may make a suggestion, madam," he said, with respectful kindness, "I would strongly urge you not to do so. Let me take your butler in the morning. He will do all that is necessary. I can promise you everything will be done with the greatest reverence."

She seemed grateful to French for his attitude and agreed about sending the butler in her place.

French promised to keep her advised of all that was done, and took his leave.

His visit to Deeping's house was not quite so painful. Here he saw the eldest son, a young fellow of about twenty. The youth was terribly upset by the news, and a frightened look in his eyes suggested that he feared greater trouble than mere bereavement. But he showed considerable self-control, undertaking to break the news to his mother and to be ready to accompany French in the morning.

It was nearly three when French reached home. He set his alarm clock for five-thirty, then creeping very quietly into bed, slept the sleep of the weary.

CHAPTER
FIVE

Newhaven

The next morning was one of the brightest and freshest French had ever experienced. His companions were waiting for him when he reached the Yard and they got away on the very stroke of the half-hour. As the car turned southwards over Westminster Bridge French felt that life was good. The sun, already well up in the sky, was burnishing up the buildings on the south side till they looked almost ethereal. The air came thin and cold to the nostrils, giving an exhilaration more intense than that of the wine to which it is so often likened. It was a morning for health and wholesomeness, a morning which made the grim quest on which they were engaged shrink back into the shadows like an evil and half-forgotten dream.

At such an hour there was practically no outward traffic and the major made good running. French sat with him in front, young Deeping between Carter and the butler in the tonneau. No one felt inclined for conversation. The major was occupied with his pipe and his driving and proved an indifferent companion. Carter and the butler took placidly what the morning brought, while to young Deeping the journey seemed a nightmare, relieved only by the quick passing of the miles.

"Our own doctor is following us down," French said soon after they started. "I rang him up this morning and he will come in his own car." It was a remark which did not seem to call for an answer and no one commented. French did not essay a second.

At Lewes Major Turnbull stopped.

"I don't know what you gentlemen feel like," he explained, "but I'm going to get some breakfast here. Better do the same, I think, French, and then you can get started right away when you arrive."

It was put to the vote and the ayes had it. Young Deeping alone would have liked to hurry on. He evidently wanted to get his hateful task done and leave the place and his companions as soon as it was humanly possible. French saw how things were and drew the young man aside. "I know how you feel," he said kindly, "but believe me a cup of coffee won't do you any harm. Come with us. We won't be long."

Breakfast over, they took the winding road along the side of the valley and were soon at Newhaven. Sergeant Heath was waiting for them, the photographs in his hand. Turnbull dealt with him tactfully.

"Well, sergeant," he said pleasantly, "between ourselves I've had rather a triumph. I've managed to shunt this whole case over to the Yard. We've nothing more to do with it and I'm sure you will be as thankful as I am. Here's Inspector French come to do the dirty work and we'll just hand over to him and let him go ahead." He turned to French. "Of course, Inspector, you may count on us for all the help we can give you. If there's anything you want, ask the sergeant and he'll do it for you."

This was just what French wanted and he gave the correct reaction.

"We'll not trouble you if we can help, sergeant," he wound up. "Now, if you would show us the mortuary, I should like to get these independent identifications and let these two gentlemen off."

"I must warn you, Mr. Deeping," French said as they followed the sergeant, "that your poor father has met with severe injuries. I'm afraid you'll get a shock when you see him. However, it is better than if your mother had to go through it."

The mortuary was a small white-washed building of the plainest type and spotlessly clean. The remains lay on marble slabs, and as the sheets, with which they were covered, were lifted off, it became apparent that French's warning to Deeping was not unnecessary. The witnesses were manifestly affected. Deeping shuddered visibly, while the butler crossed himself and hurriedly looked away.

As far, however, as French's purpose was concerned, a glance was sufficient. The two men quickly gave their testimony. There could be no shadow of doubt in either case as to identity. The deceased were the two senior partners of Moxon's General Securities.

"I'm sure you're glad that's over," French said as he left the building with his charges. "It's all that is wanted at present and you can go ahead with your arrangements about the funerals. Of course you understand that the

71

remains cannot be removed until after the inquest, but that won't mean a long delay. You'll have to be present, both of you, to give evidence of identity. The proceedings will be purely formal, as there's certain to be an adjournment."

"When will the hour be known?" Deeping inquired. "If it's soon, it won't be worth while going back to Town."

French sent Carter to inquire, then went on. "I said that the identification was all that was required, but, as a matter of fact, while we have this opportunity I should be glad if you would answer one or two questions. I should have to ask them sooner or later and it strikes me we might as well get them over."

Deeping agreeing, they retired to the sergeant's office, which had been put at French's disposal. The young man seemed numbed by the tragedy which had befallen his family and once again French sensed a hidden agony of apprehension in his manner. It was something more than sorrow for bereavement and French could not resist the conclusion that the son suspected financial troubles behind the disaster.

"When, Mr. Deeping," French began, holding out his cigarette case, "did you last see your father alive?"

The young man absently helped himself.

"On Wednesday morning," he answered. "We breakfasted together, as usual."

"You are not in the same business?"

"No, I am studying art."

"And was your father then perfectly normal? He didn't show excitement or anxiety or depression or any unusual emotion?"

Deeping hesitated and looked down. Then he answered doggedly: "He was a little depressed and anxious looking. He had looked so for two or three weeks. I took it that he probably had some business worries and I didn't, of course, comment on it."

"Did he seem more anxious on this occasion than formerly?"

"On the whole, I think he did. I could see there was something on his mind, but it never occurred to me that it could be anything really serious."

"Were you expecting him back that night?"

"No. Marvell told me — I should explain that Marvell is the butler — Marvell told me that he said that morning that he was going to a City dinner in the evening and wouldn't be home till late."

"Till late?"

"Yes, but he rang up again. About ten that same evening he telephoned to say that he had unexpectedly to go to the country and wouldn't be home for one or possibly two days."

"He didn't say where?"

"No."

"Did he take any luggage with him?"

"I asked that. Marvell said not. He had taken his dinner clothes in the morning. When he dined in Town he sometimes changed at his club and he said he would do so on this occasion. He had taken nothing for the night."

"I follow you. Now, Mr. Deeping, just one other question. Do you know anything, no matter how trifling, which might in any way throw light on this terrible affair?"

Deeping shook his head.

"I know nothing whatever," he declared emphatically.

French next turned to the butler. From him he heard a very similar story. Moxon also had left his house for the last time on the Wednesday morning. He had, however, said that he was going on a short business tour and would not be back for a couple of days. He had taken a small suit-case with night things and a change of clothes. It was an unusual, but not an unprecedented action on his part.

Moxon too, it appeared, had shown recent signs of mental strain and these had been particularly noticeable on that last morning. Normally, he was an exceptionally even-tempered man, but lately he had become irritable and nervy. For the week previous to his death he had practically given up all his social duties, spending the evenings in his study at work on figures of some kind. He had also been taking more spirits than he was accustomed to, more indeed sometimes than he could well carry. To the butler it had seemed as if he were heading for a breakdown.

At that moment Sergeant Heath put his head in to say that the inquest would be held at three o'clock that afternoon. He had seen the coroner and it had been decided that only evidence of identification would be taken, the proceedings then being adjourned.

French, having obtained all the information he could from his two witnesses, dismissed them with a cheery word of reminder of the need of their presence in the afternoon. He would have liked next to have examined the bodies, but as the police doctor had not yet turned up, he postponed this task, and calling Carter, went down to the *Nymph*.

She was still lying where she had come in, some six hundred yards down the river from the road bridge, and on the west side. On the east side the river is fronted by the usual vertical-walled quay, on which, a little lower down, is the Harbour Station and the berths of the Dieppe boats. On the west side there is no wharf in the ordinary sense, the river bank being an ordinary stone-pitched slope. Connection with shipping on this side is obtained by means of a row of separate gangways, projecting out from the bank like a series of miniature pierheads; spidery erections of timber piles. It was at one of these that the *Nymph* and launch were moored.

The two men climbed down a somewhat slippery ladder and reached the *Nymph's* deck. After a general look over the little vessel, French began one of his meticulous examinations. First, with the help of the photographs, he pictured how the deceased had been lying, then considered how they had come to fall into these positions. As he did so, a tentative theory of what must have happened formed in his mind.

The man in the cabin, Moxon, must, French thought, have been at lunch when the murder took place. On the table were the remains of his meal, an interrupted meal. Moxon had evidently finished a plate of cold meat and was actually engaged on some bread and cheese. A half-finished tumbler of beer stood beside his plate. The knife he had been using lay on the floor. A similar meal for a second person was laid, but remained untouched.

It seemed to French that Moxon had been shot from the entrance to the cabin while he was in the act of getting up from his seat. The position of the bullet wound was consistent with this idea, and the body would, he thought, have pitched forward and fallen where it was found.

As he looked about a bright object caught his eye. It was a cartridge case of fairly large bore and, he thought, of service pattern and it was still smelling of powder. It was lying on the floor in the left-hand corner, next to the companion steps and diagonally opposite the body. Its position seemed to strengthen French's theory, as it might well have been discharged from an automatic pistol pointed from the companion steps towards the dead man.

Further detailed search of the cabin revealed a second similar case. It had rolled behind the leg of the table, close to the companion steps, but on the right side of the cabin. For a time French was puzzled by its position, but when he went on deck and began to consider Deeping's end, he saw its significance.

A reconstruction of the position in which Deeping's body had been found showed him that the unfortunate man must have been coming forward towards the companion when the shot was fired. The man had not collapsed where he stood. His body had fallen forward so markedly that French was sure he must have been moving at the moment of death, possibly even running. He also was shot in the forehead, therefore his assailant had fired from the direction of the companion. In fact, French believed that he must have fired from the companion itself. This was, he now realised, confirmed by the position of the second cartridge case. Had the man been standing on the steps in a position from which he could command the deck, French saw that a shell case, discharged from his pistol, might well have fallen back into the cabin in the direction of the leg of the table.

It therefore seemed not unlikely that the murderer had gone down to the cabin and shot Moxon from the entrance as the unhappy man rose to meet him. Deeping, who was presumably at the wheel, had heard the explosion and come running aft. The murderer, swinging round, had rushed up the steps and fired his second shot as Deeping reached the companion.

If this theory were correct, something else emerged from it. The murderer must have been no stranger to his victims. Moreover, he must have been trusted as well as known. The attack was obviously unexpected.

French sat down to reconsider this idea. If he were right, it would surely represent a very important step forward in the inquiry. The number of persons who could appear on board without, as it were, upsetting the life of the ship must be very limited and it should be fairly easy to get a list of them. A list once obtained, elimination should do the rest.

It was therefore highly desirable that he should reach certainty on the point. As, however, he continued turning it over in his mind, he thought he had already reached certainty. In addition to the factors he had already thought of was another, and this other seemed to put the matter beyond doubt. These men were not ordinary travellers. They were, he believed, defaulters flying from justice. Therefore, was there the slightest chance of an unknown or distrusted person being allowed to move about the yacht unwatched? French felt there was none.

It was rather wonderful, he thought, that here at the very outset of the inquiry he should have made such progress. As he recalled other cases he had handled, in which after perhaps weeks of hard work he had not advanced so far, it seemed almost too good to be true.

It was not yet time, however, to report progress. French turned back to his attempted reconstruction of the crime.

The next point to be considered was the sinister trail across the deck. The drops of blood began at the embarkation opening in the rail and continued to the point at which Deeping's body had been lying. How had these been caused?

Failing a second wound, it was obvious that this gruesome trail could not have been made by Deeping. In such a case, who could have made it?

Only, he believed, the murderer. This had been Turnbull's theory and French thought it must be the truth. The murderer would have passed across that very stretch of deck in leaving the yacht, and if he had been injured, might have left just such a track.

French, whistling softly, went down on his knees and began to scrutinise the marks of the various drops. He was thinking that if a drop of liquid falls vertically on a horizontal surface it makes a more or less round mark. But if the source of the drop is moving horizontally, the drop itself falls obliquely and the resulting stain is more oval. Little sparks, moreover, frequently show on the forward side. He wondered if he could find any such indications in the present instance.

The result was entirely convincing. A proportion of the drops were oval or pear-shaped, very slightly, it is true, but still unmistakably. Further, the balance of the little sparklets surrounding the drops were at the end away from the companion. There could be no doubt whatever that the wounded person had been moving from the companion to the side of the yacht.

Second shot or no second shot, therefore, it was clear that the marks had not been made by Deeping. Presumably, therefore, they were made by the murderer.

Detection is very much like any other constructive work. The solution of every difficulty becomes the premise of a further problem. Such work advances by the overcoming of a never-ending series of difficulties, each of which is raised by the preceding success. In this case the conclusion that the murderer had been injured raised the more difficult question of how his injury had been received.

For a long time French could suggest no solution to this problem. Then at last he thought he saw how it might have occurred.

Deeping, at the wheel or elsewhere on deck, hears the shot fired below and at once realises that the visitor, whoever he may be, is their enemy. He seizes a knife, the only weapon he can lay his hands on, and rushes to the cabin. This hypothetical knife is probably lying in the wheel-house and may be a part of the yacht's equipment. Or Deeping may even have had a large pocket knife. At all events he seizes a knife from somewhere, reaches the companion as the murderer appears, and flings himself on him. The murderer at once not only fires, but tries to parry the blow. He does not entirely succeed. The knife catches him, probably in the left hand. His parry, however, coming with or just after the fatal shot, when the victim's muscles would be relaxing, knocks the knife out of Deeping's hand and it falls overboard and is lost. If the murderer struck inwards, as in the hurry of the moment he might, it would tend to throw Deeping's right hand across his body, and would therefore account for the fact that he was lying on it. The murderer's pause to ascertain if his evil work was properly done, would account for the pool of blood.

This, French recognised, was all the merest theory. At the same time it fitted the facts and might well be true. French put the idea aside, to be accepted or rejected in the light of future discoveries.

At this juncture Sergeant Carter, who had been ashore, reported that Dr. Hemingway had arrived and had made an examination of the remains. Though this was as yet only superficial, he had done enough to be sure that Deeping had only been wounded once.

"That's all right," French said. "Help me to complete the search of the yacht."

After another hour's hard work French was able to say positively that not only was there no weapon on board, but there was nothing else that so far as he could see threw any light on the tragedy.

It seemed then that shortly before the *Chichester* hove in sight on that fatal Thursday afternoon, the murderer, wounded, must have left the yacht. Did this, French wondered, offer further help?

It certainly implied one thing which might prove a very material clue, and that was, the presence of a boat. What boat could it have been? Was a boat seen? Surely such a boat could be traced.

Once again French whistled tunelessly below his breath as he considered these facts. The murderer was well known to the deceased and trusted by them. He was aware of the circumstances of the flight. He had a boat. He was in the neighbourhood at the time of the *Chichester's* passage . . .

The suggestion that the Assistant Commissioner and he himself had made to Major Turnbull recurred to him. Nolan was known to the deceased and presumably was trusted by them. He knew the circumstances of the flight. He had a launch. He was in the neighbourhood at the fatal hour . . .

French wondered if there would be any use in testing for fingerprints. On deck there would be none. Exposure to the weather for the most of a day and night would remove such traces, even if there had been any surface smooth enough to take records. But there were handrails at each side of the companion steps, polished handrails. It might be worth trying.

It did not take long to get the powdering apparatus rigged and make some tests. The result was embarrassing in its richness. There were prints literally all over the rails. French grunted with impatience as he settled down to photograph them all.

"A good bag," he said to Carter, who was helping with the camera. "Our friends in the finger-print department won't bless us when they see all this stuff coming in. But it's worth it. A find here might end our case."

"Got any light, sir?" Carter asked as he focused, exposed the plate, shifted the camera and focused again.

"I don't know," French returned. "I'll tell you what strikes me so far," and he explained the course of his ideas.

Carter was impressed. It seemed to him a fairly clear case. "Pretty good work, if you get it as quick as all that, sir," he considered. Then he dropped into silence and his absent manner and the lines on his forehead showed that the wheels of his mind were revolving.

"If you're right, sir," he said presently, "it shouldn't be hard to get proof."

"You think so? Go ahead then and trot it out."

"This way, sir. If Nolan was bleeding bad enough to make that track when he left the *Nymph*, he'd go on bleeding when he got into his launch. There's the launch beside us. What's wrong with a look over it?"

French laughed. "My good owl, what do you take me for? Of course we'll have a look over it. It's the next item on the programme."

The photographs completed, they moved to the launch. She was, as has been stated, decked over for some two-thirds of her length. The space beneath this deck was divided into three portions, a saloon, a tiny two-berth cabin, and a still tinier engine-room. In the cabin was a surprisingly large cupboard, locked. The key, however, was on Nolan's ring, and French found the locker contained a man's clothes, mostly yachting suits. As far as fittings were concerned, the boat was practically as well done as the *Nymph*, well above the average of her type.

Their search, however, proved disappointing. Nothing in any way helpful to the inquiry was found. Not only were there no bloodstains, but there was neither weapon nor cartridges. There were only a very few stores, fresh water and provisions, showing that a long trip was not intended. In fact, all they found seemed to bear out the statement of his movements which Nolan had made.

"I thought that theory too sweet to be wholesome," French commented when they had finished. "Come along and let's see the doctor and then we'll knock off for lunch."

They reached the mortuary to find that Dr. Hemingway had completed his examination of the remains.

"There you are," he said, displaying a couple of bullets in the palm of his hand. "Harmless looking, aren't they? But bad when they get into the wrong place. What do you make of them, French?"

French took the shell cases from his pocket.

"These have seen each other before, I fancy," he replied, fitting the one to the other. "Found these on board the *Nymph*. A Colt's Automatic, 38 bore, I think. Plenty of them about, unfortunately. We probably won't get much by trying to trace a sale."

"Those did the damage, at all events," the doctor went on. "That all you want?"

"Can you say from what distance the shots were fired?"

"No. Quite impossible with smokeless powder, except that in each case it was over three inches."

"Then the only other thing I want, doctor, is the approximate direction the bullets were travelling in."

The point was one which usually arose in cases of the kind and the doctor had obtained the information as part of his routine. His statement was in complete accord with French's reconstruction. If the murderer and his victims had been in the positions postulated by French, the bullets would have penetrated the unfortunate men's skulls as they had.

A search of the deceased's clothes gave a purely negative result. Except that the contents of the pockets confirmed the men's identity, French obtained no information.

"That's that," French grunted when he had finished his search. "Come along, Carter, and we'll see about that lunch."

CHAPTER
SIX

The Crash

In most of the cases with which French had been connected in the course of his long career, the great difficulty had been to find lines of investigation likely to yield profitable clues. Often for weeks at a stretch he had marked time, feeling himself up against a seemingly blank wall, unable to think of any method of approach to his problem which might give him a hint of the truth. In this case, so far at least, it was very different. There were so many avenues to be explored that his greatest difficulty was to decide which was the most promising. During lunch he turned the question over in his mind.

"I think," he said at last to Carter, "we've done everything here that is necessary in the meantime. The first thing is to find out more about Moxon's General Securities, whether it has really crashed, whether money has vanished, and whether any other partners or officials are missing. We'd better stay, I suppose, for this confounded inquest, then we'll take the first train to Town."

French filled the short time between lunch and the inquest by a further visit to the mortuary. There he took prints from the fingers of both the deceased. He noted mentally that he must also get the prints of the *Nymph's* caretaker, so that these three sets might be eliminated from those found on the companion handrails. Any remaining on the rails after this would form the basis of a line of inquiry of which the first step would be to obtain Nolan's for comparison.

By the time they had finished at the mortuary it was nearly three o'clock and they went on to the hall in which the inquest was to be held. The tragedy had attracted keen interest locally and a large number of the curious had assembled in the hope of a sensation. Though he thought it best to be present, French was not interested in the coroner's inquiry, and he and Carter found unobtrusive seats at the back.

The proceedings as a matter of fact were purely formal. Contrary to more recent practice, the jury elected to view the bodies. The Moxon butler and young Deeping then gave evidence of identity and the coroner adjourned the hearing to allow of further inquiries being made by the police.

When French reached Town he found it in the throes of a major sensation. The world of finance was rocking. Special editions of the evening papers were pouring out in a vast flood, only to be snatched up eagerly as they reached the streets. Everywhere were groups of anxious-looking people repeating to one another the huge scare headlines and delving in the letterpress either to learn the extent of the disaster or in the hope of finding something to assuage their fears.

86

French bought a number of papers, and going to his room, sat down to make up their contents. The best account seemed to be that of the *Afternoon Mail* and that he read thoroughly. Its editor had certainly risen to the occasion. In one-inch letters right across the top of the page ran the enormous headline:

HUGE FINANCIAL DISASTER IN THE CITY

Beneath that in three-column-width and heavily-leaded capitals were the captions:

MOXON'S GENERAL SECURITIES CRASHES
LIABILITIES APPROACH £8,000,000
FURTHER FAILURES FEARED
TRAGEDY ON TRAGEDY
TWO PARTNERS KILLED WHILE FLYING
THE COUNTRY
A THIRD PARTNER AND CHIEF ACCOUNTANT
MISSING
VAST DEFALCATIONS SUSPECTED
THOUSANDS RUINED.

Below these literary gems a paragraph of heavily leaded type followed, in which, after the manner of the yellow press, the captions were repeated in slightly different words. It read:

Moxon's General Securities this morning declared itself unable to meet its liabilities. The total deficit is believed to approach eight millions. A panic on

87

the Stock Exchange ensued, and it is feared that several other firms will become involved. Vast defalcations are suspected. Three partners and the chief accountant left London secretly on Wednesday. Of these, two partners, the chairman and vice-chairman, were the Mr. Paul A. Moxon and the Mr. Sydney Deeping who were yesterday found murdered in a yacht in the Channel. The remaining partner, Mr. Bryce Raymond, and the chief accountant, Mr. Joshua Esdale, are still missing. Thousands have already been ruined and it is feared that the tale of disaster is not yet complete.

After this summary the narrative shrank to mere large print in single column width.

This morning [it read] was announced one of the most disastrous financial failures that has ever taken place in this country, suggesting Wall Street at its very worst. Moxon's General Securities, a name which for the last fifty years has stood synonymous for everything that was sound and stable, has declared itself unable to meet its liabilities, in the midst of a panic unparalleled in this century. For some time vague rumours had been in circulation that all was not well with the firm. But yesterday, in the mysterious way in which such beliefs crystallise, it was freely stated in financial circles that the house was on the verge of a crash. All through the afternoon and evening these reports grew more and more insistent. To-day, as we have said, they were unhappily substantiated by the official announcement of the failure. The utmost sympathy is felt for the thousands of unfortunate people who had entrusted their money to the firm, and of whom many are irretrievably ruined. As we go to press it is announced that the total liabilities will probably amount to the enormous total of eight millions sterling.

For some weeks, it is now stated, the firm has been in difficulties. The times of course are bad and normal calls were heavier than had been anticipated. At the same time a succession of heavy losses had to be met, due to failures and lowered dividends from outside firms. It was believed that by judicious handling the firm would have weathered the storm, had no further disaster occurred to prevent its recovery. Unfortunately such a disaster was forthcoming.

It has now become known that the firm was heavily involved in the recent failure of Messrs. Millwater & Hooversack, of Bombay. This failure proved the straw which broke the camel's back. Half a million of soundly invested stock became worthless and Moxon's General Securities lost an asset which might have made all the difference to it in its present difficulties.

What brought matters to a head was the fact that this morning the firm had, in the normal course of business, to meet a number of heavy charges, estimated to total over a million. In preparation therefore the partners had for some time been realising securities, and a very large sum in cash was lying in the cellars. The exact amount of this sum is not yet known, but it is believed to have been not less than a million and a half sterling. The most sinister feature of the affair is that practically the whole of this vast amount has disappeared.

Coincident with this information comes the news of the departure in the small hours of Thursday morning of three of the partners, Mr. Paul A. Moxon, Mr. Sydney L. Deeping and Mr. Bryce Raymond. These three gentlemen were present on Wednesday evening at the dinner to welcome the South American Chartered Accountants' Association, of which representatives are now on a visit to this country. After the dinner the partners simply disappeared. Messrs. Moxon and Raymond had that morning informed their respective households that they would be away for a couple of days, and while the dinner was in progress Mr. Deeping rang up his home to give similar information. To this must be added the fact that Mr. Joshua Esdale, the chief accountant, left on Wednesday afternoon for Paris, with the expressed intention of bringing back certain securities, and has not been heard of since. The deduction from these facts is, we fear, only too obvious.

Mr. J. Patrick Nolan, another of the partners, has since been working might and main to minimise the disaster. He also was present at the dinner on Wednesday evening, and as he was leaving he was asked by Mr. Moxon to go next day to Fécamp, between Dieppe and Havre, to meet a French financier on the firm's business. It seems that Messrs. Moxon and Raymond had arranged to make this journey in the former's yacht *Nymph*, as after business they wished to take the financier out sailing. Mr. Moxon, however, told Mr. Nolan that his brother-in-law, who lived in Buxton, had just been killed in a motor accident while returning from the theatre, and that he must go down to see to things for his sister. Mr. Nolan agreed to go on his own launch, and it was arranged that Mr. Raymond would meet him at Dover in the morning. Mr. Raymond, however, failed to turn up, and Mr. Nolan went on alone. Inquiries this morning in Buxton revealed the illuminating fact that no accident had happened to Mr. Moxon's brother-in-law, nor had any telephone message been sent from there to Mr. Moxon.

TRAGEDY IN THE CHANNEL.

As was reported in our later editions yesterday, the Southern Railway Company's steamer *Chichester*, engaged on the day service from Newhaven to Dieppe, on Thursday, came up with a motionless yacht, which at first seemed deserted. A man, apparently dead, was then noticed on the deck and the *Chichester* stopped and sent a boat to investigate. The man on the deck was actually dead and a second man, also dead, was lying in the saloon. Both had been shot through the head. The *Chichester* left a crew on board to work the yacht to Newhaven, where it was met by members of the Sussex County Constabulary.

It happened that on the way to Fécamp Mr. Nolan crossed the path of the yacht as she was being worked to Newhaven. He recognised her as Mr. Moxon's boat, the *Nymph*, and going alongside, learned of the tragedy. He identified the deceased as Messrs. Moxon and Deeping, his two co-partners. What the unhappy men were doing on board is not yet known. Nor has any trace yet been found of Messrs. Raymond and Esdale, the missing partner and chief accountant.

The paper went on to repeat this story a number of times in different words and sequences. With extraordinary cleverness something like nine and a half columns were filled with solid and quite readable matter. Short biographies were given of the dead and missing men; a list of previous large failures was added, with dates and amounts; the consequences of these were printed; prophecies were indulged in as to the result this failure would have on finance, on trade, on foreign securities and English prestige. Heartrending pictures were drawn of the loss and ruin likely to fall on individuals, with human interest stories purporting to be details of actual cases. In fact, as French thought to himself, the editor had seen a good thing and had bit on to it for all he was worth.

French read every word, but the only other fact that seemed interesting was that the deceased Paul A. Moxon was the nephew of the Hugh H. Moxon who had founded the house in 1882.

On reaching the Yard, French went as in duty bound to his immediate superior, Chief-Inspector Mitchell. He was told, however, that the Assistant Commissioner wished to handle the case himself and that he was to report direct to him.

When French reached Sir Mortimer's room he found that a conference was in progress. At least Sir Mortimer was talking, and two of French's colleagues, Inspectors Tanner and Willis, were listening.

"Come along, French. You're just in time," Sir Mortimer said pleasantly. "The chief-inspector has to meet those representatives of the New York police, so I'll hear what you have to say myself."

French told his story as concisely as he could. The others followed with close attention.

"You've had the best of it," Sir Mortimer commented when he had finished. "This place has been like a hornet's nest all day. I suppose you've heard that another partner and the accountant are missing, as well as something like a million and a half sterling?"

"I've just seen it in the paper, sir."

"A pretty serious job this is growing into. The most serious we've had for many a long day." The Assistant Commissioner shook his head. "I should tell you, French, that we've made fairly exhaustive inquiries, and every one else in the concern, except those two, was at his work to-day. When you came in I had just made the obvious remark."

"Meaning that it certainly looks like one or both of them, sir?"

"Now you've made it too. Yes, that's what I mean. It looks so like it that we've got to find them both at once. That's why I've brought in Tanner and Willis. No reflection on you, French; it's simply that there's too much for one man. I've arranged that Tanner will take over the tracing of Raymond, that's the partner, and Willis will get on to Esdale, the accountant. You, French, will continue working on Nolan."

French was disappointed to find the plums going past him.

"You still think there's a chance that Nolan may be guilty, sir?" he asked a trifle dubiously.

"Of course, there's a chance. As I see it, the evidence is fairly similar against all three men. All were in highly confidential positions and it's difficult to see how they could have been ignorant of what was going on. And if they knew of the fraud, we may take it they knew of the get-away. In fact, Raymond's and Esdale's disappearance proves it. And Nolan's turning up and coming back to London may be just his way of throwing dust in our eyes."

Sir Mortimer paused, looking interrogatively round his audience.

"That's certainly true, sir," French said tactfully, "and, of course, Nolan's tale that Moxon had asked him to go to Fécamp, which constitutes his explanation for his trip, is just the kind of tale he would invent to account for it, as it cannot be disproved owing to Moxon's death."

"Quite. It means then that the cases of all three must be gone into equally completely. And that's what I want you men to do. The case, as a whole, is yours, French. As soon as you have reached certainty about Nolan you will take over from Tanner, and as soon as you have reached certainty about Raymond you will take over from Willis. I should tell you that I've also got a finance expert from the Home Office at the headquarters of the firm, going into the question of what exactly is missing. Mr. Honeyford, it is. I think you've met him, French? Probably you'll have to retain Honeyford, but the sooner you can release these other two, the better pleased I'll be."

French said he would do his best.

"It'll take it," Sir Mortimer returned dryly. He paused, then went on, "Anything else any of you can think of?"

No one spoke for a moment, then French asked if it was actual cash that had disappeared.

"Yes, notes."

"The numbers should be known."

Sir Mortimer made a whimsical gesture of admiration.

"Do you know that the same profound idea struck me? As a result, one of Honeyford's first duties is to send in a list of all the numbers that he can learn. You'd better see him about that, French, and get the necessary advice out to the banks as soon as possible."

"I'll see to it at once, sir."

Sir Mortimer nodded. "I'm not sentimentally inclined, as you know, French," he went on presently, "but really when I think of all the innocent people who are going to suffer through these dirty scoundrels, I'd give a big bit of my salary to know they were safe in Dartmoor. I know a case in point. Two old maiden ladies living close to us, friends of my wife's. I happen to know they had invested their whole worldly goods through Moxon's General Securities. What is there for them now? The poorhouse? And their case will only be one of thousands. And even where the whole livelihood is not gone, it may still be bad enough. Think of all the people who will now have to give up sending their sons to a decent school. And all that will have to do without their holiday and little pleasures they had been counting on perhaps for years. I tell you, French, it'll not be the fault of this department if those fellows have any more happiness in this world." French wholeheartedly agreed.

"But weren't there other partners, sir, besides these three? What were they thinking about?"

"Figureheads, the whole of them. At least, that's the excuse now. Knew nothing about what was going on. It's a lovely system! They were got in because they had handles to their names, to create public confidence. Public confidence! Remember Carlyle's 'mostly fools'? Sometimes you think he wasn't far wrong."

"But that doesn't apply to Nolan?"

"No. Nolan is the dark horse at present. He's supposed to have been alive to things. However, that's your job."

"Yes, sir."

The Assistant Commissioner swung round in his chair and the three inspectors, taking the hint, rose. "I'll go along to the head office now, sir," French added. "I'll see Mr. Honeyford and get things moving."

It was a long time, French thought as he drove towards Threadneedle Street, since he had seen Sir Mortimer so moved. The Assistant Commissioner was a man who, while utterly relentless in his war on crime, not infrequently showed a surprising sympathy with the criminal. He always deplored the punishment of the out-of-work or the poorly paid, who, seeing his family in want, had stolen to relieve their immediate needs. Even on occasion he had surprised French by expressing regret as to the fate of murderers. Murderers, he held, were by no means necessarily hardened criminals. In their ranks they numbered some of the most decent and inoffensive of men. But for the wealthy thief who stole by the manipulation of stocks and shares and other less creditable methods known to high finance, whether actually within or without the limits of the law, he had only the most profound enmity and contempt.

A constable stationed at the side door of the Moxon's General Securities building admitted French. Though it was close on eight o'clock there was still a buzz of activity in the great offices. It was true that most of the clerks and all the juniors had gone home, but the heads of departments remained at their depressing task of estimating the losses. To most of them the crash had come as a hideous and devastating

97

surprise. While few of the subordinate officers doubted that they could have managed the business better than those who were actually in charge, this was only in the nature of things, and none at bottom had any but the most profound confidence in its prosperity. The failure was for them an overwhelming blow. Not only were their cherished beliefs thus rudely shattered, but the same cataclysm took from them their means of support. Small wonder was it that pale anxious faces and hushed voices were the rule.

French found Nolan and Honeyford poring over ledgers in Moxon's room, a large ornately furnished chamber, evidently intended, like the titled partners, to inspire confidence in the lay mind. With them were a couple of the higher-grade officers, with a girl stenographer to take down the figures and conclusions as these were reached. At French's appearance Nolan threw down his pen and sat back in his chair. His face looked gray and drawn and there were dark rings under his eyes.

"There's eight o'clock," he said in a dull voice. "I'm through. I can't go on any longer. I've had no sleep for the last two nights and practically no food to-day and I'm done. You people can either carry on, or better, go home and leave the cursed thing till to-morrow."

Honeyford also sat back.

"I agree with Mr. Nolan," he declared. "I think we've had enough. I propose that we adjourn till the morning. Let us leave all these books exactly as they are and get a couple of policemen in to see they're not interfered with." He rose slowly, looking at French. "Aren't you

Inspector French from the Yard? You remember we met years ago over those Mincing Lane frauds? Do you think you can get us a couple of men to watch these books to-night? It's quite a job putting them away."

"Good-evening, gentlemen," French said, advancing into the room. "Glad to meet you again, Mr. Honeyford. I'll arrange the constables, of course. I'm in luck to find you and Mr. Nolan here. I wanted a word with you both."

"I'm afraid it'll only be a short word you'll get with me, Inspector," Nolan declared, "unless talking in my sleep would be any good to you." He got up and stretched himself wearily. The attendant officials, after a moment's hesitation, did the same. Honeyford was left seated alone.

"Better than nothing, Mr. Nolan," French smiled. He sat down beside Honeyford and went on in a lower tone, "I've just seen the Assistant Commissioner and he asked me to get in touch with you about this affair. There is one point, Mr. Honeyford, that he's very keen on, and that is, the numbers of the missing notes. Is that going to be an easy thing to get?"

"It's not going to be easy at all. I've not had time to go into it thoroughly, but so far as I've been able to learn, there are no records of these numbers here. The only chance of getting them is by tracing the payments at the various banks at which they were obtained, when the tellers' memoranda would be available."

French shrugged. "It doesn't sound too hopeful," he admitted, "if there's no note of the payments."

"There isn't. The whole thing was evidently done secretly."

"That's only to be expected. All the same, Mr. Honeyford, I must get it under way. If I came in here to-morrow morning, could you spare me time to discuss it?"

"I take it, Inspector, that's what I'm here for."

"Right, I'll be round about nine-thirty. Goodnight, Mr. Honeyford. I'll send you those constables. Now, Mr. Nolan, if you're ready perhaps we might go together and we could talk on the way."

They reached the street in silence, French pausing to give instructions as to the watching of the books. Then he turned to Nolan.

"I'm really sorry, Mr. Nolan," he said, "to trouble you to-night when you are so tired, but there are a few questions I must ask, as my investigation is being held up for want of information. Look here, would you come and dine with me? I suggest a room at the Orleans. It's a quiet place and we can talk in peace. During dinner I should think you could give me everything I want."

Nolan hesitated. It was evident that he would have preferred to go home. However, under the circumstances he could not very well help himself, and with not too good a grace he accepted the invitation.

CHAPTER
SEVEN

What Nolan Had to Tell

The Orleans was a small French restaurant in King Street which made a speciality of simple, but extremely good food. A private room was vacant and before many minutes French and his victim were installed therein.

"A drink, for the love of Mike!" said the victim as he flung himself down on a couch which ran along one wall in place of a sideboard.

Here was an unexpected opportunity, far too good to be missed.

"I'll order it," French said swiftly, and left the room before his guest could ring the bell. In the passage outside some shillings changed hands, with the result that the drink arrived in a specially cleaned glass, which when being cleared away was handled by the rim, and which, carefully packed, afterwards found its way to the Yard.

In the next five minutes Nolan had disposed of three of the Orleans' specialities, the principal constituent of which seemed to be neat brandy. They had an immediate effect. A drain of colour came back to his face, the drawn look relaxed, and he sat up comparatively briskly.

"Lord, I wanted that!" he exclaimed. "Ghastly job down in that office! Fairly takes it out of you."

"I believe you," French answered. "All the same, whatever things may be actually, they look worse when a man's hungry. You've had a bad three days, Mr. Nolan."

Nolan had no words to describe how bad. He simply made an imprecation indicative of the *ultima thule* in badness and let it go at that.

French changed the subject. "You're an Irishman, surely, Mr. Nolan?" he essayed. "Irish name, isn't it?"

"Limerick," the other returned morosely. "And I'm wishing I'd stayed there."

"I've got a friend who's been working near there for the last couple of years — at Ardnacrusha, the power house of the Shannon hydro-electric scheme. Ever seen the workings?"

Nolan had never seen the workings nor did he care a blanked Continental if he ever did see them. In fact, Nolan was in a thoroughly unhappy frame of mind and French was glad when the *hors d'œuvres* appeared.

However, under the mellowing influence of good food the man's outlook improved, and by the time black coffee was tempering the soporific influence of a good cigar, it had become almost normal. French waited for a suitable opportunity, then during a lull in the conversation he returned to business.

"What I really wanted to ask you, Mr. Nolan, was for some general information as to the running of the firm and a more detailed account of your own movements during the last three days. Your statement to Major

Turnbull was quite sufficient for the then requirements, but I have to get every detail on paper and I want more now. Would it be too much to ask you to give it to me to-night?"

Nolan sighed. "I'd be as well to get it over, I suppose," he said in resigned tones. "That dinner of yours has made me a new man anyway, so forge ahead and tell me what you want to know."

"First I'd like a short account of your firm and its partners."

Nolan, who seemed no longer unwilling to talk, settled himself at full stretch on the couch and in the intervals of drawing at his cigar, held forth.

"Moxon's General Securities is, as you know, a very big concern. It deals literally in millions and its ramifications spread all over the Continent and to America as well. It was started by Moxon's uncle about fifty years ago. He built it up from small beginnings and as it grew he retained the controlling interest and he became chairman. The late Moxon, my co-partner, succeeded him in this capacity. Deeping was at one time the cashier. He put his savings into the concern, was taken into partnership, and later became vice-chairman. These two, as I told you, acted as sort of joint managing directors.

"There were twelve partners altogether. Of the other ten, myself and Raymond were really executives. We were whole time workers in the concern and did practically all the supervision. Three other partners, Sir Garnett Chislehurst, Lord Melby and Mr. Arthur Grantham took an occasional and desultory interest in things. They did nothing towards the actual carrying on of the business and only occasionally attended the board meetings. The remaining five were purely sleeping partners. The others concerned, Esdale, the accountant, Knowles, the chief clerk and the rest of the officials, were officers pure and simple, who attended to their own departments, did what they were told, and had no voice whatsoever in policy. Is that all you want about the firm?"

"Yes, that's very clear. I'd like to know something now about this big cash realisation."

"We were all in that. It's been going on for several weeks. To-day, as you know, the firm had to meet very heavy payments, and cash was being accumulated for the purpose."

French nodded. He knew little about finance, yet this turning of securities into actual money scarcely seemed to him to ring true. However, that was where Honeyford came in.

"We've always done it in the same way," Nolan went on, as if he thought some justification was necessary. "We've gradually accumulated what would be wanted to meet our outpayments. Usually the money has been lodged in the bank at intervals and the debts discharged by cheque."

"That wasn't done in this instance."

"It was not," Nolan admitted despondently, "and I'm afraid we're seeing the reason for it now."

"The failure to lodge this realised cash in the bank didn't rouse your suspicions at the time?"

"I didn't even know it hadn't been lodged. Moxon and Deeping were looking after it. I wasn't worrying about it at all."

"Very good, Mr. Nolan. Is there anything else that you can tell me that you think might help my investigation?"

"Not a thing. Sure you know all the rest. I've told you already about my going to the dinner on Wednesday night and about Moxon asking me to see Pasteur at Fécamp; also about my starting off there and coming up with the *Nymph*. That's the lot."

"Yes, that's all quite clear. Your story now takes us up to yesterday, Thursday mid-day. As you say, I know what happened then. You returned to Newhaven, reported to the police, came to Town with Major Turnbull, and I saw you last night at the Yard. Now just give me an idea of what happened to-day."

Nolan ground out the stub of his cigar and carefully selected another.

"To-day was hell," he announced. "I went down to the office about eight. Knowles was there before me as white as a sheet — I had rung him up and asked him to come in early — and in a few minutes Melby and Grantham came in, both looking scared and shaky. The first thing was to get the strong-room opened. It took two directors to be present, you understand. I had a key, but the only other keys in existence had been Moxon's and Deeping's, and they were held by your people at the Yard. So we rang up the Yard and the keys were sent at once. We opened the strong-room and then the fat was in the fire."

"Did you know how much was gone?"

"It was all gone, Mr. French. We didn't know, not at first, how much there had been, though we knew there must have been hundreds of thousands. I went to my office with Knowles, who was the only man who knew anything about our position, and we talked it over. Our cash was nearly out and a telephone to the directors of one or two of the big banks showed us we weren't going to get any outside help at all. I decided to close down. My faith, Mr. French, it was a terrible moment! But there was nothing else I could do."

"Then you started in to find out the worst?"

"That's exactly what we did. We soon learned that there must have been over a million in that strong-room, and by the afternoon it had gone up to a million and a half."

"Pretty desperate."

"And that wasn't all," went on Nolan despairingly. "Other debts began to come out, then assets that we had been counting on were found to have dwindled down to half-nothing — I mean the returns from investments and so on. Altogether in one way or another we were down hopelessly. Eight millions, more or less."

"Terrible," French commented absently. He was favourably impressed with this statement of Nolan's. It certainly rang true and the man's way of telling it inspired confidence. French could see in imagination the entire action, and he felt that Nolan's conduct during the day was just what it should have been. He ran over the story in his mind and then began to ask questions.

"I think you said that the first thing you heard about going to France was at the dinner?"

"After the dinner, just as we were getting ready to go home."

"Quite so. Mr. Moxon told you. Now did any one overhear your conversation?"

"Part of it. We, Moxon and I, wondered how we could let the office know I wouldn't be there. We thought of Garnett Chislehurst, who was also at the dinner. I told you he was another of our partners. We sent a boy to find him. Moxon explained the thing to him and asked him would he put in an appearance at the office next day in case his signature might be wanted. Sir Garnett said he would and that he'd explain what had occurred."

"What is the name of Mr. Moxon's boatman in Folkestone?"

"John Hurley. I don't know his exact address, but he lives a couple of doors from the Angel Tavern, just going down to the Inner Harbour."

"And of your own man at Dover?"

"John Squance, 17B Pilot Street."

"Good. Now, Mr. Nolan, I don't think you actually said it, but I rather gathered it was in your mind that all three of the missing partners had gone on the *Nymph?*"

Nolan moved uneasily. "The thing did pass through my mind," he admitted, "but, of course, I had no reason at all to think so. Really I know nothing about it."

"Were you not surprised all the same to find no trace of Mr. Raymond aboard?"

"I was not. I was so much surprised and horrified to find what I did find that I didn't think of anything else."

"And since?"

"Since, of course, I have wondered where Raymond disappeared to."

"You never had a suspicion?"

"I had not. What are you getting at, at all?"

French sat forward and lowered his voice confidentially.

"I suppose you never thought of Mr. Raymond as the author of the tragedy?"

Nolan started. "You mean that Raymond murdered the other two?" he asked sharply. "No, I never thought of that, and neither would you if you had known Raymond. Sure the very idea's absurd! No, if that's the line you're going on, Inspector, you'd be better leaving the job to some one else."

French was pleased rather than otherwise at his vehemence.

"I merely asked a question," he pointed out mildly. "I made no accusation."

"Well, it was a darned silly question," Nolan retorted, adding, "If that's all you want, Inspector, I'd like to get home. I've an idea that bed would be about my ticket."

"I still only want two things. The first is the addresses of your remaining partners, accountant, and head clerk."

French noted these, then continued: "The second thing is that I've had instructions that every one connected in any way with this affair must be examined

108

by a doctor. The point is this. For certain reasons we believe the murderer was wounded aboard the *Nymph*. Any one bearing the mark of a recent wound would therefore come under temporary suspicion. Have you any objection to being examined yourself?"

Nolan stared.

"Does that mean, Inspector, that you're suspecting me of the crime?"

"It means nothing of the kind, as I'm sure you know very well. It's a precaution which we have to take in connection with every one concerned."

Nolan continued to stare. Then he shrugged lightly.

"Does the converse apply?"

"You mean that if a person has no wound he must be innocent? Not necessarily, but it would tend in that direction."

"Then," Nolan said decisively, "I'll be examined by all means. If it's going to preserve me from a new trouble it'll be worth it. Do you want it done now?"

"If you please, sir," answered French, who believed in striking while the iron was hot.

Nolan grumbled for a moment, then agreed. French immediately rang up a police doctor, and in twenty minutes they were at his house. The examination was carried out at once, the doctor reporting that Nolan bore no scar nor sign of a wound, and that bleeding leaving the traces which had been described, could not have come from him.

This at least was progress, if negative, but, of course, it only confirmed the conclusion suggested from the examination of Nolan's launch.

It was getting on to eleven when French said good-night to his victim. He, French, had no illusions as to the efficacy of bed in his case also. He had been at it since five-thirty that morning, and he was tired. At the same time it was not only a very important case, but also one in which time was a vital factor. A good deal might depend on the way he handled it. Inspector Tanner did not live so far out of his way, and he thought he would call for a last pipe and learn what his colleague had been up to during the day.

Of all his colleagues, Tanner was French's greatest friend. They had worked together in many a case, and though wild horses would not have dragged it from either, each had a lively admiration and regard for the other. Not once only had they risked their lives in a common effort to lay by the heels some dangerous criminal. The adventure with the Mills' bomb in the refreshment room at Waverley Station, Edinburgh, at the dramatic close of the Starvel Hollow tragedy, was only one occasion of many where the prompt help of the one had saved the life of the other. With the passing of the years this friendship had only grown stronger. Indeed it had survived perhaps the greatest test which could have been imposed on it, a walking tour in the Scottish highlands lasting for ten days, nine of which were wet.

Tanner and his wife were deep in a couple of novels at the open window of their sitting-room when French appeared. They smilingly drew up another chair and for a few moments the three sat chatting. Then Mrs.

Tanner discreetly became sleepy and the men were left alone.

"So I've had to do another of your jobs for you," Tanner said wearily. "Disgusting habit, not being able to look after your own cases."

Tanner dearly loved what he called a joke, and particularly made efforts worthy of a better cause in trying to take rises out of French, usually with but poor success.

"Well, you can't spend your whole life in idleness," French retorted. "If it wasn't for my letting you do small routine jobs for me, you'd lose the power of movement."

For a moment they sparred amicably like two great children, then French turned to business.

"I wondered how things were going on the job?" he inquired.

"I wondered the same," Tanner answered dryly.

"I've had a decent excursion at all events," French told him. "Newhaven. Went down this morning with Turnbull in his car. Yachts, launches, inquests, bodies; quite an entertainment."

"D'you get anything?"

"The usual thing; plenty of suspicions and no proof."

Tanner began moving about the room, getting out whisky and a siphon. "Say when," he invited, adding sepulchrally, "That Raymond did it."

French sipped his whisky.

"Nolan doesn't think so," he countered.

"Of course Nolan doesn't think so. How on earth would he, and the two of them supposed to be friends? But it's Raymond all the same."

111

"Why do *you* think so?"

"Why? Elimination. There's nobody else."

"Talking through your hat, son," French said genially. "Tell me what I want to know and let me get to bed. Been at it since five-thirty."

Tanner, when at last pinned down to facts, had not a great deal to tell.

"The A.C., as you know, put me on to tracing Raymond. I've not done it, but I've found out that he started as a clerk, came into money, put it into the business, and two years ago was made a partner. He is now aged thirty-three, has a pleasant manner, and is a general favourite. So much for the man himself."

"No bad traits?"

"Not that I've heard of."

"So you deduce he's a murderer. Good. Go ahead, old man."

"Then I went along to his rooms. He has a rather tiny little flat in Half Moon Street, small, but everything very much so. Man and wife in attendance. Decent looking couple. The man said that late on the Tuesday evening, the evening before the dinner, Raymond told him that he'd be out of Town for a couple of days. He would be leaving the next morning, Wednesday, and would want his evening things as well as a suit of yachting clothes. He did not say where he was going or when exactly they might expect him back. He seemed perfectly normal in every way and was in excellent spirits. In the morning the man packed for him and got him a taxi. He left after breakfast at his usual time.

"The taxi had been taken from a nearby stand and I found it without any trouble. Raymond had been driven to the office. He had gone there straight, without stopping or paying any calls *en route.*"

"Looks as if he hadn't anticipated trouble," French suggested. "He could scarcely have been normal in manner if he had all this business on his mind."

"So you might think, but you couldn't really be sure. I went back to the office and made some further inquiries. Raymond had had his suit-case taken up to his room, where it had stood all day. He had worked late with Moxon, then they had both changed at the office and had driven to the dinner. They had gone in Moxon's car and both had taken their suit-cases; I found the porter who had put them in. Next I went round to Hallam's, where the dinner was held. The function broke up about midnight and Moxon and Raymond went off in Moxon's car."

French was impressed.

"In Moxon's car?" he repeated.

"In Moxon's car."

"By jove, Tanner, that gives you something to think of right enough! If Raymond went with Moxon and Moxon cleared out on his yacht, what's wrong with Raymond going in the yacht also?"

Tanner grinned.

"And if," French went on, disregarding him, "Raymond went on the yacht — Why, I can tell you, that's pretty suggestive."

"Go on," said Tanner.

"If Raymond went on the yacht, well, he has disappeared, same as the money; and his companions are dead. You're right, it's certainly beginning to look as if Raymond might be our man."

"You shouldn't commit yourself too irrevocably," said Tanner anxiously. "You know you're really only guessing."

"Well, we've got to find Raymond and make sure. I should get on with it, if I were you, and not hold the whole case up."

If Raymond really had left Folkestone in the *Nymph*, and if there had been some means whereby he could have got away from her in mid-Channel, there would certainly be a pretty strong circumstantial case against him. The inspectors agreed that these possibilities were vital to the inquiry and must be gone into at once.

"You didn't find out anything about their actual start?"

"I phoned to the Folkestone sergeant and he replied that the *Nymph* had put to sea at five-fifty on that Thursday morning, but he didn't know who was on board and I've not had time as yet to go into it personally."

French agreed that a visit was necessary.

"I'll try it to-morrow," Tanner wound up the conversation. "I'll go down to Folkestone first thing and get the details of the start. If I can find that Raymond joined the others, it will be something."

French whole-heartedly agreed. Then he repeated that it was getting late and that he was sleepy and was going home.

Half an hour later he was in bed.

CHAPTER
EIGHT

The Start of the Launch

After a visit to the yard next morning to report progress, French went on to Threadneedle Street to keep his appointment with Honeyford.

The great building with its closed doors and empty windows seemed already to have taken on a woebegone appearance, as if the very stones and glass knew that calamity had touched its inmates. French, ringing at a side door, obtained admission and in a few minutes was seated with Honeyford in the late Paul Moxon's room. For some moments they talked of the case generally, then French got to business.

"What I want to discuss with you, Mr. Honeyford, is how we are to get the numbers of the notes and bonds which have disappeared."

Honeyford repeated that it would not be easy. Not only had no note of the numbers been kept in the Securities office, but he now strongly suspected that the records of the various realisations had been destroyed. If so, it meant that he would have no way of finding out from whom the cash had been received. He could not go round to the banks and ask them for a list of the numbers of the notes of such and such a payment, as he himself did not know what payments had been made.

"Awkward," French agreed. "Could it not be done the other way round?"

"How d'you mean?"

"Ask a number of likely banks what cash or bond payments, if any, they had made to Moxon's within the last few weeks. See if you can get anywhere near the total that way."

Honeyford smiled pityingly.

"I did that yesterday; almost the first thing after I came over. But I'm not hopeful of the result."

"Why not, Mr. Honeyford? To me it seems a pretty sure line."

Honeyford lit another cigarette.

"I'll tell you why I don't think so," he answered slowly. "If these people were going to make a break such as we suspect, they'd never collect that cash openly. It would be got in with the help of some misleading trick and probably only in small amounts. Possibly it may have only been obtained from banks in the provinces and foreign capitals. However, as I say, I'll do what I can, and if you are not satisfied you can take a hand yourself."

French tactfully thought that if Mr. Honeyford had the matter in hand, nothing else would be needed.

"Pretty deliberate, the whole thing?" he went on, accepting a cigarette.

About this Honeyford was non-committal. "Yes and no," he said, "if 'yes and no' constitutes an answer. It seems to me, again tentatively, as if the failure was quite genuine. I mean that it was unavoidable and that the partners tried to prevent it to the best of their ability and in perfectly good faith. I think they were in a ticklish position as a result of the generally depressed conditions, the aftermath of war, over-production, unemployment, and all the rest of our present troubles. Then before they could get right there came the Wall Street crash and after it the Hatry case. Their losses from each of these were enormous, and they cannot be blamed for it."

"It's the way most of these frauds begin, isn't it?"

"Quite. I'm sure they did their best for a while. But where I think they went wrong was that when they saw the crash coming they didn't go into liquidation at once and so minimise it."

"Hoping always for the best?"

"I don't think so. I think by then it had got past that. I think they saw ruin and disgrace coming and they could do nothing to stave it off, so they said in effect: 'Charity begins at home; we'll save ourselves and get out with what we can. What we take will make little difference.'"

"If they were going to start a new life, they might as well have an income to do it on."

"Quite, and once they had taken that view the thing went from bad to worse. If they were going to take enough to live on, why not take enough to live comfortably? And if enough to live comfortably, why not enough for luxury for the rest of their lives? And particularly for safety. They wanted money for safety. In

117

fact, once the first wrong step was taken, the rest would follow almost inevitably."

There was silence for a few moments, both men smoking thoughtfully.

"Somehow it doesn't seem so bad, put in that way," French said at last. "Not that I'm trying to whitewash them."

Honeyford threw his cigarette into the grate.

"Nothing is so bad as it seems to the man who is ignorant of the inside circumstances," he declared. "Surely, Inspector, a man of your experience ought to know that?"

"Well, well," French returned, rising and stubbing out his cigarette, "life's too short to get metaphysical. I've got to go and earn some bread and butter. Many thanks, Mr. Honeyford. I'll come in and see you again shortly."

It seemed to French that now that he was in the Securities building, it would be a suitable time to interview Knowles, the chief clerk. He did not expect to get much information from him and the interview need not therefore take up much time.

He had for some reason unknown to himself formed a mental picture of Knowles as a benevolent, white-haired old man of timorous mien, a man more of the old-fashioned retainer type than of the wide-awake business expert of to-day. It was therefore with an unreasonable feeling of surprise that he found the chief clerk to be as complete a contrast to his preconception as was well possible. A medium tall, middle-aged man with a dark saturnine face, sallow skinned and lantern

118

jawed, and with a pair of the shrewdest eyes French had ever seen, set close under a high, narrow forehead. Too shrewd to be quite wholesome, those eyes. French felt that this was a personality and not an attractive one at that.

Knowles, however, proved himself anxious to help. He answered French's questions fully and without evasion. Unfortunately the result of his examination was surprisingly meagre.

According to Knowles, Moxon, Deeping, Nolan and Raymond each spent the whole of their time at the office, and all worked hard and efficiently. The other partners were a negligible quantity. Knowles, however, refused to confirm or deny the statement that Nolan and Raymond were in ignorance of what was going on. Knowles stuck to it that in their position as partners they had access to all the facts, though to what extent they had availed themselves of their position he did not know. He had received orders from each and all of the four and that was all he could tell about it.

In Knowles' opinion, Esdale, the chief accountant, had also every opportunity of knowing how things stood, and whether anything underhand was in contemplation. But here again Knowles could not tell the actual state of Esdale's knowledge. All he knew was that the critical books were posted by the partners and the chief accountant, and were kept locked up.

"Now, Mr. Knowles," French went on, "I want to know something about yourself. I have to get details about every one connected with the concern. You were knocked up at the time?"

Knowles had had 'flu. He had been off for nearly a week when the crash occurred, but was getting better. Indeed, he had intended to return to the office on that very Thursday. He had, as a matter of fact, got up and dressed, but he had felt so ill that he had had to go back to bed again. He went up to Town, however, on the following day, the Friday. Yes, Mr. Nolan had telephoned for him. Oh, yes, he was in the hands of the doctor, Dr. Swayne, who lived close by. No, the doctor had not called on the Thursday. He had been on Wednesday and had told him, Knowles, to lie up for a day or two longer. Owing to Nolan's message he had felt that he just must go to Town on the Friday, though his wife had been strongly against it. The Inspector would understand how thankful he was that he had done so, when he found out how bad things were. It was terrible and an appalling shock to him. Not only the loss of his employers — indeed he might say friends, for both the deceased had shown him many kindnesses — but he feared for his own job. However, that was not what the Inspector wanted to hear. No, their servant had not been at home at the time. She, too, was ill and had gone on leave a few days before. His getting laid up was hard lines on Mrs. Knowles, as she could get no help and had to do everything herself. But that was always the way things happened. With this French duly sympathised.

It was close on eleven o'clock when French, considerably disappointed with the result of both his interviews, left the Securities building and returned to the Yard. His presence was not required there and he decided that the next most urgent business was to begin the checking of Nolan's statement.

The first thing was to see Sir Garnett Chislehurst and get his account of the conversation between Moxon and Nolan after the dinner on Wednesday night. At first shot French ran him to earth in his club.

Sir Garnett was slow, elderly and pompous, but he was sure of his facts. He confirmed Nolan's story in every detail. Moxon had stated that he had just had a telephone message from his sister in Buxton saying that her husband, while returning from the theatre, had been knocked down by a car and killed. Moxon had seemed much upset. He had said that his sister would be alone and that he must go down first thing in the morning to see her through. Nolan was going to France in his place. Moxon had asked Sir Garnett to call at the office next morning to explain Nolan's absence, as well as to be at hand to sign any papers which could not lie over.

This, French considered, was an important point in Nolan's favour. It had occurred to him that this story of Moxon's request was just the kind of tale Nolan would have invented, had he been guilty. So far as it went, however, it was no invention, but the sober truth.

To complete this section of the investigation French next sat down and went carefully through the papers in Nolan's despatch case. Here, he saw, was ample evidence that financial negotiations on a large scale had been in progress between the Frenchman, Pasteur, and the firm. There was also correspondence arranging Moxon's visit to Fécamp on the Thursday. Proof of this

121

part of Nolan's statement was therefore complete. At the same time, to make quite certain that the file had not been faked, French took it to the Securities building and ascertained from Knowles that the critical letters it contained were genuine.

The next business was at Dover. French took the first train there and was soon walking through the small streets near the harbour, looking for 17B Pilot Street and John Squance. The man was out, but his wife described him and French picked him up without difficulty at the harbour.

Squance was an elderly man on whose statement French felt he might rely. He explained that he lived by hiring boats and that for the past three years he had been in Nolan's employment as caretaker to the launch, which Nolan kept lying up in the Granville Basin. His business was to see she was always clean and the motor ready for running. He believed that in this he had given satisfaction.

At about half-past twelve on the previous Wednesday night a boy from the Lord Warden Hotel had knocked him up to say that Mr. Nolan had telephoned that he wanted the launch to be ready for him about seven-thirty next morning and to have stores aboard in accordance with card E.

Nolan, Squance explained, had a number of typed cards aboard with different sets of stores on each. When Nolan wanted certain requirements he simply mentioned the card covering them. Card E was for sufficient food-stuffs for a two-day trip for two persons.

Squance had hurried down to the Basin, for, as the tide was beginning to ebb, he feared the gates would be shut before he could get the launch out. However, he was just in time, and he got her through and tied her up to the steps on the Crosswall Quay, just outside the dock mouth. There was little to be done with her, as Nolan had had her out on the previous Sunday, and Squance had given her a good cleaning on the Monday morning, filling up the various tanks. He therefore had a sleep aboard, and in the morning set out to try to get the stores. He couldn't get all that were required as the shops were not open, but he was able to borrow enough to keep Nolan going.

At a few minutes past seven all was ready. The launch, clean and fairly well equipped, and with the motor ticking over, was moored at the steps. Squance waited with her and about quarter past Nolan turned up. He seemed just as usual, quiet and self-contained and not excited or in a hurry.

He began by telling Squance he had left his car near the bridge at the end of the quay and that he, Squance, was to go to Holsworth's Garage after he started, and get a man to drive the car there. Squance was to ask them to keep it till his return in a couple of days. Then he asked if Raymond had turned up. Squance knew Raymond's appearance, as he had seen him with Nolan on previous occasions. He answered that Raymond had not arrived. Nolan then said he would wait for a short time.

He did wait — till eight o'clock. Then he said he had an appointment across the Channel and he was afraid he must get away. He told Squance to watch for Raymond, and if he turned up to explain that he, Nolan, had gone on, and for Raymond to follow by one of the boats from Dover or Folkestone. Squance had watched, but there had been no sign of Raymond.

"Then do I understand you to say that Mr. Nolan was alone in the launch when he left?"

"Yes, sir, 'e was alone."

"You say also you filled her up with petrol and paraffin. Can you tell me just how full? I want to know how much was gone out of the tanks when we found her."

"Yes, sir, I can tell you. There's a hindicator on each tank and they was both filled right up to the 'ighest mark."

"Now, Squance, you said that Mr. Nolan waited until eight o'clock for Mr. Raymond. Was it exactly at eight that he left?"

"Between three and four minutes after eight, sir."

"How are you so sure of that?"

"This way, sir. Mr. Nolan, 'e started to get ready when 'e 'eard the clock strike eight, and 'e left the steps three or four minutes later."

French was considerably impressed with Squance's statement. The man was transparently honest, and he seemed to have his head well screwed on and to be sure of his facts. French felt he might implicitly believe every word he had heard. All the same, corroboration was always useful.

"Any one else see her start?" he concluded.

It appeared that several persons had, among whom were a pavior who was doing a job on the wharf, a policeman named Hogarth and two boatmen. French considered the fixing of the time of the departure so important that he took the trouble to interview the two former. From the pavior he got an approximate confirmation and from Constable Hogarth an absolute one.

All this testimony seemed to be conclusive proof of the truth of Nolan's statement. There was still, however, the matter of the launch's speed to be checked up. For a moment French thought of taking Squance to Newhaven to run her over some known distance, then he decided this should be done by strangers who could not by any conceivable chance be interested parties. Accordingly he put through a telephone call to Sergeant Heath at Newhaven to know whether there was a first-rate marine motor establishment in the town from which he could borrow a mechanic. Heath's reply being satisfactory he took the next train to Newhaven.

It was too late to carry out any experiments that night, but he called on the proprietor of the firm at his home.

"Certainly, Mr. French, I can let you have a good man, or two if you prefer it. Unless you're well up in the job yourself, I'd advise you to have the two. It's not easy to take accurate readings from a moving boat."

French said he didn't propose to undertake it. The information might be required in court and must be obtained by experts who would be prepared to swear to its accuracy.

"Then you'd better have Bateman and Lancashire. They're both tip-top fellows and you may have every confidence in them."

"Right. I'd like them to-morrow, Sunday, at nine in the morning."

"I'll see to it. They'll be there on time."

CHAPTER
NINE

Distance Over Time Equals Speed

When at all possible French was, so far as duty was concerned, a strict Sabbatarian. He did not believe in working seven days a week, nor, to give them credit, did his superiors. Nearly always, when the weather permitted, he and Mrs. French took a Sunday excursion. Both loved the country and these visits counted for a good deal in their lives.

This Moxon's General Securities case, however, clearly required an exception to be made to the rule. It was too urgent for any time to be lost. Every hour that passed would make more difficult the task of tracing the missing men and recovering the money. French, therefore, felt that he must arrange the trials for the very first moment possible. That this should prove to be a Sunday was his misfortune.

According to some schools of thought his Sabbath desecration should have been rewarded by a wet and stormy day. As a matter of fact he was favoured with perfect weather. A clear sky and a bright sun gave a feeling of exhilaration, while a light breeze, not strong enough to raise the sea, was still sufficient to keep the air fresh and cool. In spite of the expedition being strictly "work," French had something of the feelings of a schoolboy on a holiday as he joined his new colleagues on the gangway.

"I did say nine," he greeted them, "but I'm sorry I'll have to ask you to wait. I see the *Chichester's* at the other side there and I want a word with the skipper before we start."

"We'll run you across, Inspector. Get in."

They moved slowly across the harbour to near the *Chichester's* berth. French climbed ashore and going aboard the steamer, asked for Captain Hewitt.

At that moment the man himself turned up. "Come along to my cabin," he invited cheerily. "I can guess what it's about. You people have got your work cut out for you now and no mistake. I little thought when we raised that yacht that it was going to stir up all this dust. Will you smoke, Inspector?"

"Thanks," French said, accepting a thick brown cigarette and taking the comfortable chair to which the other pointed. "In a way it's a peculiar case. Though murder is the most serious crime in the calendar, in this instance the arrest of the murderer is not so important as the finding of the cash. Even though the failure is so large, a million and a half sterling would make sizeable difference to the creditors."

"Yes, poor devils," the captain agreed, holding out his lighter. "But don't you think, Mr. French, that the two problems are one? If you find the murderer, you find the cash?"

"Not necessarily, though it's certainly likely. I'm hoping, captain, that you can give me some help."

Captain Hewitt didn't think he could add anything to his report, which he had made as exhaustive as he had known how. All the same he was quite at his visitor's disposal.

"It's like this," French explained. "I've formed the idea, rightly or wrongly, that a third person started from Folkestone with Moxon and Deeping on that yacht. Admittedly we've not proved it, but let that go and assume it for argument's sake."

Captain Hewitt nodded.

"Again purely for argument's sake," went on French, "let us call this person Raymond." The captain whistled. "No, captain, it's only speculation. However, let's assume it. Let us suppose that Raymond sailed with the others to where you found the yacht, that he there committed the murders, took the cash, and cleared out. Now, captain, how could he have done it? You see what I mean? Did you happen to notice any boat or launch or vessel that he might have been on board?"

Again Captain Hewitt nodded.

"I get you," he said. "I hadn't thought of that, though I should have. As a matter of fact there was a French fishing boat not far away at the time. Mr. Hands, my second officer, and I both saw her. One of those small mackerel luggers with an auxiliary motor and a crew of about three. It was too thick to see her letters."

"Could she have done the trick, do you think?"

"Conceivably she might. She was three to four miles nearer France and was heading sou'-sou'-west, pretty well in the direction of Fécamp. We picked her up immediately on leaving the *Nymph* and passed about a mile astern of her."

"If she had been at the *Nymph* when the murder was committed, could she have got to where you saw her in the time?"

Captain Hewitt looked doubtful.

"She could have got a darned sight further; out of sight altogether if she'd wanted to. There's another thing: she wasn't steering away from the *Nymph*."

"Worth looking into all the same?"

The captain did not reply for some seconds.

"Since you ask me," he said at last, "I think it's a bit far-fetched. Are you suggesting she fell in with the *Nymph* by accident or design?"

"I don't know; either."

The captain shrugged.

"To my mind, you might rule out accident. Apart from the unlikely chance of her turning up like that just when she was wanted, I don't see any murderer risking such a secret with three or four strangers: particularly men of that type. On the other hand, if you assume she was there by arrangement, it means long preparation as well as some jolly decent seamanship on the part of your amateurs."

"I wish your reasoning wasn't so sound," French declared. "You raised my hopes when first you mentioned a lugger. I agree with you, captain, that nothing is likely to come of it. All the same I wish you'd give me a description of her."

Captain Hewitt pressed a bell and directed that Mr. Hands come to him immediately.

"My second officer, Mr. Hands," he introduced him. "Mr. Hands, this is Inspector French of Scotland Yard. It's about those yacht murders. He wants a description of the French lugger we saw after we left the *Nymph*."

"I wish you'd make a sketch of her, showing her sails, will you?" French begged.

The second officer did so like an artist born. "Black hull about thirty feet or more long," he murmured as he worked. "Stern raking so, with an outboard rudder. A white line here with registration number here. Masts stepped about a foot from each end, the foremast the higher. The mast here in the stern is set right out to starboard to allow room for the tiller. Masts nominally upright, but actually leaning towards each other, so. Brown lugsails on both masts. A small dinghy on deck amidships. That's about all, I think. Probably she was decked over with a couple of hatches and a sky-light shaped cover for the motor, though I couldn't see that. That's it, sir, isn't it?"

Captain Hewitt said the picture was lifelike and that he would get Mr. Hands to do another for his cabin.

"Why did you observe her so carefully?" French asked curiously. "Surely you must see these little boats in scores?"

The two sailors grinned at one another.

"Well, you should guess that," the captain declared with the suspicion of a wink. "We had a sort of idea some busybody might come around afterwards asking silly questions, and we thought we'd better be prepared for it."

French laughed.

"Some sense, you two, haven't you? I wish you'd show more of it by telling me how to find that darned lugger."

"Your best plan, to my way of thinking," Captain Hewitt answered seriously, "is to go on the time she was seen. These luggers generally work at night and go in any time from six to ten in the morning. Not always, but generally. Now she was seen at least thirty miles from home at two o'clock in the day. That should help you."

French's ardour was somewhat damped as he returned to the launch. This had at first seemed a promising line of inquiry, but the captain's objections to it were discouragingly sound. Of course the fact that the officers had not seen a boat did not prove that there was none. But it made its existence less likely.

He found the launch motor ticking over.

"I've been running her," the mechanic explained, "and she's nicely heated up. She'll develop full power now and we can get right ahead with whatever trials you want."

"It's a very simple matter," French returned. "I want to know her maximum speed. Later I'll want to find out the same in the case of the *Nymph*. I leave all details to you. Only remember that you may have to give evidence on oath as to the speed. What do you suggest?"

The men consulted in low tones. French could hear phrases, "Seaford Martello Tower," "Beachy Head," "seven and a half miles," then Bateman, the navigator, turned round.

"What about a run from the breakwater light to the pier at Rottingdean and back?" he suggested. "That would give us two trips of about five miles each way. We can get the exact distance off the chart when we go in."

French considered. It was the speed over a long distance that he wanted.

"I'd like a longer run," he decided.

"Then we'll go to Brighton," the man answered. "Nine miles or more each way."

"That's better. Now there's another thing. I want a note of the quantity of petrol and paraffin in the tanks before we start and after we get back."

The readings taken, French gave the word to start. In a few seconds they were gliding down the river, past the *Chichester* and her sister, the *Steyning*, and through the outer harbour to the end of the breakwater. They kept well to the east, then with a big sweep turned right round towards the west. Both French and Bateman took careful time readings as they passed the lighthouse at the end of the breakwater. Then, with the motor humming merrily, they headed for Brighton.

French, chatting with Bateman in the well, felt that had he been allowed a choice of his Sunday excursion, he could not have made a better selection. The bright warm sun, the clear exhilarating air, the blue sparkling water, the easy roll of the launch over the tiny swells, all were a delight. They kept close to the shore, interesting, every yard of it, with its bold white chalk cliffs, its stretch of shingle fringing the water, and where the cliffs were low enough to see it, the smooth green grass of the downs running back from their summits. Soon

133

they were abreast of Peacehaven with its endless array of bungalows. Then Rottingdean came in sight, drew abeam, and dropped astern, and then at last appeared the long "front" of Brighton with its vast sequence of Victorian buildings and its two great piers.

As they reached the centre of the first of these French and Bateman read their watches, and a rapid question showed that they were agreed as to the time of the run. Then making another semi-circle, they once more passed the pier, and the starting time of the return journey was taken.

The sail back was not quite so pleasant. The wind had freshened and was now against them. All the same it was an enjoyable trip and French was sorry when once more they reached Newhaven breakwater. Having again read the time, they turned up the river.

The two trips gave surprisingly close readings, due, Bateman explained, to the wind and tide having been in opposite directions. Having worked out the distance on the map, they found the speeds were 9.62 and 9.47 knots respectively.

"If you want maximum, Mr. French, you may make it the even ten and you won't be far wrong," Bateman concluded, "though the average run would be just about the nine and a half we've been doing."

"Fine," French answered. "Now if we had the same information about the yacht we'd be through."

They locked up the launch and transferred their activities to the *Nymph*. Here the same proceedings were gone through. Lancashire insisted on running to Seaford and back before starting the test, so that the motor might be well heated. Then they retraced their course to the pier at Brighton and back again to Newhaven.

As Nolan had stated, the speed of the *Nymph* was lower than that of the launch by about two knots. After making allowances for the tide — the wind by this time had dropped — they found that the *Nymph* would do an average of eight knots or a trifle less.

"That," French said to Bateman as they re-berthed, "finishes our tests. Now for our deductions. I wish you'd come below and check me up on these figures." He had found a large-scale chart of the Channel in the wheel-house and with this he led the way to the cabin.

"These two boats," he went on when they were settled side by side at the table, "Moxon's yacht *Nymph* and Nolan's launch ran on Thursday morning last from Folkestone and Dover respectively to the point at which the tragedy occurred. The *Nymph* went first and the launch followed pretty well in her tracks. I've had a statement about the movements of these two boats which I want to check."

Bateman was supremely interested. He had read detective stories and was mildly amused by the *coups* of the famous detectives of fiction. But this was very different. This was seeing Scotland Yard at work, and from the inside. French might count on his enthusiastic help. He got out a scale and a sheet of paper, pointed his pencil, and waited with an air not far removed from reverence.

"The first thing," French went on, "is to fix the point of the murders. Let us call it Point M — Point of

Murders. We have a good many checks on that. We'll begin with the captain's report. He gives the position as fifty degrees fifteen minutes north by no degrees forty-one minutes west. Will you plot that?"

Bateman calculated and scaled, finally making a dot with his pencil.

"Now," said French, "that's on the route of the steamer. Therefore if you're right it should be on the direct line joining Newhaven and Dieppe. Just draw it in, will you?"

The line passed through the point.

"Right so far. The next thing to find out is when the *Chichester* got to Point M. How many sea miles do you make Point M from Newhaven?"

"Thirty-nine," Bateman answered presently.

"What speed does the *Chichester* run at? Let's see, I have it here. Newhaven, depart, 11.45; Dieppe arrive, 2.55; that's 190 minutes. What do you make the total distance between the ports?"

"Sixty-seven sea miles."

"Then it's an easy sum in proportion. If she goes 67 miles in 190 minutes, how long will she take to go 39 miles?"

"One hour fifty minutes," Bateman returned.

"I agree. Therefore the *Chichester* should have got to Point M at approximately half-past one. This checks in with the captain's time of 1.33. So we may take it that we are right so far."

"Not much doubt about that, Mr. French."

"We can't afford to make mistakes," French pointed out. "Some one's life may depend on these figures.

Now for our final check. My theory is that these people were making for Fécamp. Will you rule a line from Folkestone to Fécamp and see if it goes through Point M?"

French watched with a scarcely veiled eagerness as Bateman worked.

"A bull's eye again," the latter said a moment later. "Within a mile or so of it. That's as near as you could possibly expect. Good enough navigation."

"It's certainly very reassuring. One's usually afraid of a number of checks, but when they work in it makes you feel good. Now, I've not finished. The doctor got aboard the Nymph shortly after half-past one. He estimated that the deceased had probably been dead about an hour. The watch of one of them had stopped at 12.33. Finally, from the heat of the motor it was estimated that the launch had been stopped about an hour. All these, I think, are sufficient to prove that the tragedy occurred about half-past twelve. The Nymph, then, reached Point M at about twelve-thirty. You follow me?"

"Correct, sir."

"Very good. If the Nymph reached Point M at twelve-thirty, at what hour did she leave Folkestone?"

This involved scaling the distance, which Bateman made 54 sea miles, and dividing it by the 8 knots they had just found by experiment. It worked out at 6¾ hours, and this gave 5.45 a.m. as the time at which Moxon left Folkestone.

"By Jove," said French, "that's not bad. I've had evidence that she actually did leave at 5.50."

Bateman's enthusiasm grew. This information, reached bit by bit by ordinary commonsense methods, the soundness of which he could himself appreciate, was before his eyes transforming a series of mere unsupported statements into definite ascertained facts. His respect for the work of Scotland Yard rose by leaps and bounds. A case built up in such a way was unshakable.

But he had not appreciated the great question to which all this had been leading up. It still remained unsolved. Could Nolan have been guilty?

"I want to check up that launch now," French went on. "We'll do it in the converse way. I've found that it left Dover at 8 a.m. Tell me at what hour it should have reached the *Nymph*?"

"That's easy," Bateman answered. He scaled again. "Dover to Point M is about 57 sea miles. The question is therefore, How long would a launch, running at 9½ knots, take to do 57 sea miles? The answer is, 6 hours. Six hours after 8 a.m. would bring it to 2 p.m."

The result was no surprise to French. He had, in fact, expected it. He had never really believed in Nolan's guilt.

"Two p.m.! Near enough as not to matter to the time she actually did turn up. But wait a minute," he added as Bateman began once more to express his admiration, "let's go the whole hog when we're at it. Supposing the launch had reached the *Nymph* at the time of the murders, at what speed must she have travelled?"

This was another easy sum. 8 a.m. to 12.30 p.m. was four hours and a half. The distance was again 57 sea miles. The answer was, therefore, about 13 knots. French asked his crucial question.

"Is it conceivably possible that by any means whatever that launch could have travelled at such a speed?"

It did not require the assurances of the two men to convince him. It was not possible; not within three knots. As French had for some time believed, Nolan was out of it.

"Now," he went on, "there's only one thing more. I want the oil checked up."

"I've got the figures, Mr. French," Bateman declared, and once again they buried themselves in calculations.

The problem was different for each little vessel. In the case of the *Nymph* they had as yet no reading of the tank levels at the beginning of the trip, but they had them at Point M. They found, however, that had the tanks been full at Folkestone, the run to Point M would have lowered them exactly to the position in which they were found. This seemed good enough corroborative proof that the *Nymph* had simply made the direct journey, as Nolan had stated.

In the case of the launch they knew the tank level when she left Dover. They had no reading at Point M, but they had when she reached Newhaven. Here again they found that the oil used just accounted for the whole run between Dover and Newhaven. In the nature of the case these results could not be taken as absolutely correct, but they were as accurate as the rather rough measurements permitted.

This at least was progress, though it was negative progress. But it was satisfactory to French in that he had now completed his immediate job.

Nolan was the first suspect, and though his guilt was improbable from the first, his case had necessarily to be dealt with. The Assistant Commissioner had said that if and when French cleared it up, he could take over from Tanner or Willis. Things looked blackest against Raymond, and Raymond's case French decided he would next follow up. Tanner had not had time to go very far with it. He would see Tanner that night, take over from him, and start on the Raymond trail in the morning.

His thought reverted to Nolan and the investigation he had just completed. Suddenly he saw that to a considerable extent he had been wasting his time. There was a further consideration which he had overlooked, but which proved Nolan's innocence quite as convincingly, though a good deal more simply.

The swag!

The money was a factor to which he had not given sufficient attention. Now, as he thought over it, he realised that it dominated the situation.

In the first place, he now saw that it must have been obtained in notes of small denomination. It was simply impossible that notes of high value could have been got rid of, certainly not in any number. Banks, even if they would change them for a stranger at all, would observe any one offering them pretty closely. The numbers of such notes would be taken. The notes would be traced and their connection with the frauds would become known. In a few days every bank would be on the lookout for further applications. The next unknown man who wished to change a large note would be detained in conversation until the police could be called, and when he left the bank he would not be lost sight of. If he were connected with the fraud his last days of liberty would have dawned.

But if the notes were of comparatively small denomination their bulk must be considerable. What space, French wondered, would notes for a total value of a million and a half take up, if in denominations of, say, five, ten, and twenty pounds? He did not know, but he thought at least that of a good-sized suit-case or even suit-cases.

French pursued this line of thought. Suit-cases had figured in the case. Two suit-cases had been taken to the Securities building on that Wednesday morning. They had lain there all day. In the evening their owners, Moxon and Raymond, had worked late; alone in the offices with the suit-cases; within reach of the strong room. Those suit-cases had been removed in Moxon's car. Moxon — and probably Raymond — had gone aboard the *Nymph* at Folkestone. Was it conceivable that the suit-cases had been left behind? It was not. French felt absolutely convinced that those suit-cases, containing thousands and thousands of low value notes, had gone out of Folkestone Harbour on the *Nymph*.

And now came the point to which all these considerations had been leading, the point which demonstrated Nolan's innocence apart from times and speeds. The money had disappeared, but Nolan had not taken it. It was on neither the *Nymph* nor the launch when these reached Newhaven, nor did Nolan bring it ashore. He had no bag nor suit-case, nor was it possible that such a bulk could have been secreted on his person. On the other hand, it was not likely that any one would commit a murder for a million and a half sterling, and then forgo the reward!

French turned to the two men and thanked them for their help.

"That's all I want," he ended. "I suggest that we lock up now and make the best of what's left of our Sunday."

French caught the evening boat train and after supper made his way once more to the Tanners'. Tanner was alone, Mrs. Tanner having gone to see her married sister. He was evidently bored and greeted French with delight.

"Hallo, old son! This is getting chronic. Stuck again and wanting some more help?"

"No," said French, "I called to say that I can't wait any longer while you muddle around with the thing. I see that if the work's to be done I'll have to take it over and do it myself."

"Ha, ha!" Tanner laughed. "So John Patrick Nolan, Esquire, is, so to speak, a washout. Why didn't you believe me when I told you that?"

"Experience. I've heard you talking before."

"Huh. Tell me about it."

French related his adventures. He had brought the chart with him and he demonstrated each step on it as he went along.

Tanner listened with close attention. "Seriously," he said when French had finished, "you might have saved yourself all that trouble if you had known what I know. But though I suspected it, I didn't prove it till to-day."

"You were working to-day?"

"Well, what do you think, with a case like this and the A.C. like a cat on hot bricks. Of course, I was working, and I've got something, too."

"Tell me."

Tanner busied himself getting out whisky and soda. Then after waiting till French's pipe was going satisfactorily, he told his story.

CHAPTER
TEN

The Man with the Suit-Cases

"It's nothing very spectacular," Tanner began, "but I think it's fairly conclusive. I'll tell you what I did and you'll see how it came about.

"I had the fact that Moxon and Raymond, each with a suit-case, had been at Hallam's restaurant for the dinner on Wednesday night. I had the fact that Moxon was found dead on the *Nymph* in mid-Channel at one-thirty on the following afternoon. I had the fact from the Folkestone sergeant that the *Nymph* had left Folkestone Harbour at 5.50 a.m., and I had the fact that Raymond and the suit-cases had disappeared. I took these in order.

"I told you that I went round to Hallam's, and that there I got a useful bit of information out of the porter? He had seen Moxon and Raymond start, and they had gone together, in Moxon's car. What's more, he had seen the two suit-cases on the back seat when he opened the door. The time was close on half-past twelve. So that was something to begin with."

"You told me."

"Next I thought a visit to Folkestone was indicated and I went on there. Before starting I rang up Nolan to see if he could give me the address of Moxon's boatman. He did so."

"John Hurley. Lives a couple of doors from the Angel tavern."

"Oh, you know that, do you? Lives at 3 St. Michael's Lane, to be more correct. I found the place and the man without trouble. Hurley is an old man, but is still fit and seems reliable. He makes a job out of looking after people's boats. He's had charge of Moxon's for five years; keeps it clean and provided with stores and goes out if required. A useful sort of man.

"He'd had a letter from Moxon on last Tuesday, he told me. Moxon said he would want the *Nymph* on the next day, Wednesday, and to get her ready. Also he wanted stores put aboard for three people for three days. He was coming down, he said, about midday on Wednesday, to see that all was right.

"Hurley did what he was told. He cleaned the yacht, tested the motor, filled up with petrol and paraffin and got the stores on board. About twelve Moxon arrived in his car. He went aboard the *Nymph* and examined everything, even starting the motor to make sure it was running freely. The *Nymph* was lying moored bow and stern in the Inner Harbour and he also tested the slipping of the moorings.

"Moxon said he was going over to France next day, but owing to a dinner in London, he couldn't get down till, say, three in the morning. He would go aboard the *Nymph* at once, sleep for three or four hours and leave about six for France.

"Hurley said he would sit up and be on the lookout for him, but Moxon replied that this was not necessary, that all he wanted him to do was to tie the dinghy up to one of the wharf ladders, so that when he arrived he could get aboard. Hurley then asked if he could do anything about the car, but Moxon said no, that he would put it into the Harbour Garage, which was open all night."

"Sounds all right," French commented.

"Of course it sounds all right; the man was no fool. Well, I thought that was all I'd get out of Hurley, but it wasn't. The best was yet to come and it came practically by chance.

" 'That dinghy you spoke of,' I said. 'That's your own boat, I suppose?'

" 'No, sir,' Hurley answered, 'it belongs to the *Nymph*.'

" 'Oh,' I said, 'and where is it kept when the *Nymph* is out?'

" 'She takes it with her,' he said.

" 'Do you mean to tell me that when she left on Thursday morning that dinghy was with her?' I asked.

"He said he assumed as a matter of course that it was. He hadn't actually seen it, but he was sure it must have gone as it had disappeared from the harbour. So there, French, seems a discovery. Pretty important, what?"

French was vastly interested. This was what he had been looking for. The dinghy supplied the missing link in his theory. With its help Raymond could, after shooting his companions, have got away with the all-important suit-cases.

"By Jove, Tanner, that would be a lift to us and no mistake! Were you able to prove it?"

"Yes, after a bit of time, I was. I asked Hurley what time the *Nymph* left on Thursday morning and he said ten minutes to six, same as the sergeant. I asked how he knew; had he seen it? He said no, but that some other men, friends of his, had.

"They were fishermen and I lost a lot of time finding them. They had all noticed the *Nymph* going out, and all had seen the dinghy towing behind. So that's that."

French was much impressed. To find the dinghy would now be essential and he feared it might prove no easy job. In all probability it had been taken on Thursday night to a deserted point on the French coast and there scuttled. However, cases were not made for the police, but the police for cases.

"That's good, Tanner. You might let me have those men's names."

He added them to his notes, then Tanner resumed.

"The next thing was to find out who went aboard the *Nymph*. I tried the obvious people, the various night watchmen and the police on night duty. But I couldn't get any luck. I went on till six o'clock, then I decided I would drop that line and go for the car.

"There I had no trouble. The man on night duty at the Harbour Garage knew Moxon and remembered his putting the car in. Moxon had turned up about three in the morning and had left the car without any explanation except that he had been unexpectedly delayed on his way from London."

"Strange his doing all that so openly."

"It was a matter of time. So long as he got to sea so many hours before the alarm was raised, he didn't care who knew about it."

"Probably you're right."

"That," Tanner went on, "brought me to dinnertime last night. I thought I'd had enough, so I went to an hotel and got a bit of well-earned rest. This morning I started in again, trying to find some one who'd seen the parties going aboard the *Nymph*. Lord, it turned out a job! But I got it at last."

"Good. How?"

"From two firemen from one of the Channel boats. It seems they had been at a friend's house and they had got a bit lively; dancing and a bottle or two. They broke up about three in the morning and came down the Strade and under the railway so as to get round the Inner Harbour. D'you know the place?"

"Fairly well."

"Then you know that there's a wall bounding the Inner Harbour on the Harbour Street side. The two firemen were walking beside this wall, just coming into Harbour Street, when a car passed down from the town and stopped near the Harbour Garage. A tall man with two suit-cases got out and turned along the side of the harbour in front of the Royal Pavilion Hotel. Then he stopped and stood waiting, while the car went across the road into the garage.

"The firemen were in the frame of mind in which any trifle is a matter of personal interest. They stopped behind the wall to see what would happen. In a few moments a man came out of the garage and joined the first; a shorter and fairly stout man. Both then with the suit-cases climbed down one of the ladders into a dinghy that was tied up at the bottom. They paddled the few feet across to the *Nymph* and went on board. So what do you think of that?"

"By Jove, Tanner, you've done well! Moxon and Raymond, and with proof enough to go into court."

Tanner swung round and struck his fist on the table.

"But that's just what it's not, French," he retorted. "You're convinced that it was Moxon and Raymond and so am I. But we can't prove it. It might have been Moxon and Deeping."

French made a gesture of annoyance.

"Curse it, so it might! I had forgotten Deeping. Those firemen couldn't see his features?"

"No; he was too far away."

French smiled.

"I should like to see those firemen's faces when they realise that that night they stood and watched thieves carrying one and a half millions in banknotes out of the country."

"That's what I thought. It occurred to me that if they'd had any inkling we'd have had our murders at Folkestone instead of mid-Channel."

"Shouldn't wonder," French returned. "What you've got is very fine and all that, Tanner, but if we're right that that was Raymond, there's something missing."

"Missing?"

"Yes: Deeping's arrival on the scene. When did he go aboard?"

Tanner shrugged.

"Don't I know that, you silly old ass. I didn't stop when I found the firemen. I went on till I had exhausted every inquiry I could think of. But the *Nymph* was lying only a few feet from the shore. If Deeping had gone down and called out, Moxon could have picked him up in a few seconds."

"Well," said French, "anyhow it's jolly good. What are you going to do now? Carry on or hand over to me?"

"Hand over to you if you can manage. I'm really on that St. Albans case. I'd like to get back to it."

"Right, I'll carry on your line in the morning. Now just a couple of points. First, I'd like a description of the dinghy."

"Got it here." Tanner took a leaf out of his note-book and passed it across. "It appears she's a surprisingly big boat for the job. Good in a choppy sea, Hurley says."

"Has a general call for Raymond been put out?"

"Yes. That was about the first thing I did."

"That's fine, Tanner. I suppose you haven't heard what Willis is up to?"

"Only that he left for France after the accountant."

"I expect he's having the best of it over there. Well, old man, I'll make tracks for bed. About this time in the evening I get a sort of feeling that a pillow and sheets would help my work."

"Lazy dog. Cheerio, then."

When French reached the Yard next morning he sought out his friend, Inspector Barnes. Barnes was the Yard's nautical expert. He did the shipping cases and advised generally on matters connected with the sea. A smart man was Barnes, and because of his genial disposition, a general favourite.

"The Channel murders?" he said when French button-holed him. "I thought some one would be round about that before long. What's it like? A teaser? Or all clear?"

"Part of it is clear enough," French told him, "but there's a deal to be done before we're through. You know the details?"

"Only what appeared in the papers. I've been at Southampton over the mail-bag robbery from that Union Castle liner."

"I didn't see about it."

Barnes shrugged. "A simple case enough. It was the three postal men in charge. We got some of the stuff at their houses. This case of yours looks more interesting."

"I'll tell you all that matters," and French gave him a brief summary of the facts.

"A newspaper case," Barnes commented. "Big money; thousands directly hit; dramatic story of the sea. Fine copy! Been much troubled by the newspaper folk?"

"Not too badly. Now, Barnes, I want to find that dinghy. If you have a brain wave you don't want, you might as well pass it on."

"My dear chap, how can I help you? You know as much as I do about it."

"I agree," French said dryly. "All the same, two heads, and so on." He unrolled his chart and explained

151

what he had done. Now Barnes, my theory is that about twelve-thirty that day the murderer left Point M, the Point of the Murders, you understand, in the yacht's dinghy, which is a surprisingly large and heavy boat. What I want you to tell me is this: What steamers or other vessels might have passed close by at that time? If I knew that, I would get in touch with them. One of them might have seen the dinghy."

Barnes whistled thoughtfully between his teeth.

"'Pon my soul, French," he said at last, "I don't believe that if you had searched the whole of the seas about Britain you could have found a place with less shipping. I doubt if I can help you. See here, let's pencil on some of the shipping routes. Now first, all up and down Channel sailings opposite this place are near the English side. That's because the coast of France from Calais to Cherbourg forms a huge bay and the shipping crosses the mouth of it in a straight line. Your Point M is well inside the bay, therefore off the track of shipping. See?"

French saw. It didn't look very hopeful.

"The only regular steamer path that would suit you is from ports north of Cap Gris Nez to Havre. But so far as I know, there's no regular passenger service on such a route. There are freight boats, of course, and I suggest that your best way would be to slip over to Havre and find out just what was running on that day."

"I'll do it," said French.

"Then," Barnes went on, "there is always the chance of coasters, fishing boats and pleasure yachts; little boats going into such places as le Tréport, Dieppe, St.

Valéry or Fécamp. If you want to make sure, you'll have to go over. In fact, you'll have to do that in any case if you want to trace that lugger the *Chichester* saw."

"Lloyd's couldn't help me?"

"Might, but I scarcely think so. I should plump for a personal visit."

"Very good, Barnes, I'll go. It won't take so very long."

For a moment Barnes did not answer.

"What exactly is your idea?" he asked presently. "Are you assuming that the murderer left the *Nymph* in the dinghy and was picked up by some passing vessel?"

"Either that or rowed himself ashore."

Barnes shook his head.

"I shouldn't build on it," he advised. "First, take rowing ashore." He turned back to the chart and began scaling. "Your Point M is about twenty-four sea miles from the French coast, the nearest land. That's farther than from Dover to Calais. Over all this distance strong tides run up and down the Channel. This would increase the virtual distance by many miles. It is not so bad here, of course, as up in the Straits. There, you remember, it is the tides and not the distance that have beaten the majority of the swimmers. But even here the tides are a big item. Now you're not going to tell me that a man could row all that distance; certainly not an office man, still less in the heavy boat that you describe. You may put that out of your mind, I'm afraid, French. It would be quite impossible for your murderer to escape by rowing himself ashore."

"Something to know that anyhow."

"Then with regard to his having been picked up," Barnes went on, "I question very much whether any master of any tramp or fishing boat would pick up a man in a dinghy and say nothing about it. Even if he took a bribe to keep it dark, when he saw about the murder he would think better of it. You see, to keep the thing quiet might be to make himself accessory after the fact. He'd want a deal to compensate himself for the risk. Then there's the crew; these difficulties multiplied four or five times over."

French sighed. "There's certainly a lot in what you say, Barnes. And it brings me to my next point. I'm going for publicity. Will you tell me if this is O.K. so far as the boat is concerned?"

He handed over a slip on which he had transcribed Tanner's notes.

Moxon's General Securities Case.
Murder in English Channel.

Missing. English built dinghy. 12ft. 6ins. long by 4ft. 3ins. beam. Very stoutly built. Carries four persons; square stern; small three-pronged grapnel with five fathoms of rope; additional two-fathom painter; two 5ft. 6ins. light sculls. Built of American elm, not new, but freshly varnished and in excellent order. Believed to have been in lat. 50° .15′ N., long. 0° .41′ W. about 12.30p.m. on Thursday, 26th June, and to have had on board one man and two suit-cases. See below.

Also Missing. Norman Bryce Raymond, partner in Moxon's General Securities. Aged 32, 6ft. 0ins. in height, slight, athletic build, square face, lean but healthy looking. Red hair cut short, light blue eyes, clear sun-burnt complexion, straight nose, small mouth and strong chin. Probably dressed in yachting clothes, white trousers and white or blue jacket and cap.

Probably has with him two suit-cases, both of good quality leather, one brown with silver fastenings and the letters P. A. M. in 2in. black letters, the other yellow with brass fastenings and marked N. B. R. in brown 2½in. letters.

This man and the suit-cases are believed to have been in the dinghy mentioned above.

Barnes said that so far as the boat part was concerned, this document read quite intelligently. French thereupon went to the Assistant Commissioner to report progress and to have his inquiry sent to the French police.

"This is all very well, French," Sir Mortimer said when the matter had been discussed, "but I fancy you'll have to go over. Why not get an introduction to the French authorities and go now?"

"I was going to propose it, sir."

"Right. By the way, what about those finger-prints you found on the companion handrail?"

"Nearly all Moxon's, sir. There were a few of Deeping's, one or two of the caretaker's, and one or two that I've not identified."

"The interesting ones."

"Unfortunately that's so, sir. I may say, however, that I got Nolan's on a tumbler one night we dined together, and they were not represented."

"That's at least something. Very well, French, trot along and see what you can pick up in France."

CHAPTER
ELEVEN

M. Fiquet of Dieppe

Before starting for France, French called at the Securities building and asked for Honeyford.

"I came, Mr. Honeyford," he said, "to know whether you had succeeded in getting any of those numbers yet?"

For answer Honeyford produced some sheets of foolscap bearing endless columns of figures: thousands and thousands of numbers. French gasped.

"Good Lord!" he said weakly, contemplating this array. "What in thunder am I going to do with these? Get 'em printed and published in book form?"

Honeyford snorted. "Huh, that's my thanks for sweating myself to the bone for you! Right, Inspector, you needn't have 'em if you don't want 'em."

French grinned as he sat down and took up the sheets. As he had imagined, most of the numbers represented five and ten pound notes. Though there must have been some hundreds of twenties, these still remained a small proportion of the whole. The figures were grouped under the various banks which had issued the notes.

"Some job getting these, Mr. Honeyford. How did you manage it?"

"Simply enough. I began by writing to all the banks with which the firm was known to have had dealings during the last three or four months. There were twenty-seven of them. I asked each what recent payments in cash they had made to the firm. I totalled the figures of the various replies, and as these reached a sum not far short of the million and a half which had disappeared, I assumed that I had succeeded so far."

French nodded.

"The next thing was obvious. I simply wrote back to the banks asking for the numbers of the notes paid on these occasions, and there you are."

"Pretty useful, that. It lets us get on to the critical step — to watch for them coming in again. Our friends are bound to get rid of some of them shortly, for making get-aways like theirs is an expensive amusement."

"They took thousands of singles as well."

"Oh, they did, did they? That's not so good. Then they have thousands of untraceable pounds to play with?"

"I should say so."

French rose.

"I'll add to my circular to report cases of strangers paying in large sums in singles, but I don't suppose it'll get us much. They'll spread their payments over too many banks. However, it's all we can do. Well, I'll get along to the Yard and get my book published."

His "copy" ready for the printers, he sat on at his desk, considering his visit to France.

He had three separate and distinct tasks in view, though if he were lucky, the accomplishment of one might fulfil the others also. He had to find Raymond, he had to find the money, and he had to find the lugger. Of these, he believed that the easiest, and possibly the most urgent also, was the finding of the lugger.

After Barnes' remarks, French had practically given up the theory that Raymond might have rowed ashore. Therefore if the man had reached the French coast at all, he must have been picked up by some vessel. Up to the present the lugger was the only known craft which could have done such a thing. If she had not done it, she might have seen some other vessel which had. Hence find the lugger and make sure. He decided that he would take the 8.20 from Victoria that very evening.

Having obtained his passport, some money, and his letter of introduction to the French police — with whom Sir Mortimer Ellison had already communicated direct — French set off. He reached Dieppe shortly after two in the morning, and going to one of the hotels fronting the Plage, did his best to make up for the sleep he had missed in the early part of the night. After *petit déjeuner* he presented himself with his papers at the *Commissariat de Police*.

The officer in charge had already had telegraphic instructions from Paris and received him with every courtesy. *Mon Dieu, oui, monsieur!* A case indeed of an importance! It would be an honour to assist. Would M. French have the complaisancy to state his requirements and he, the officer in charge, would see to it that, so far as the resources of the French police would permit, they would immediately be met?

French, suitably overwhelmed, declared that nothing was further from his thoughts than to put the officer to inconvenience; assured him that all he wanted was to trace a certain French lugger which might in all innocence have aided the English scoundrel concerned in the murders to escape; and tactfully begged the officer's advice as to how this object might best be achieved.

The officer declared once more that he and his entire staff were at the disposal of his distinguished colleague. It was evident, French saw, that the man was not going to have any *sacré anglais* roving unchecked over his territory. And so it turned out. M. Jules Fiquet, the most distinguished member of the local detective force, would "assist" M. French in his labours. As a matter of fact this was an arrangement entirely satisfactory to French, who with the language difficulty could scarcely have handled the affair alone.

There was nothing Gallic about M. Fiquet's outward appearance. Tall, fair and blue-eyed, it was evident that his stock came from the north. His traits were English, or what French believed were English. He was unemotional, thoughtful, sparing of conversation and highly efficient — all of which French considered sterling British qualities. But to these he added a cultivated imagination admittedly French. Altogether a thoroughly good man for his job, and as he spoke very fair English, just the companion French would have chosen.

160

Having achieved an impressive farewell to the officer in charge, French and his new acquaintance adjourned at French's suggestion to a convenient café to cement their friendship over a couple of bocks and to draw up their plan of campaign. Fiquet had read all that the papers contained about the case and was deeply interested in hearing of it from the inside. He rapidly grasped the significance of the lugger and agreed that it must be found without delay.

"It is necessary that the coast be searched, yes," he said when French had finished, "but by us, *non!* We confine ourselves to Dieppe. The local police can do the other work, each in his own district. We write the needful particulars; then we ourselves are free to act as we think best. Is it not so?"

Seated on their little buff-painted iron chairs at their little buff-painted iron table in the U-shaped space in front of the casino, they drafted their notice. It was a bright, sunny day, warm, but delightfully fresh. Though the season had not yet fully set in, Dieppe was already full and even at this hour in the morning the Plage was gay with people. The noises of the town, the muffled roll of tyres on smooth pavements, the snore of gears starting up, the hoot of a steamer in the port, all came faintly to their ears.

The circular drawn up, they returned to the *commissariat* to have it despatched to all the police stations along the coast from Boulogne to Le Havre. Then they turned down to the harbour, and passing along the Quai Duquesne, halted at the Darse de Pêche. It was a basin entered from the Avant-Port, from

161

which the Newhaven boat started. In it lay a number of fishing luggers and one or two small steam trawlers. On the quay were some groups of longshoremen, and Fiquet, idly sauntering with French, approached one of them.

It consisted of three men, of whom the most salient feature was the atmosphere of garlic in which they seemed to live. Fiquet evidently knew them, greeted them as old friends, and drew up for a chat. This was his friend, Monsieur French, from London, come to spend his holidays in Dieppe. They were looking for a good boat to do a bit of fishing. Could any member of the trio put him on to one?

Fiquet's manner was excessively leisurely. He seemed to suggest that here was this infernal nuisance of a visitor who had to be amused, and the longer he talked on the quay, the less time there would be to put in elsewhere. The three men, evidently suspicious, were not over responsive, but they were civil to the representative of the police and the conversation did not quite languish.

Fiquet passed round cigarettes as he leant against an iron rail and continued chatting. From the hire of a fishing boat for pleasure — which, as Fiquet well knew, none of them could supply — the talk turned to fishing as a business. Seemingly by accident it touched on the hazards of the sea and the hardness of the life, then on what Fiquet considered its most objectionable feature, that it was carried on at night. From this a little gentle suggestion led to examples of long hours of work, e.g. late returns in the mornings. Hopefully Fiquet tried to introduce a spirit of emulation into tales of long hours worked. He himself told an impressive story of how he had recently seen a boat arriving at nearly five o'clock in the afternoon; terribly hard lines on the crew; but surely an exception? . . .

But Fiquet landed no fish from these turgid waters. When the date of the alleged late arrival was established, it produced no answering enthusiasm. The men hadn't seen such a boat, nor had they heard of one arriving late on that day.

"Do you think they are telling you the truth?" French asked as they sauntered to the next group.

Fiquet threw out his hands expressively.

"Ah, but certainly," he exclaimed. "Here they do not lie to the police unless there is some reason." He repeated his gesture. "Why should they?"

"Some men do it on general principles."

Fiquet shook his head decisively.

"*Non, non,* my friend, not so. They like to keep — how do you say it? — on the sunshine side of the police. They lie, yes! But only when they think it pays. Why should they here?"

Fiquet then extended the range of his inquiries. Any one who by chance or in the course of his business was known to have been in the neighbourhood at the time was interrogated. The men in the lighthouses on the *jetées*, the harbour-master and his staff, workmen who were carrying out repairs to the Quai du Hâble, the skippers of any Dieppe boats that were in the harbour, even taximen and employees at the Gare Maritime, all were asked, but none answered. For quiet systematic thoroughness, it was a piece of work after French's own heart. All day the inquiry continued and it was after six o'clock when Fiquet confessed himself beaten.

"We can't be absolutely certain," he declared, discussing the result, "but it is hundred to one chance that your boat did not come in here. Same time, if we do not learn of her elsewhere, we shall see the skipper of every lugger on the coast and make him prove the hour of his arrival on that day. But I make the bet that we learn of her elsewhere. *Allons!* We have done enough. You will meet me for dinner in a little, will you not?"

French would gladly meet him for dinner, but Fiquet must be French's guest. But no! M. French was the visitor. When he, Fiquet, came to London . . . The affair at last arranged itself.

"We shall not, I think, have to wait long for our information," Fiquet remarked when at last it was time to say good-night. "If the boat is found, it will be at once. I hope for news to-morrow, but if not, there is much to see in Dieppe and I think you could pass a pleasant day looking round."

French thanked him and they parted with a friendship in the making.

Fiquet proved a true prophet. Next morning they found that a despatch had come in from Fécamp. It was believed that the boat had been found.

"*Bon,*" said Fiquet. "I have a car. Let us depart."

French enjoyed every minute of the drive. The country was interesting, well wooded and undulating, not unlike, French thought, parts of Surrey. It was a longish run, indeed something over an hour and a half had passed before they came to a steep hill, which wound backwards and forwards down into the valley at the bottom of which lay Fécamp.

CHAPTER
TWELVE

The F711

Fécamp proved to be a larger and very much better town than French had expected. As a matter of fact, he had never heard of the place before, and it came to him with a sort of mild surprise that a place of which he had never heard should be so important. It lay on a bay at the mouth of a river between two great hills. There was the usual concrete plage stretching along the sea almost from hill to hill, perhaps half a mile long, with the usual line of hotels behind it. At the mouth of the river a harbour had been formed. Inside the moles was a good sheet of water with many fishing boats, while farther up were wharves at which half a dozen steamers were discharging. The place was full of summer visitors, and French promptly added it to his list of places at which he would like to spend holidays.

Fiquet, seeing that his guest was interested, took on the rôle of showman and insisted on driving round the town and pointing out its beauties before going on to business. At last, however, they reached the police station.

The sergeant had not much to tell. On receipt of Fiquet's circular he remembered that a local lugger, which answered the given description, had remained at sea during the whole of the Thursday in question. It had left at its usual hour of eight o'clock on the Wednesday night and it had not returned till nearly six o'clock on the following Friday morning, twenty-four hours longer out than usual. The skipper, however, had explained to the curious that his auxiliary motor had broken down and that he had not been able to get it right for several hours. Thursday had been a day of complete calm and they had found themselves unable to make port under sail. By the time the motor was repaired it was evening and they decided to remain at sea rather than miss a night's fishing.

The sergeant could not say that this was the lugger Fiquet required. He had made it his business to verify the facts without approaching the fishermen, who had therefore no idea that inquiries were in progress. He might mention, however, that the men were considered *des mauvais types* who might well be guilty of any kind of villainy.

Fiquet commended the sergeant's discretion. The two men talked quickly in French and then Fiquet said: "All right, bring them in and we'll put them through it."

The sergeant hurried off and for half an hour French and his companion sat smoking in the little police station. Then the sergeant returned and with him three men, the skipper and his crew of two. True enough they were an evil-looking trio. French felt as he looked at them that their purposes would not be hampered by any nice points of ethics.

"One at a time," said Fiquet.

The crew were hustled away, leaving the skipper standing facing the three police officers. He looked acutely uneasy.

"Name?" Fiquet asked sharply.

"Jean Martin, monsieur."

Fiquet stared at him fiercely. "Now, Martin," he went on, thrusting out his face aggressively, "I have to warn you that this is a serious matter. You attempt any tricks and you'll find yourself —" His gesture was more threatening than any words. "Your only chance is to tell the truth. See?"

Martin nervously indicated that anything less than the truth, the whole truth and nothing but the truth was anathema to him. Fiquet went on without heeding him.

"You don't want to be arrested on a charge of conspiracy to murder, do you? Conspiracy to murder would mean the Devil's Island. I warn you that if you hold anything back you may go there."

For some time Fiquet continued in the same strain, creating his abominable atmosphere. Martin evidently took it all seriously and his uneasiness grew more pronounced. He blinked piteously at Fiquet out of his shifty, close-set eyes and swore that he had done nothing wrong and that he didn't know what all this was about.

"Oh, you don't, don't you?" Fiquet returned, apparently satisfied that the ground by this time had been properly prepared. "We'll see about that." He swung round suddenly and fixed his victim with a still more intense regard. "Tell me this, Martin, where did you set the gentleman ashore on last Friday morning?"

French's opinion of his temporary colleague's tactics, which had been rapidly dropping during this scene, reached zero at the question. Much too crude, he thought, and not even quite fair. A sudden thrill therefore ran through him as he noted Martin's reaction. The man started and for a moment terror showed in his eyes. To all outward seeming the question had got a bull's eye.

But if so, the result was disappointing. Martin wasn't admitting anything. He denied with oaths that he understood what the detective meant and declared that he had seen no gentleman that morning, still less brought one ashore. Fiquet pressed him hard, but without result.

"Where were you at half-past twelve on last Thursday?" went on the inquisitor.

"Half-past twelve, monsieur? We were out in the Channel, nearly half-way to England." He considered. "About off Dieppe, I think."

"Did you see the Newhaven steamer?"

"Yes, monsieur, but not at that hour. It was later, nearer two o'clock."

"Where was she?"

"She was going to Dieppe. She passed a couple of kilos behind us."

As Fiquet put these questions Martin's face began to register relief. The suggestion was that a danger which he had feared, was receding.

"Did you see her when she was stopped?"

"No, monsieur, she was going at her usual speed."

"You saw the yacht *Nymph* at the same time?"

Martin had not seen the *Nymph*. He was absolutely certain that he had seen neither the *Nymph* nor any other yacht. Nor a dinghy. Earnestly he called his gods to witness that he spoke the truth. As Fiquet hesitated his relief grew more marked. A hint of truculence crept into his manner.

"Take him out, but hold him," Fiquet said presently in disgusted tones.

Martin was hustled from the room and one of his crew took his place. This was a heavy, stupid-looking man with a vacant expression, by name Maurin.

Fiquet began by asking him whether the young man they had picked up on the previous Thursday had red hair or black. But if Maurin knew the answer, he did not give it. His lay was ignorance. At every question he stared bovinely at Fiquet, slightly shaking his head and disclaiming all knowledge of the matter at issue. After wearisome iteration he confirmed in general his skipper's statement, except on one point. Under strong pressure he admitted that he had seen the *Chichester* lying motionless before she passed them, but he denied absolutely that he had seen the *Nymph* or its dinghy, still less that he knew anything of a young man or of suit-cases.

In his turn Maurin was taken out and the third member of the trio, Malot, brought in. This man was a contrast to the last in almost every particular. A mere rat of a man, his face was still full of a low-grade intelligence. Fiquet began as before by asking the

170

colour of the hair of the young man they had taken aboard.

Malot's cunning little eyes twinkled mockingly as he asked with exaggerated innocence to what young man his questioner was referring. Fiquet pressed him hard on the point, but without result. Then he asked whether he had seen the *Chichester* when she was stopped. This seemed more of a problem to Malot. For a moment he paused, evidently considering. Then he said the *Chichester*, travelling as usual, had passed behind them about two o'clock, but he had not seen her at rest.

"Then," said Fiquet, "if the skipper and Maurin say they saw her standing still, they're both lying?"

But Malot was not to be caught so easily. He declared, still with that mocking light in his eyes, that he was speaking neither for the skipper nor for Maurin, but for himself alone. He wouldn't say that the *Chichester* had not been standing still, only that he personally had not seen her do so. He had not heard either of the other men remark on the subject; in fact, he knew nothing whatever about it.

The result of all this inquiry was to make French increasingly suspicious that something illegal had taken place, about which the three men had made up a concerted story for use in case of need. They had, however, overlooked the point about the *Chichester*. It was a more significant point than it seemed at first sight, because a knowledge of the tragedy could alone make it important enough to hedge about. Fiquet apparently took the same view. He began to press Malot about small irrelevant details. Malot apparently saw what his questioner wanted, for the mocking assurance disappeared from his manner and he grew wary and nervous. His memory, which up to now had been perfect, became immediately tricky and unreliable. However, Fiquet accumulated a number of odd statements which he wrote down and forced Malot, much against his will, to sign.

On calling the other two men back one at a time and putting to them these same questions, agreement manifested itself on some points, while on others a difference of opinion became revealed. In the end the only thing that seemed certain was that the motor had really broken down, though whether the damage was accidental or intentional could not be ascertained. The men were agreed as to the nature of the mishap and the hours at which it had occurred and at which the repairs had been completed. But when Fiquet attempted to make a time-table covering the actual repairs, a hopeless divergence of testimony resulted. Thus Malot said it had taken nearly two hours to remove the cylinder head, while Maurin, who was supposed to be assisting him, said it had occupied some fifteen minutes. Other estimates varied similarly.

When Fiquet had done his worst, he turned to French.

"I think we'd better have a look over the smack. If the unlikely happens we may find a cigarette end on board of the exclusive brand your friend smokes."

Followed by captain and crew, they walked down to the outer harbour. There the lugger, F711, was subjected to the closest scrutiny that it had received since it left the builder's yard. But the unlikely did not happen. They found neither a cigarette end nor anything else to suggest that Raymond might at one time have been a passenger.

Baffled, but intensely suspicious, the two police officers dismissed Martin and his crew and withdrew to an hotel on the Plage for refreshment and discussion. Both held the view that while the men might be innocent of active participation in the *Nymph* affair, they knew something about it.

"I must see this man, Pasteur," French observed. "I dare say this would be as good a time as any. Will you come along?"

French felt there could be nothing to learn from the financier, as at the request of Scotland Yard he had already been interviewed by the local police. And so it proved. Beyond confirming what French had already heard as to his negotiations with Moxon's, Pasteur could tell them nothing.

"If I were on this job in England," French said after they had unfruitfully considered their next step, "I should make a cast."

Fiquet looked puzzled. "A cast?" he repeated questioningly. "A model of plaster? What? I do not understand."

French smiled. "No, not a model," he explained. "The word has another meaning. A cast is what we call dropping out one or more difficult links in a chain and leaping or casting forward to one which should be easier to deal with. For instance, in following footsteps we come to a hard patch of ground which has retained no marks. We therefore make a cast, drop out the hard, and look for tracks on the next soft piece."

Fiquet smiled in his turn. He was pleased. He had learned a new English phrase. "To make a cast" represented a process with which he was very familiar.

"Yes, my friend," he answered, repeating the phrase with unction, "we make the cast. *Bon!* And then?"

"Let us assume for argument's sake that Raymond somehow came ashore in France. That is Step Number One. Step Number Two is how he did it. That we've not been able to find out. Let us drop it and make our cast to Step Number Three — where he went to after landing. In other words, I propose we search the coastal towns and villages for traces of him. He must have had food, and getting it must have brought him into contact with people."

"But already we have a circular out about him."

"I know, but let us intensify the search over this area."

Fiquet did not think that a second circular would help matters, however, he agreed, and the document was drafted. Fiquet presently went to telephone it to Dieppe, from where it would be sent on to all stations in the district.

"When we're here, we may as well start the sergeant on it at once," he said on his return. "Come back to the police station."

There being nothing more to keep them in Fécamp, they presently started their return journey. By the time they reached Dieppe the afternoon was well advanced. Fiquet excused himself on the ground of business, leaving French to amuse himself exploring the little town. He liked these narrow old streets with their ancient buildings, in some ways so like his own, in others so foreign and different. Dieppe he found more interesting than he had expected, and he had no trouble in filling all the time at his disposal.

Next morning he was early at police headquarters. Fiquet greeted him with a little whoop of triumph.

"Ah, *mon ami*," he cried, waving two flimsy pieces of paper. "Behold, I have here two replies! We have not been idle? *Non?*"

French made suitable sounds of interest and congratulation.

"The first is this. About seven on the morning of last Friday a young man who answered with exactness to the description was seen at a place called Senneville. He walked from the shore past a labourer who worked in the fields. My friend," Fiquet became impressive in his solemnity, "it was Raymond!"

To French this sounded credulous.

"How is that known?" he asked sceptically.

"Known?" Fiquet shrugged eloquently. "I know it because of the place. Senneville! It is the place of the smugglers; nowhere could a man more easily come ashore unseen. You will agree. But that is not all."

He put the report back on his desk and picked up the second with the air of a conjurer about to perform an exceptionally fine trick. "Behold," he said somewhat unnecessarily, "the second message. Also it is from our friend at Fécamp. The sergeant reports that on that same morning of Friday, a young man also answering well the description, arrived about eight o'clock at the Hotel des Étrangers in Fécamp and ordered *petit déjeuner*. Now, my friend, listen to me. From Senneville to Fécamp it takes to walk, one hour. Seen at Senneville at seven and at Fécamp at eight — one hour! The same young man? *Hein?*"

French nodded. It was certainly promising.

"*Bon!* The young man, he had *le petit déjeuner*. Afterwards he left. The sergeant tells us so much. He still makes inquiries."

"Jolly good, Fiquet. Congratulations on your men's response to your training."

Fiquet made a deprecating gesture, but he was evidently delighted by the Englishman's approval. "Ah," he said, somewhat contradicting his earlier attitude, "we must not be too sure. It sounds good, but it may be that we — how do you say it? — strip the bark from the wrong tree."

French agreed, while gently setting the other right as to his metaphor.

"Ah! It is the voice of the dog and not the covering of the tree? Strange! 'To bark at the wrong tree.' It is good."

French stopped suddenly.

"But look here," he said, "you've not mentioned the suit-cases. What about them?"

Fiquet threw out his hands with an expressive shrug.

"The reports, you have heard them," he pointed out. He knew no more than French. They would inquire. All would be made clear.

French hoped so. "I suppose then, our next excitement will be another drive?"

"But yes! We repeat the journey of yesterday. The car is waiting. *Allons!* Let us go."

"I would make the wager that this indeed is our man," Fiquet went on as they drove up the hill out of Dieppe. "I would make the wager that he landed at Senneville and lay hidden till the morning. You think so?"

French thought so. His views on the affair were changing and he was becoming optimistic. It seemed to him to grow increasingly likely that the man was Raymond, that Raymond was the murderer, and that he, French, was on his track.

CHAPTER
THIRTEEN

A Well-Marked Trail

The Fécamp sergeant, in answer to a telephone message, was waiting for them at the tiny village of Senneville. "We'll see the labourer first," said Fiquet.

They turned down a narrow road, a mere lane, towards the sea. At first it led through well cultivated country with labouring class houses spaced at intervals. But soon they came to wilder country, with only an occasional house of the poorest type. At one of these they stopped and the sergeant in a stentorian voice called "Jules Marquet!"

A tall, strongly-made young man, who was working in a field close by, somewhat unwillingly came forward. Slow and not too intelligent, thought French, but tenacious and reliable. The best possible kind of witness.

Marquet's story was simple. About seven o'clock on the morning in question he was working in the field behind his house when a tall young man with red hair and dressed in white flannels with a blue jacket, walked up the lane from the sea. Marquet was surprised at seeing any one there so early, though he was accustomed to strangers passing, the approach to the sea at Senneville being something of a show place. The young man did not see Marquet, but passed along up the lane. Marquet declared he would recognise him if he saw him again. He was carrying neither suit-cases nor anything else.

"Ah," said Fiquet delightedly as they returned to the car, "did not I tell you? Raymond, without a doubt!"

They drove on down the lane, which here had shrunk to a mere track. It fell continuously, winding down a narrow valley. Then suddenly they turned a corner and came in sight of the sea, framed in the V of the gorge.

The lane terminated on a little plateau some sixty or eighty feet above the beach. From this point to the beach itself a narrow zigzag footpath had been cut. This grew steeper and narrower the lower it went, until, some eight or ten feet from the bottom it all but disappeared. A branch, securely pegged at the upper end, had been laid along the slope for these last few feet, and this acted as a rope by which the adventurous could raise or lower themselves. The three men scrambled down on the beach and looked round.

It was certainly true that a place more suitable for a secret landing could scarcely be found in any part of the world. The coast consisted of a line of vast chalk cliffs, absolutely sheer and unbroken from top to base. This overpowering wall stretched away in an almost straight line into the distance in either direction, this little winding path up to the gap at Senneville being the only visible access to the land. The place was wild and forbidding, utterly lonely, overlooked by no human eye.

A paradise, French was sure, for the smugglers of old time.

"What do you think? *Hein?*" Fiquet asked with the air of a showman presenting a star item. "Behold!" he pointed westward along the coast, "not more than five kilometres to Fécamp. They bring in their smack, those fishermen, they set Raymond ashore here. None see. They go themselves to Fécamp. All is in order."

"It's likely enough," French admitted. "But you could only land here in calm weather."

"But certainly! But forget not that Thursday night was calm weather. Come, my friend; you have seen. We go on to Fécamp and the sergeant shall take us to the hotel of the second message? It is good?"

It was good. They climbed up from the shore and once more took their car.

"It is true," Fiquet explained as he drove carefully up the narrow track, "that this is not the only way to the sea. There are many valleys — Fécamp itself is in one of them, Dieppe in another — but the others are overlooked, there are houses. There are near here les Grandes Dalles, les Petites Dalles and others — all with roads down to the sea through valleys, but all with houses. Les Petites Dalles is quite a town."

"We have valleys like that on our side too," said French. "We call them chines. Same kind of coast as here, but these cliffs are steeper."

The road led back through the little hamlet of Senneville and then across open level pasture land on the top of those terrible cliffs to the edge of the valley in which Fécamp lay. Picturesque the town looked, spread out far below, with its long plage, its church spires and its river formed into a series of basins in which lay lilliputian ships. At the side of the road over the sea was a little church.

"The church, see," said Fiquet, pointing upwards, "it is to there that they come to make the thanks when the boats return after a storm."

A terrible light on the life of a fisherman on this iron coast! French looked with interest at the little building with its stunted spire. How close to the bedrock of human nature those gray old stones must have got. Life, death, widowhood, these were the things with which it dealt.

But Fiquet did not leave time for moralising. In his self-constituted capacity of showman he had stopped the car at a steep bend in the road.

"See, monsieur," he exclaimed, getting out and leading the way across a patch of grass towards the sea. "I show you another view of the cliffs. Behold."

The grass ran on for some fifty yards, sloping slightly upwards. Then it stopped. It stopped so suddenly that there was here a complete grass sward, running evenly with the general contour of the ground, and an inch further there was nothing.

"Look over," said Fiquet.

Resting his hands gingerly on the edge, French did so.

There was the grass on which he was leaning and then — the waves breaking some five or six hundred below. An absolutely sheer drop. No rocky buttresses or crags or even a slope at the bottom to break a fall. A vertical line from his eye to the shingle. He shivered and drew back.

"No coming ashore there," Fiquet chuckled.

They returned to the car and after a long drop down a winding road, crossed the swing bridge over the harbour and reached the Hotel des Étrangers.

A few seconds and the great question of identity was settled. The proprietress had met the young Englishman on his arrival, and both she and the waitress who had attended him at breakfast picked out Raymond's photograph from those of the half-dozen of other young men of similar type with which French had provided himself.

As to details, however, they had but little fresh information. The young man had entered the hotel about eight o'clock. Madame had gone forward to meet him and he had asked for *petit déjeuner.* This had been provided and had been paid for with French money. When he had finished the man had sat reading a newspaper. He had then asked the waitress at what hour the next train or bus left for Dieppe. She had told him there was a bus at 10.40. For some twenty minutes longer he had remained in the *salle á manger* reading his paper, then had gone out. He had seemed very much perturbed and upset. He had no suit-cases or other luggage.

French was extraordinarily pleased. He had come to France on the mere suspicion that Raymond might have reached the country, and here after only three days he had got on the man's trail. Jolly good! Of course, these French police had helped him, but he had no doubt that he would have got on all right without them, though perhaps more slowly owing to the language difficulty. Raymond had reached France! On arrival in the country he had immediately disappeared. Though he must have known his place was in London, he had remained hidden. Was it possible under these circumstances to doubt his guilt?

After a lot of thought French came to the conclusion that it was utterly impossible. If the man were innocent he would unquestionably have hurried back to London with his story. The fact that he had not brought the suit-cases to Fécamp was no argument for his innocence. He could easily have hidden them along the shore or among the bushes along the path leading to it. In fact, French now saw that he would have to do so. To carry them about would have been dangerous. Through some accident they might have been opened, which would have been the end of everything for Raymond. If he had hidden them along the shore he could have bought a second-hand car in Fécamp and gone back the next night and collected them.

At all events, whether the suit-cases had been hidden or not, there wasn't much chance that they were still in the neighbourhood. French discussed the point with Fiquet, but, rather to his surprise, Fiquet took the view that a search for them should be made. Some accident, he held, might have prevented Raymond collecting them. French naturally was not going to stand in the way of anything which might throw light on the tragedy and the sergeant was instructed to organise a thorough search in the whole Senneville district.

About half-past five the Satos bus was due from Dieppe. Till then the two detectives killed time over a multiplicity of bocks. When it arrived they met it and while it waited they questioned the conductor.

But here they drew blank. The bus on the journey in question had been well filled and the conductor could not remember whether a young man resembling Raymond had been a passenger.

Before leaving Fécamp Fiquet sent once again for Martin and his men, told them that the man about whom he had been inquiring had been put ashore at Senneville, and pointed out that only by means of their smack could this have been done. But it was no use. All three fishermen persisted in their vigorous denials.

It was late when the detectives reached Dieppe, and tired from their long day, they knocked off work and after dinner spent a couple of hours trying their luck at the casino. But early next morning they were at work again.

"I don't think," said Fiquet, "there is any use to go out along the coast again. We remain, I suggest, here in Dieppe?"

French said his idea was a look round the garages. "I was thinking also," he went on, "that Raymond might have made another call here. When, or rather if, he reached Dieppe that morning he was an undoubted Englishman. No one wanting to lie low in a French town would look as he did. I imagine, therefore, that his first care would be to get French clothes. What about trying the ready-made shops?"

Fiquet thought it a good idea. "That red hair also," he added, "he would not find a help. Red hair is not common in France and dye is. We'll include the hairdressers."

The inquiry opened well. The men had not been at work an hour when there was a message for Fiquet and French that their presence was required at M. Lemonnier's shop in the Rue St. Jacques.

In ten minutes they reached the building, a large establishment devoted to men's outfitting. A constable was waiting for them at the door and led them at once to the proprietor's office. At his desk was M. Lemonnier, a stout consequential individual, while in front of him on the edge of a chair sat a rather frightened looking young man. The constable effected introductions with an air.

"I think," M. Lemonnier said when all had been accommodated with seats, "that we have some information for you. This gentleman, M. Gaillard, is one of my salesmen. He served an English gentleman who may be the man in whom you are interested. Tell them, Gaillard, what you told me."

The young man shuffled nervously.

"It was on the morning of Friday last, messieurs," he began, "about one o'clock that the gentleman called. He said his luggage had gone astray and that he wished to buy a small outfit. He chose a suit, collars, tie, underwear, a hat, shoes and a light overcoat, in short, messieurs, a complete outfit. I fitted him with all these, he put them on, paid for them and left."

Fiquet nodded encouragingly.

"That might be the man we want, M. Gaillard," he said pleasantly. "Is he among those?" and French's photographs descended in a little shower on the desk.

Without hesitation Gaillard selected that of Raymond. Fiquet beamed.

"Excellent, M. Gaillard. You are a man of observation. Now will you describe the clothes you sold so that we may tell our people what to look out for."

Gaillard did so in detail. The detectives exchanged glances. "Suit-case," French prompted.

"You say, M. Gaillard, that the gentleman bought underclothes. Also there was his old suit. How did he carry these away?"

"He had a suit-case, monsieur."

"Can you describe it?"

Gaillard was afraid he could not do so very well. His description, however, was good enough to make sure that the suit-case was neither of those which had left England with the money.

"He must have bought it second-hand here in Dieppe," French suggested.

This information enabled the detectives to put out a corrected description of Raymond, and they went back to the *commissariat* to start the men on the *quais*, stations and hotels. The garages they reserved for themselves, and soon they were driving round from one to another, propounding their questions.

But all at once the luck seemed to have deserted them. Nowhere could they find the slightest further trace of Raymond. If he had vanished into thin air he could not have left less trace than he actually had. All day the men worked and by evening had to confess themselves beaten. Before going off duty they held a meeting at headquarters to summarise the position.

Only two further facts had emerged. At a small shop in the Rue Victor Hugo a man resembling Raymond had bought a secondhand suit-case of dark brown leather. The second fact was that a man of the same appearance, but dressed in clothes like those bought at M. Lemonnier's, had called at a hairdresser's in the Rue de la Barre and bought a bottle of brown hair dye.

With these two exceptions it was clear that the thorough combing given to Dieppe had been absolutely without result.

At this point Fiquet was called to the telephone. The sergeant at Fécamp rang up to say that a very complete search had been made of the country in the neighbourhood of Senneville, without obtaining any information whatever as to the suit-cases.

"I think," said Fiquet, when they had talked for some time, "that he has made for Paris. The bigger the town, the easier to lie hidden in it. Take my word for it, French, he's gone to Paris. He'll go into rooms in some small street on the south side and wait till things quiet down, perhaps till he's grown a beard. Then he'll make for his final hiding-place, possibly Brazil or Chile."

French was doubtful.

"I'm not sure that I agree with you," he returned slowly. "Raymond has been a lot in Paris and he must know plenty of people there. He must also have English friends who would be there often. I should say that in Paris he'd be afraid of being recognised."

"What then do you think he'd do?"

French shrugged. "That's not so easy. I think on the whole he'd try to get out of France as soon as he could. He might hope to leave by some of the southern ports or to get into Spain or Italy before his description was circulated. I agree that South America would be a likely enough destination, but I imagine he'd try to get there at once."

Finally it was arranged that the French police as a whole would take over the search, while French returned to London to report progress.

French was bitterly disappointed. Fiquet saw something of what was passing in his mind.

"This is no longer a job for one man," he pointed out consolingly. "Neither you nor I nor any one else, working alone, could find your man. It's a case for the organisation. Hundreds of men are required, thousands in fact, and through the organisation is the only way you can get them."

French agreed, though the argument did not remove his disappointment. But a telephone in the late evening from the Yard to police headquarters consoled him somewhat. Fresh news had come in on the English side and he was wanted back as soon as possible. He, therefore, took an impressive leave of the French officials and travelled back to London by the night service to Newhaven.

CHAPTER
FOURTEEN

A Change of Venue

French reached Victoria at 6.5 next morning and after a visit to his home for breakfast, went on to the Yard. There he found an instruction awaiting him to report immediately to the Assistant Commissioner, and as soon, therefore, as Sir Mortimer Ellison had come in, he presented himself at his room.

"Well, French, you didn't get your bird in France?"

French shook his head despondently.

"Not so far, sir," he said. "But everything's in train for a detailed search of the country."

"You think he's still there?"

"We haven't been able to trace his leaving."

"Not what you might call an absolute demonstration, is it? Let's see what you did get. If I've read your reports correctly, you found that Raymond landed at Senneville, near Fécamp, during Thursday night, that he went to Dieppe and disguised himself, and that he then disappeared? That all?"

"That's about all, I'm afraid, sir," French admitted ruefully. "But that may lead to something," and he explained the steps which had been agreed on.

"You were worried about not getting the suit-cases?"

"That's so, sir. It seemed to me that if the suit-cases were not forthcoming, the whole motive for the murders was gone."

"The search for them is still in hand?"

"Yes, sir."

Sir Mortimer shrugged. "Let our French friends amuse themselves with it. There's something more important here for you."

French was surprised. This was not the attitude the Assistant Commissioner usually took up in such matters. He waited expectantly.

"We had some news yesterday afternoon and as it seemed promising, I thought it better that you should handle it from the beginning. Hence your recall."

Sir Mortimer went on to say that on the previous evening the Chancery Lane Branch of the London and Northern Bank had rung up stating that they had come on some of the notes referred to in the Yard's Circular No. F174D of 30th June, and suggesting that a representative should be sent down to get the details.

French was highly pleased.

"The very thing we wanted," he declared. "We're much more likely to get something from that end of it than from any other."

"Well, off you go to the bank and get it."

The bank occupied a large Victorian block of buildings at the Fleet Street end of Chancery Lane. Everything was massive, ornate and old fashioned. French was shown into a waiting-room while the porter took his name to mysterious regions remote from the vulgar. At last he was ushered into the holy of holies.

There the manager, Mr. Craven, from his bearing a very great man indeed, awaited him. With condescension he requested French to be seated. It seemed to French that so lofty an individual would be unable to bring himself to deal with the sordid details of mere finance, but in this he was speedily undeceived.

"Sit down, Inspector, won't you?" the great man began. "You know, I take it, what I want you for? Three of the notes your people wrote about have come in. One of our tellers found them in his cash last night."

"Very good news for us, sir," French replied. "I suppose you know that it's in connection with the Moxon's General Securities case?"

"I didn't know definitely, but I suspected it from the large number of notes involved. A terrible business, that, Inspector! I know three men, well-to-do they were in a small way, nice little houses, sons at college and all that, and now — ruined, every penny of their savings gone. Elderly men, having to start life again. And heaven knows where they'll get jobs. It's terrible to think of."

French whole-heartedly agreed.

"That's three among my own personal acquaintances," Mr. Craven reiterated, "and there must be thousands of others. And it's not only here," he went on, warming to his subject, "but the same thing is happening abroad. Only this morning I've heard that the Schneider-Hummel Company of Berlin is down. And it's by no means the first in Germany. And you know Bollini's of Milan crashed on the third day. And some of the French firms are so badly hit that it's doubtful if they'll recover. I tell you, Inspector, your people must get hold of these fellows. It's not that I'm vindictive, though when it comes to actually decamping with the money there's nothing too bad for them. But so many people are ruined by this sort of speculation in higher finance that it must be made very definitely not to pay. I suppose it's not a fair question to ask you if you've made any progress?"

French hesitated. There could be no harm in giving a little information.

"Don't let it go beyond you," he said, "but we've learned that Raymond landed in France. We're following him up, but we've not got him yet. Of course we've so far no proof that he's guilty."

Mr. Craven became more confidential.

"Do you know, I've been rather surprised to learn that Raymond was mixed up in this thing? I should have thought he was one of the best of them. But you never know. Right, Inspector, I'll keep what you've said to myself. Now you want to hear what we have to tell you. I think we'll have Mr. Blake in. He is the teller who found the notes."

He touched a bell and presently a solemn-looking young man with a round face and round tortoise-shell spectacles like a brob-dingnagian owl, entered the room.

"Sit down, Blake. This is Inspector French from Scotland Yard You might tell him about those notes."

The young man blinked at French.

"It was yesterday afternoon that I noticed them," he said. "It was after the doors were shut and when I was squaring away my cash after the day's work. It occurred to me that the number on a ten pound note was one of those on the Yard's circular. I got the circular and found I was right."

"Good," French said heartily.

"It occurred to me," the young man continued, "that if there was one, there might be more and I looked all through the notes I had. There were two others, both tens; that is, three tens altogether. I immediately reported the matter to the manager."

"And I in my turn rang up your people at the Yard," Mr. Craven added.

"Quite so, sir," French returned. "Very satisfactory." Then to Blake: "Now, Mr. Blake, here is the important question: Can you tell me where these notes came from?"

"Yes, I can. As you know, we keep a note of the passing in or out of all notes of five pounds and over. These were paid in by Mr. Samuel Thompson of Covent Garden. He paid them in in person."

French was delighted. As fast as a taxi could take him, he reached Covent Garden.

Samuel Thompson was a little old man with a goatee beard and a shrewd eye. French explained his business, asking the other where he had obtained the notes.

Thompson remembered the transaction, but with a distorted sense of humour, pretended to be annoyed at French's questions.

"Ah," he mocked, "you'd like to run me in for 'avin' forged notes in my possession, wouldn't you? Or is it stolen notes?"

"Stolen," said French cheerfully.

"Aye, stolen. You'd like to run me in, wouldn't you? Well, you ain't a-goin' to. I've kep' out o' the clutches o' you an' your like all my life, an' I ain't a-goin' to fall into 'em now."

The man's face was solemn, indeed outraged, but there was a twinkle in his eye.

"Sorry," said French. "I'd have liked your company to the Yard, but if I can't have it I'll just have to get a broken heart mended elsewhere. Well, what can you do for me, Mr. Thompson? Can you help me to get on to those notes?"

"Aye, I can 'elp you, since you're not goin' to do the dirty on me. Those notes, do you know where I got them?"

"It's what I want to know."

"Well, you wouldn't be likely to guess, so I'll 'ave to tell you. I got them from the bank."

"The bank?"

"You may well say 'The bank.' Aye, but it was the bank all the same."

"What bank?"

"W'y the bank in Chancery Lane. The same bank as wot I paid 'em into."

French smiled.

"Is that the way you do your business, Mr. Thompson? Take them out and watch them grow and then put them back again?"

"Well, it was like this 'ere. I 'ave a daughter wot keeps apartments. Well, the 'ouse was dirty and wanted doin' up. She was losin' 'er boarders along of it, an' the

194

landlord —" Mr. Thompson's vocabulary failed him and he spat in deepest contempt. "So I thought as I'd send 'er thirty poun' for the job. I got the thirty poun' out o' the bank an' kept it to send 'er, but before I got it away I'd a letter from 'er that an uncle of 'er 'usband's 'ad died an' left 'er 'undred quid. Not often a thing like that 'appens, is it?"

French breathed sympathetic congratulations.

"Aye. Well, that kind o' saved me my thirty quid. I didn't want to 'ave the money lyin' about 'ere, so I paid it in yes'day afternoon; the same notes as wot I got out nearly a fortnight before."

"That," said French, "should be easy to check. The banks keep a note of what they pay out."

"If that's so," the old man returned, "it's durned strange they didn't tell you themselves, without your comin' to me abaht it."

French entirely agreed, though he didn't say so. As a matter of fact he was considerably disappointed with the interview. While he thought that Thompson believed what he had said, French felt sure the man must be in error. The notes had been paid to Moxon's General Securities and almost certainly had left England in one of those suit-cases with Moxon and Raymond. And now this old fellow said he got them out of the bank before the date of the crime. A mistake here surely.

Twenty minutes later French was once more closeted with Blake in the vacant room in the Chancery Lane bank.

"According to that Thompson man you people paid the three notes out yourselves," he explained. "He says he got them from you on last Wednesday week. That was the day before the murders. Can you check it up?"

Blake was not away many minutes.

"Paid out to Thompson on the 25th of June," he declared, "just as the old man says."

"Who paid them out?" French demanded.

"I did."

For a moment a sarcastic reply hung on French's lips. Then he remembered that so far from reprimanding the young man for his carelessness, he should compliment him on his efficiency. These notes were paid out before the Yard circular was drafted.

But the circumstance produced a quaking at the foundations of French's world. His whole case was that these notes had been paid out by the bank to Moxon's General Securities and had been taken out of the country by Moxon and Raymond. In the case of these three notes this manifestly had not been done. The question, therefore, immediately arose, Were these three notes exceptional, or had others been dealt with similarly?

French thought first of calling on Honeyford and getting his views on this disturbing phenomenon. Then he saw that the views of neither Honeyford nor any one else mattered two hoots. Facts and facts only were required, and facts it was his duty to obtain. His next step was obvious. He must issue a new circular to the banks asking them to find out if any of the notes in question were at present in their strong-rooms, and if so, when they had come in and from whom they had been received.

He went back to the Yard, drafted his circular, and arranged for it to be put out with the minimum of delay. Then to save time he rang up Mr. Craven and the managers of a number of other banks in the neighbourhood, explaining the point and asking if it could be looked into at once.

He had scarcely finished when there was a reply from Blake. The young man had found some more notes and suggested that the inspector should return to the bank and hear the details first hand.

When French arrived he found the owl-like clerk in what must have been as nearly a state of excitement as his temperament would allow.

"The strong-room's full of them!" he exclaimed, his eyes rounder than ever. "Just full! I've got nearly four thousand pounds' worth of them already and I've not finished going through the tens! Will you sit down and wait a few minutes, Mr. French? I've two men helping me and we won't be very long going through the rest."

French was rather overwhelmed by the news. He was not sure whether to be pleased or otherwise. If these notes had been paid by the absconding partners, either in France or through some English agents, it would mean additional clues at his disposal. On the other hand, if they had left Moxon's General Securities before the crash, it would mean that their value as evidence was gone. All, he saw, would hinge on the date on which they had been received back into the bank.

Anxiously he sat waiting, while he continued turning the matter over in his mind. The whole orientation of his case might be altered by this discovery. He wished Blake would hurry up.

It was over an hour, however, before the young man reappeared. He carried an open note-book and his look of excitement had not diminished.

"There, Mr. French," he said, planting the note-book down on the desk. "What do you think of that? 141 twenties, 153 tens and 327 fives! £5985 altogether, and if you add the three tens found originally, over £6000! Is that any good to you?"

French was very much puzzled. Except on the general principle that all information must be useful he didn't see that this was going to help. "When was it paid in and by whom?" he demanded. "That's what we must get. How soon can you let me have it, Mr. Blake?"

Blake, who by this time had got over his awe of French's position, smiled.

"It'll take the deuce of a while to get out. I shouldn't wait for it if I were you." He was proceeding to explain how much work there would be in the operation, when a porter looked in.

"Beg pardon, sir, but is Mr. French here? Wanted on the 'phone, sir."

"That you, French?" came over the wire. "Ellison speaking. Are you nearly through there?"

"Yes, sir, for the time being. Just this minute."

"Well, go along to the Oxford Street branch of the Western Counties Bank. There's more news there of the same kind."

"That was the Yard," French said as he rang off. "I'm wanted elsewhere. Well, Mr. Blake, I'm much obliged for what you're doing and I hope you'll push on with getting out this other information."

History slowly but steadily repeated itself in the Oxford Street bank. It was after hours when French arrived, but he was expected, admitted, kept waiting, and then shown into the manager's office. The case was stated, a teller was called, and details were given. It might have been the same episode over again.

Like Blake, the teller stated that on receipt of the telephone from the Yard, he had been instructed to make the required search. He had not gone far when he found that a large number of the notes mentioned in the circular were actually in the strong-room. He had reported the matter, obtained assistance, and counted the notes. Here also they ran into a considerable sum. In twenties, tens and fives, it amounted to no less than £9025.

French swore weakly. Then pulling himself together, he put his questions. When had these notes been received, and from whom? He wanted to trace how they had got back to the bank. His remarks were received without enthusiasm, but the information was promised in due course.

It was not likely, French thought, as he walked slowly towards the Yard, that both these banks should have made a mistake in their figures. It surely must mean that these criminals had been extraordinarily efficient in their organisation. Here it was, not a fortnight from the crime, and in spite of all the precautions taken, large amounts of the stolen money had been got rid of! To French it seemed almost incredible. He had made a list of all those who could by any possibility be suspected.

The descriptions of these people were in the hands of every policeman in the country, indeed almost of every policeman in Western Europe, and yet some of these persons had presumably walked into banks or shops or money exchanges and planted thousands of pounds' worth of the stolen notes! Thousands of pounds' worth of stolen notes under the eyes of the police and with the bank clerks warned against that very thing! French could scarcely bring himself to believe it possible.

But if it hadn't happened, it meant that his case had gone very fundamentally adrift. Indeed, it meant nothing less than that the Yard's theory was wrong and that no theft had taken place at all. Was this the explanation? Had all this missing money vanished in more or less legitimate operations on the Stock Exchange? Honeyford had seemed certain enough about the thefts. Was Honeyford wrong?

On the other hand, if there had been no theft, what was the motive for the murders? Where were Raymond and Esdale? Where were the suit-cases?

French felt it was a case for coffee. He had a strong brew after supper, but though he spent the evening racking and re-racking his brains, he obtained no light. During the next morning, however, he got a fresh start. Some further information came in.

CHAPTER
FIFTEEN

Clear Currency

A great deal of information, in fact, came in. Some of it was merely an amplification of what had already been received, some was entirely new. Of the former, four additional banks had rung up to say that numbers of the notes in question had been found among their cash. The amounts varied. In one bank there was over three thousand pounds' worth, in another only a few hundreds. Adding the amounts in the whole six, it meant that some twenty thousand pounds' worth of the money had been accounted for.

Of the new information there were two distinct items. First, all of the four new banks mentioned that the notes on the Yard's list were circulating among the public. In each case, one or two had been paid in during the day. In each case, happily, the tellers had noted the person presenting them.

French gave a grunt of satisfaction. Here at least was something he could get on with. It would indeed be hard luck if he failed to trace these notes back to Moxon's General Securities.

The other piece of news was due to his friend, Blake. That estimable young man had completed his list of the persons who had paid in the notes lying in the strong-room.

In half an hour French was once more at the Chancery Lane bank and had the list in his hands. At once he received a further shock.

The very first item he looked at, one for £547 10s. had been paid in on June 5th!

Three weeks before the tragedy! Impossible, he thought.

Then as his eye ran down the columns his amazement grew. The notes had been presented on varying dates, it was true. But every single one of them had been lodged before the date of the crime; most of them weeks before it!

French was staggered. It was beginning to look as if there couldn't have been any robbery at all. Curse the confounded thing!

Then in a moment he saw the explanation. These dates referred to some previous occasion on which the notes had gone to the bank. It must have been *after* this that they had been sent to Moxon's General Securities.

This appeared obvious, but French thought it well to have it confirmed. He got Blake to look up the point forthwith.

But he was wrong. The notes had in every case been sent to Moxon's before these dates of return to the bank. Moreover, since their return they had lain in the bank's strong-room.

French's brain whirled. But he had not time to sit down and think things out. For the next two days he was fully occupied in visiting the original six banks, as well as seven more which afterwards rang up, and in getting the details from each collated. This mass of information at least left no doubt as to the facts.

For some considerable time, it was now proved, Moxon's General Securities had been cashing cheques and drafts in notes of comparatively small denominations. They had obtained, apparently in April, May and early June, considerably over a million in this way. Shortly after getting it in, they had paid it out again. Of these outward transactions there were no entries in the firm's books.

For some time French worried over the problem without obtaining a glimmer of light. At last he put it aside and turned to see if he could learn anything from the list of those through whom the notes had returned to the banks.

The first was that of Messrs. Paul Malet & Co., Jewellers, of Regent Street.

At this suggestion that there might be women in the case, French mentally sat up. If these men were making gifts, it should certainly help him by widening the basis of the inquiry.

The second name was also that of a jeweller, and French noted with satisfaction the growing prominence of the feminine side of the affair.

But when he came to the third name and found that it also was a jeweller's, he stopped abruptly, staring at the paper before him and whistling softly through his teeth.

Then at last an idea flashed into his mind, and hurriedly he began examining the names, taking them at random.

Yes, he was right! They were practically all jewellers!

French swore as he rose from his chair and began pacing the room. By Jove, yes! He saw it now. At last he understood these strangely contradictory facts. A fool he had been! Now that he saw it, the thing seemed obvious. He should have guessed it long ago.

The partners were buying jewels. Jewels in the rough, French dared swear. He had wondered how they had intended to get rid of these vast sums of money without leaving a trail of numbered banknotes which would lead to their goal the detectives who would inevitably be put on the case. Here was the explanation.

It was not true, of course, to say that jewels, presumably uncut diamonds, could not be traced. Experts could identify stones almost as readily as tellers could banknotes. But French knew that the difficulties of tracing the stones would be much greater than that of following up the notes, had the "swag" been retained in that form. In all probability the thieves would get the stones cut as soon as they could, and if so, all hope of direct identification would be gone. Everything would then depend on the cutters, and even were there no unscrupulous cutters in the world, in the nature of things adequate evidence would be hard to obtain. In fact, the move was highly astute. By it the partners had changed a dangerous commodity, banknotes, into a comparatively safe currency, diamonds. At least, so French now suspected.

As he continued turning the matter over in his mind, he saw that it might well have even more important consequences. The suit-cases! Until now he had believed the suit-cases to be a vital part of the affair. Without them, or something like them, so much wealth could not have been transported. But in the form of uncut diamonds a million and a half sterling could be carried in a man's pocket. Not only was there safety in the use of such a medium; there was portability also.

This consideration led a step further. Raymond, escaping without the suit-cases, might still have carried the whole of the booty with him. French realised once again that the finding of Raymond was absolutely essential and must be prosecuted with the utmost energy that the combined forces of the English and French police could put into it.

He swung his thoughts back to the immediate present. Obviously his next job must be to call on the jewellers in question. A rich vein this, he felt sure! If he couldn't make something worth while out of the jewellers, he felt that he should resign his job.

It was too late to do anything that night, but next morning saw him hard at it. He began with the first on the list, Messrs. Paul Malet & Co., of Regent Street.

On sending in his card, he was received by Mr. Malet in the latter's private room.

"I hope you're not coming as a stormy petrel, Inspector?" began the proprietor. "Your official visits are almost as unsettling to a man in my position as to a criminal."

"You've nothing to be afraid of this time, sir," French returned. "I'm after thefts, certainly, but not thefts of jewellery. All I want is a bit of information."

Malet looked his question.

"On May 23rd," French went on, "your firm lodged £547 10s. in the Chancery Lane Branch of the London and Northern Bank. I want to know what this sum represented."

"What's it all about?" Malet asked curiously.

"This Moxon's General Securities case. As you know, a vast sum has disappeared, about a million and a half, so far as we can make out. You know that?"

Malet nodded.

"At first we thought that it had disappeared in cash. Now there is reason to suspect that before the crash it was changed into jewellery," and French went on to tell what he had learned from the banks.

"It doesn't affect me."

"I told you, sir, it didn't. But I'd be obliged for the information all the same."

Malet frowned, summoned his manager, Mr. Dulap, and asked him could he obtain the information.

Dulap thought he could. He disappeared, returning in a few moments with a story which French received as a thirsty land receives rain.

It seemed that on the date in question a man had called and asked to see some uncut diamonds of good quality. He explained that he was considering setting up in business as a dealer and wished to have a small stock in hand before doing so. He carefully examined the stones shown him and at last selected four. The price came to £547 10s. Somewhat to the salesman's surprise, he paid for these in notes of comparatively small denominations, chiefly fives and tens. He was unknown to the salesman, but gave his name as Mr.

Septimus Birrell, of Dungeness, The Dunes, Farnham, Surrey.

This was all highly encouraging, but it did not go far enough. French asked to see the salesman.

"Have a look at those," he invited, spreading out his photographs on the table. "Is the man among them?"

They made in all a rather large collection. Not only were all the partners and chief officials of Moxon's included, but there also some two dozen more of as similar looking men as French could find.

There was some slight tenseness in the atmosphere as the salesman slowly turned over the cards. Failure to identify the purchaser would not necessarily mean failure in this line of inquiry, but a recognition would be a great step forward. Therefore French watched, almost holding his breath.

The salesman got to the end of the pile, then began to look back. For a time he compared two pictures, then finally discarded one. He held the other up, put it back, and finally picked it up again.

"It's like him, that one is," he declared, "but I'm not just sure of him. Couldn't swear to him, if you understand me."

French seized the card. Esdale! Esdale, the missing accountant! Esdale, who had vanished to Paris on the day before the crime and who had not been heard of since. This looked a bit of all right. If French could only get this confounded salesman to be sure of his identification, it would be a step forward and no mistake.

But the man would not commit himself. One thing which confused him was the fact that the customer had worn heavy-rimmed tortoiseshell spectacles, whereas the man in the photograph had no glasses. French tried covering the eyes on the photograph, but still without result.

At last, however, by asking what approached very nearly to leading questions, he got what he wanted. The salesman had noticed that the little finger of the man's left hand was crooked — permanently closed in towards the palm. This was one of Esdale's peculiarities, ascertained by Willis. The purchaser was then definitely Esdale. Not only so, it was Esdale disguised.

French felt fully convinced as to the identity and was correspondingly delighted as to his progress. To make assurance doubly sure, however, he borrowed Malet's telephone and rang up the police station at Farnham. The sergeant there was able to answer his question off-hand. There was no house named Dungeness at the Dunes, nor was any one in the entire locality named Septimus Birrell.

So that was that. Esdale was definitely a party to the frauds. French turned to Malet.

"There is only one thing that I have still to trouble you with," he said, "but it's a very important one. We've got to recover these stones. Can you give me a description of them so that I can circularise the dealers?"

"I can give you a description of them as they were when we sold them," Malet returned. "But if your friends have any sense they won't sell them as they got them. They'll have them cut first. No one on earth could identify them then."

"We'd circularise the cutters also."

Malet shrugged.

"Perhaps they might cut them themselves."

French thought this over.

"Well," he said at last, "we can only do our best. You might let me have those descriptions at all events."

French determined that the affair must be pushed with the utmost energy. He returned to the Yard and obtained a number of helpers. Between them during the remainder of the day they visited the remaining twenty-six jewellers, putting to them the same questions as French had asked Malet. As a result French's stock of information was considerably increased.

So far as he could make out, Moxon, Deeping, Raymond, and Esdale had all been concerned in the diamond buying. Several of the salesmen picked out the photograph of one or another of the four, but none of them were quite positive that it really represented their customer. The only thing about which a number were absolutely certain was that one purchaser had a crooked finger, like Esdale's. All this confirmed French's idea that the men must have disguised themselves before making their purchases.

French was surprised at the excellence of the records of stones which were kept by the various firms. The descriptions he obtained were so complete that he had no doubt that if any of the stones came on the market they would at once be recognised. The important thing now was to prevent the fact that the market was being watched from becoming known. To this end French swore all his witnesses to secrecy.

Though he had done so well, French could not but remember that while a million and a half was the total sum in question, he had traced only some fifty thousand pounds' worth of diamonds. That was to say that only one stone in every thirty would be watched for. However, when he reached the Yard there were further replies from banks, with the result that he spent several busy days squaring up the information received. This showed that the firm's operations had been wider than he had at first suspected. By far the greater number of purchases had been made in Amsterdam, where both Moxon and Deeping had been round most of the dealers. When French had finished he had traced purchases up to the value of nearly half a million.

This, of course, was all very well; it was getting valuable results. From the bank clue he, French, had established that the crime had been premeditated; that it had been decided on at least three months earlier, and that its details had been worked out with the utmost care. Even more important, he had got in train a line of investigation which would tend to cut off the profits of the criminals, if it did not indeed lead to their apprehension.

All very well, truly, but still not enough. Both Raymond and Esdale *must* be found and found quickly. This was now the absolutely essential feature of the case.

French had completed his visits to the jewellers on a Saturday. Over the week-end, which for once he spent at his own home, he continued at intervals to wrestle with his problem. He determined that on returning to the Yard on Monday he would concentrate on this matter of finding Raymond and Esdale. At the earliest possible moment he would have a chat with Inspector Willis, who was supposed to be following up Esdale. If there was nothing that he could do in that line he would go back to France and take up again the search for Raymond.

But when he reached the Yard the Fates stepped in to annul his plan. A constable knocked at his door. The Assistant Commissioner would be pleased to see him at the earliest possible moment.

CHAPTER
SIXTEEN

The "Goldenfinch's" Fireman

"Well, French. Ever hear of a thing called a banknote?"

French, who knew his chief, groaned. Sir Mortimer chuckled.

"Case of 'It never rains but it pours'? That's what they say in the North of Ireland to denote a superfluity, isn't it?"

French wasn't sure. He could not recall the phrase.

"Well, what's the good of spending years on Sir John Magill and not knowing a little thing like that? What are you doing now?"

"I was just considering what to go on with next, sir. I've gone as far with the notes and the diamonds as seems necessary at the moment. Everything on those lines is in train, dealers warned and so on. I was considering following up either Esdale or Raymond."

"Two of those things which seem easier said than done. Neither Willis nor the French police are making much of it."

"I don't see for the moment what else there is to work on."

The Assistant Commissioner smiled.

"Perhaps I can help you there. Let me see. You traced Raymond to Dieppe, where he had been buying clothes and hair-dye, didn't you?"

"Yes, sir."

"That was on Friday, wasn't it? The Friday of the crash in London?"

"Yes, sir."

"About what time in the day did you lose sight of him?"

French considered. "He left the ready-made clothes shop about one. He went direct to the hairdresser's, a street or two away. We traced him up to about ten minutes past one, sir."

Sir Mortimer grunted.

"That works in," he said. "In fact, French, there's been a bit of news since I saw you." He picked up a telegraph form. "Look at this. It came in on Saturday afternoon, but, as you'll see, there was no need to move about it till now. If Captain Quayle is correct it explains why you lost Raymond in Dieppe."

With a sudden growing interest French took the paper. It was a radiogram and read:

TO SCOTLAND YARD. Believe missing Bryce Raymond is aboard my ship as fireman. Please have ship met at Swansea on arrival Tuesday morning. Quayle, master, S.S. *Goldenfinch*.

The message had been despatched from the North Sea at 2.55p.m. on Saturday.

"By Jove, sir! Crippen over again. Did you learn where the *Goldenfinch* sailed from?"

"Yes, we called up Lloyd's first thing. The *Goldenfinch* is one of Workman & Newnes' boats, a thousand-ton tramp employed irregularly in the European coasting trade. She left Dieppe on the Saturday after the crime in ballast for Oslo. There she loaded pit-props for Newcastle. At Newcastle she changed her pit-props for coal and returned to Oslo. At Oslo she unloaded her coal and took in another cargo of props. She left Oslo early on last Thursday morning for Swansea. It works in all right?"

"It certainly does, sir. If the *Goldenfinch* left Dieppe on that Saturday morning she would be lying there on the Friday and Raymond might have got his start that afternoon. If so, and if he had slipped aboard quietly, it would explain how we missed him."

"This fellow Raymond's head seems to have been properly screwed on," Sir Mortimer went on. "I don't think I can see a much better way of leaving the country; though how he got round the captain to take him passes my comprehension. However, we needn't worry about it. You make it your business to meet the ship at Swansea and then we'll know. You've met Howells, haven't you?"

"The superintendent at Swansea, sir? Yes, I met him when I was on that Pyke affair at Burry Port."

"I thought so. I'll wire him that you're going. Better see him to-night, lest that boat should get in in the small hours."

Shortly after four that afternoon French walked into Superintendent Howell's room at police headquarters in Swansea. The superintendent greeted him warmly.

"Hallo, French! I thought you'd be back before long. No one who has breathed the atmosphere of South Wales can keep away for long. More sea mysteries?"

"Not as bad as the last time at all events," French assured him. "I come here when I want work done, because I find that you collect your men and do it for me. That's what you did the last time, and that's what I want you to do again."

"I know. It does take a bit of outside help to keep the Yard on its feet. What's the trouble this time? The Assistant Commissioner was giving nothing away. Said you'd have all particulars. I forget if you're a cigarette man?"

"Thanks," said French, helping himself from the box the other held out. "It's this Channel case; Moxon's General Securities, you know."

"Good Lord! What on earth has that got to do with us down here in Swansea?"

"So you might say," French returned. "As a matter of fact, it may have nothing. I'm here purely on spec. That'll explain it to you." He held out Captain Quayle's radiogram.

"Quayle? I know Quayle. A real good sort and reliable as they're made. If Quayle says he's got Raymond aboard, French, you may just take it that he has."

"That so? Well, superintendent, I want your help to bring him ashore. I've got two men with me, Knowles, the chief clerk of the firm to identify him, and Sergeant Carter to travel up with us, but I'd like the loan of a couple of men while I'm making the arrest. I've a notion all the exits from the ship should be covered."

"You're right. While you're sailing ahead in the captain's cabin he might be slipping into a boat from the stern."

"That's the idea. Will you fix it up?"

Howells picked up his telephone and put through certain calls.

"Hard luck," he said smiling. "That was the harbour-master and your ship is due about five in the morning. She might be in earlier, but not possibly before three. So it looks as if you'll have to spend your time from three o'clock on down in the docks." He rang up again. "Send in Jones and Lloyd."

"These are the men I'll send with you, Inspector," he explained as two constables entered the room. "See here, you two. You remember Inspector French, don't you?"

The men saluted. Details were soon arranged and French then found himself with time on his hands.

"Come home and have a bit of supper," Howells said hospitably. "We could either sit in the garden and have a chat or if you like we can run round a bit in the car."

French enjoyed his evening so much that he did not think of bed till after one. It didn't seem worth while thinking of it then, so Howells made him comfortable on the sofa in his sitting-room, with a powerful alarm clock on the table beside him.

The clock did its duty, with the result that a rather cold and sleepy French appeared shortly before three at the wharf at which the *Goldenfinch* was to tie up. With him, looking extremely unhappy, was Knowles. Carter, Jones and Lloyd made a little group close by.

"Unpleasant business this, Mr. Knowles," French remarked, feeling that a little judicious sympathy was desirable. "It's unpleasant for me; I hate making an arrest; but for you it must be ten times as unpleasant. Particularly as you know Mr. Raymond so well."

Knowles thawed under this treatment. He admitted that he loathed what was in front of him. He and Raymond had been good friends and he felt as if he were playing the part of a traitor.

"You must remember that if Mr. Raymond is innocent, this will do him no harm. Unpleasant for him, of course, but not really hurtful. On the other hand, if he's guilty, even your former friendship wouldn't make you wish to shield him."

Knowles agreed that this was reasonable. At the same time he would have preferred the job was some one else's.

They strolled up and down, smoking and trying to kill time in conversation. French found that the chief clerk was a well-read man, full of all kinds of unexpected information. His chief subject seemed to be history and he surprised French by the depth of his knowledge of the evolution of modern society. Even though finance was partly his profession, he seemed better up in its theory than French would have expected. He appeared to have read all that had been written on modern astronomy, physics and radiation, while his talk on the subjects of relativity and the quantum theory left French gasping.

It proved fortunate that the man was such a fund of information, for it was all needed. For four and a half hours the five men kept their dreary watch until, at half-past seven, the *Goldenfinch* condescended to put in an appearance. Then they slipped behind sheds and cranes and waited while she berthed.

Directly a gangway was lowered French went on board with Knowles and Carter, the two Welshmen locating themselves where they could command the other approaches to the ship. As French reached the bridge Captain Quayle came down. "Inspector French, C.I.D." French said in a low voice. The captain nodded and motioned towards the chart room. They sat down.

"I have him busy doing a bit of cleaning up under the Chief's eye," the captain began. "He'll have no chance to make a break for it, so you may make your mind easy on that. The only trouble is whether he's your man."

French took out his photographs.

"See him there?"

The captain turned them over rapidly, yet without haste. An efficient man, French thought. Then he picked out Raymond's portrait and looked at it keenly.

"That's him," he said with more conviction than grammar.

"Sure?"

"Quite."

French found it hard to hide his excitement. Raymond! The finding of Raymond bid fair to be the end, or practically the end, of the case. A triumph this, perhaps not so much for him, French, personally, but still a triumph! One at all events with which he would be chiefly associated. Good old Captain Quayle!

"Has he been quiet on board?"

"No complaints of any kind."

"You come from Oslo, don't you?"

"Yes, left on Thursday about 3 a.m."

"And he didn't try to break ship there?"

"No, nor at Newcastle, where we were before that. I didn't suspect him then, what's more, and I had no watch on him. He was perfectly free to leave the ship."

"How did you come to suspect him?" French asked.

"I'd better tell you from the beginning," Quayle returned. "We were in Dieppe unloading a cargo of Welsh coal from this port. We'd got in on the Wednesday night of that week and were due out again in ballast for Oslo early Saturday morning. I was going ashore after dinner on Friday when this fellow stepped up to me on the wharf. He asked me civilly if I was the master and I said I was. Then he said he was in a tight hole and kind of begged me to give him a helping hand. I liked the look of the fellow, so instead of telling him to go to the devil as one usually would, I asked him what was the trouble. He said he'd been making a heluva fool of himself. He'd been over on a holiday and he'd been to the casino and got caught with the gambling. He'd gone ahead amusing himself till every blessed penny was gone. He was alone, knew no one, had no money and had sold his return ticket. In short, he'd heard one of the men say I had a vacancy, and if that was so, he'd take it as an almighty favour if I'd let him sign on. He'd either work his passage back or he'd sign on for any reasonable time I liked. Well, as I said, I liked the look of the fellow and I believed his story. He didn't come making a whine, but just asked straight out for what he wanted. He was a good well-built likely looking chap; just the man for a fireman. I was a fireman short and the chief had been kicking up hell about it. So I thought I might as well give the beggar a start, and I did."

Quayle paused, opened a cupboard and produced a bottle. "Finest old French brandy," he explained. "Have a drop, Inspector?"

"I can't resist it," French admitted "But only a drop. I daren't delay till I've got this man safe."

"Don't you worry. He's safe enough. Well, I was telling you, I took him along. He signed on as fireman; came on board and started in right then. He worked with us to Oslo, to Newcastle and back to Oslo and the chief reported well of him. Then on the second visit to Oslo I came across an old *Mail* that said Raymond was wanted in connection with that Moxon's General Securities business and that he was believed to be somewhere in the north of France near Dieppe. It gave a photograph of him, and there on the sheet was my new fireman. I called the chief and we studied the picture together. He kept the chap busy aboard and when we were getting near the Channel I radioed the Yard. And here we are."

"All I can say," French declared, "is that if you've got the right man you'll be the most famous ship's master in the world. Remember the capture of Crippen? It's the same thing over again. Now, captain, I want this witness I've got to see him first. How can we fix that?"

Captain Quayle stepped out on to the bridge and blew down a tube. "Tell him to dress, that you're going to send him ashore for some stores or something. When he's ready send him up to me." He turned to French. "Put your witness in here in my state-room," he suggested. "Leave the door partly open and he can sign to you. Then you can do the needful."

The small dispositions were soon made. Knowles was placed in the captain's state-room, so that he could see into the chart-room. Outside on deck French and Carter took up their positions where they could see a signal through the porthole from Knowles. If he identified Raymond, these two would advance and make the arrest. The two local men were stationed ashore, one at each end of the *Goldenfinch*, where they could deal with any unexpected attempt to escape.

Ten minutes dragged slowly, then a tall, strongly-built, athletic young man appeared, sprang lightly up the bridge steps and knocked at the captain's door.

"Come in," French heard as he bent forward towards the porthole.

For a moment nothing happened. Knowles bent forward, peering through the narrow chink of the open door. Then he stepped quietly back and nodded his head decisively. French made a sign to Carter and the two men slipped quickly round the deck-house and entered the chart-room. As they did so Raymond swung round with the fierce expression of a trapped man.

"Bryce Raymond," French said immediately. "I am an officer from Scotland Yard. I arrest you on a charge of murdering Paul Arthur Moxon and Sydney Laurence Deeping in the English Channel on Thursday, 26th June. I have to warn you that anything you say may be given in evidence against you."

The young man had grown deadly pale, but he remained quite collected. Evidently, thought French, the scene was not unexpected. "If you come with us quietly, Mr. Raymond," French went on, "things will not be made more offensive than they need."

Raymond nodded quickly.

"I only wish to say without delay," he declared earnestly, "that bad as I know the circumstances appear, I am absolutely innocent of this crime."

"You will get every opportunity to put your case forward," French assured him. "Meanwhile we must get to London as soon as possible. Send one of those local men for a taxi, Carter, and we'll get the 8.55."

In the train Raymond turned to French.

"I've been thinking this business over, Inspector, not only since you arrested me, but also before it, for, of course, I knew the Yard was after me, and I've decided that I'd like to make a statement. It may not be wise, but as I've decided to tell the exact truth, the sooner I get it off my chest, the better I'll be pleased."

French looked at him doubtfully. He had heard this kind of opening before, and from men who were afterwards proved guilty beyond possibility of doubt. In fact, it was a favourite gambit.

"If you wish to make a statement, Mr. Raymond, I'm bound to hear it. I've already warned you officially that what you say may be used against you in evidence, and I now tell you unofficially that you would be wiser to consult your solicitor first. However, just as you like."

"Thank you, Inspector, I think you mean that kindly. All the same I'd prefer to make the statement now. It would be easier telling you here privately than it might later, and as I'm going to tell the truth in any case, it doesn't make much matter about the solicitor."

"Well, I repeat my warning, but just as you like."

"I'll tell you. Where shall I begin? Just what do you know?"

"Begin," said French, "at the close of the dinner on the Wednesday night before the crime. If you leave anything out I shall ask you. Carter, sit close here and take this statement down. Right, Mr. Raymond."

For a moment the young man hesitated, then with a gesture as if throwing everything to the winds, he began to speak.

"I shall have to begin a little bit earlier than that," he said, "in order to explain my actions on that Wednesday. On the previous afternoon, the Tuesday, Moxon called me into his room. He said that on Thursday and probably Friday he had to meet an important client, a French financier of great wealth. This man was staying near Fécamp and Moxon hoped to do big business with him. 'He's a yachtsman,' went on Moxon, 'so I think the best way to his heart will be to take him out in the *Nymph*,' his own yacht, as, of course, you know. 'I want you to come with me,' continued Moxon, 'so that if we do get down to brass tacks you can take the necessary notes. I don't want to have a stenographer with us. It would look as if we were trying to rush the man into things against his will.' Moxon explained that we were to dine with the Frenchman on Thursday evening, when he would propose the yachting excursion for Friday.

"I said it wouldn't be very easy to attend the Wednesday dinner and get away early enough in the *Nymph*. Moxon answered that he knew that and that he intended to go down to Folkestone, where the *Nymph* was lying, that night, to sleep on board, and next morning to start early for Fécamp. He advised me to do the same and I agreed. Then he said he was taking his car down and asked me to join him. I agreed to this also.

"On the next morning, Wednesday, I therefore packed my things for the couple of nights Moxon thought we should be away. I put in evening things for the dinners as well as yachting things for the day. To be strictly correct I should say that my man packed these, but you know what I mean."

"Since you're making a statement, you should be as accurate as possible, Mr. Raymond."

"I know. I'll be careful. Well, after the dinner we started off in Moxon's car, he driving. It —"

"Where did you dress for the dinner?"

"In a room we sometimes used for that purpose in the Securities building."

"Why did you not go to your rooms?"

"Moxon was working late and wanted me to help him. There was a lot to be done. It worked out very awkward, being away on the Thursday and Friday, on account of the Friday settlements. But Moxon thought it was worth while to suit the convenience of the Frenchman, in view of the business it might bring. Well, as I was saying, we ran to Folkestone in Moxon's car. There Moxon garaged the car and we got aboard the Nymph. We —"

"I'd like you to go slower, please, giving much more detail. When you reached Folkestone, for example, where did you get out?"

"At the corner of the Inner Harbour opposite the Harbour Garage, if you know the place."

"I follow. Had you any luggage?"

"Yes, I thought I said that. I had my suit-case containing an evening and a yachting suit; also night things, of course. Moxon also had a suit-case."

"What did you do with these suit-cases?"

"I took them out of the car and put them down near the ladder we should use. Moxon drove into the garage."

"Was he long away?"

"No. Three or four minutes, I should think. The dinghy was tied up to the ladder and when he came back he pulled it in and we got aboard. That was about three o'clock, I should say."

Raymond paused and a peculiar expression passed over his features. It was as if he had said to himself, "That was all easy; now we're coming to the trouble."

French wondered if he had determined to lie. Up to the present he had told the truth; French had already obtained confirmation of practically every statement. What was coming next?

"I hesitate to tell you what happened next," the young man continued at last, "because I can see it doesn't sound likely. I can only assure you it is the absolute truth. I cannot explain it myself, but it happened exactly as I'm going to tell you."

Again he paused and French nodded.

"When we got on board the *Nymph* Moxon said he was tired from the drive and wanted a drink. He asked me to join him and, of course, I did so. Then we got into our bunks and went to sleep. Or at least I did.

"Now here is the point which I hesitate to tell you. While I was asleep I had a sort of confused dream, or else the thing that I thought I dreamed really happened. I thought it was a dream at the time, but now I think it really happened. Someone woke me up and gave me another whisky and soda. At least I think so. I couldn't say who it was, though it was my impression that it was Moxon. Now, Inspector, whether this really happened or not I don't know, but I think it did. As I say, my remembrance of it is quite confused."

"I follow," French said as the young man paused expectantly.

"Then," Raymond went on, "here is the extraordinary thing. When I woke I was not in my bunk. It was dark and I was cold and stiff. I had a terrible head, a morning-after head, and my mouth was parched and tasting horribly. For a long time I wasn't able to move

— I think I slept again, but when at last I sat up it was light and then I saw where I was. I was lying on the sea shore on a sloping pathway which led down to the beach. It was a terrible coast with great white cliffs rising sheer for hundreds of feet. The path I was on led up to the entrance of a chine or valley. I supposed it was somewhere south of Folkestone, but I didn't recognise the place.

"For a long time I lay there unable to move, but gradually I grew stronger and at last I managed to get up on my feet. There was no use in going down to the sea, so I began to struggle up the path into the chine. Soon the footpath turned into a lane and I could see the wheelmarks of cars. I had no idea of the time, as my watch had stopped, but from the general look of things I guessed it was early morning."

Once again Raymond paused, but French made no comment and he continued:

"As I went on, the surface of the lane improved and at last it turned into a tarred road. I passed several houses, and from their appearance I began to think I must be in France. But I saw no one to ask and I did not want to knock at any of the houses in case it should still be very early.

"I pushed on slowly and passed through a tiny village and out on to the bare country above the cliffs. Almost at once I came to a milestone, one of those square white-washed stones with round reddish brown tops that one sees in France. Then I saw where I was. My side of the stone said 'Fécamp 4 kilos,' the other side 'Dieppe 61 kilos.'"

That at least this part of the tale was true was beyond question. French indeed remembered himself seeing that very milepost at the entrance to Senneville.

"I knew Fécamp was a good town and I decided to walk on there. By this time I should say that I was feeling a good deal better, but I was thirsty and wanted some coffee. In due course I reached Fécamp. There I went into an hotel and had *petit déjeuner.*"

"Where did you get the French money to pay for it?"

"I had changed a fiver when Moxon told me about the trip." He paused for a moment, then went on:

"I can scarcely describe to you how amazed I was at the whole thing. That I had been drugged I hadn't a doubt, but why was an absolutely hopeless mystery. It must, I supposed, have been done by Moxon. There must have been a drug in the whisky he gave me when we got aboard. But why had he done it? I couldn't form the faintest idea.

"The coffee cleared my brain and I began to consider what I should do. I picked up a paper idly, and then I got the shock of my life. It was dated Friday. At first I supposed it was a week old, but I saw that I was wrong. I could scarcely believe my eyes. I had gone to bed on Wednesday night, or rather early on Thursday morning, and now it appeared I had slept for twenty-four hours. It was then I began to believe that my dream was no dream at all, but an actual reality. I felt convinced I had been wakened and given more dope."

French was once again experiencing that exasperated disappointment which he had so often felt previously under similar circumstances. This tale of Raymond's hung together. If it continued as well as it had begun it might be very hard to shake it. In fact, it might even be true. And if it were true the most promising line of inquiry in the whole case would go west. He did not wish the young man evil, but to have one of his two possible clues peter out like this was too much for human nature to take without a protest. Then he remembered the disguise and his spirits rose again. That disguise would take some explanation.

"This made the whole thing more puzzling still," Raymond resumed. "Idly I turned over the paper, and then I got a second shock, ten times worse than the first. There was an account of the finding of the *Nymph* and of the murdered bodies of Moxon and Deeping!

"I needn't try to describe my horror. The more I thought of it, the more terrible the affair seemed. And the more puzzling too. How had Deeping got aboard the *Nymph?* How had I got off it? Who had committed these murders? How had they escaped? I couldn't see a ray of light anywhere.

"One of the things which bothered me most was the question of time. It was clear to me that I could not have lain during the day on the shore where I found myself. I should certainly have been seen. Therefore I had not been put ashore till the Thursday night. In this case, where was I on the Thursday? I was not on board the *Nymph*, because it was in charge of the mate of the *Chichester*. I could form no guess.

"Strange as you may think it, Inspector, it was not till later on that the horrible position I myself was in struck me. I had, of course, determined to return to London by the first boat, and I had asked the hotel people how I could get to Dieppe. They had advised the bus, and it was while I was sitting waiting for it that I saw my own position. Who would believe my story? I reviewed it and I got into an absolute panic. I saw that no one would. Moreover I could offer no proof of any material part of it. I had started in the *Nymph*; I was sure that would be proved. I had escaped to France. Would any one believe that I had not first committed the murders? No one, I felt sure. I became despairing.

"And that, Inspector, was where I made my mistake. I was convinced I would be accused of the crime, and be convinced too. I didn't think I had a chance. I lost my head and funked going back."

French was more disgusted than ever. The other critical point had been covered. His case seemed to be slipping away from him. "Continue, please," he said shortly.

"I took the bus to Dieppe. There I thought I should disappear. I bought some French clothes and dye for my hair. Then I hung about the Gare Maritime until in a lavatory I managed to change and dye my hair. While I was killing time I heard a boatman say that the tramp, *Goldenfinch*, lying further up the harbour, was short of a hand. I went round and watched for the skipper coming ashore. I pitched him a yarn about my having got gambling at the casino and losing all my money. He was very decent and told me to go aboard and report to the chief engineer. I got a start. That's about all, I think."

"What did you intend to do, I mean eventually?"

"Well, I didn't know. In Oslo I saw about the defalcations and that the police were after myself and Esdale. I realised what a blunder I had made, but I saw that whatever chance of being believed I might have had if I had gone home at once, I had none now. Another difficulty was, of course, that I had to earn some money to get along in the meantime, and I intended to stick to the *Goldenfinch* as long as I could. I was in hopes all the time that the truth of the Channel affair would come out so that I could get home."

French whistled softly between his teeth. Then he asked another question. "Tell me, Mr. Raymond, did you buy any diamonds on behalf of the firm?"

"Yes, many," the young man answered promptly. "We all did. An Argentina millionaire to whom we owed a lot of money asked us to pay him in that way. It was out of our line really, but because of the amount of business we had done with him Moxon agreed to oblige him."

"How do you know all that?"

"Moxon told me. Deeping also, I think."

"And did it not occur to you to doubt the bona fides of such an extraordinary arrangement?"

"Oh, no, not when Moxon said so. It wasn't my business. If Moxon wanted it done, I did it, that's all."

French nodded and said that Raymond's statement would be forwarded to the proper quarter. Then he relapsed into silence. There was a lot to think over in what he had heard and the remainder of the journey was as good an opportunity for consideration as he would get.

CHAPTER
SEVENTEEN

The Exploits of Willis

French began in the orthodox way by considering Raymond's story from the alternative points of view of its truth or falsehood. First, supposing it to be true.

In itself, the story was eminently possible. Everything could have happened exactly as described. It was no strain to one's credulity to suppose that Moxon, Deeping or the actual murderer wanted Raymond out of the way, though wishing to avoid his murder. Raymond might not have been admitted fully to the deceased partners' councils, and yet might have been a source of danger to them. Had he heard any of the rumours which were in circulation on that fatal Thursday, he might well have put two and two together and reached the truth. If, then, he were really the honest man so many appeared to think him, he could scarcely have kept silence, with the result that the hue and cry might have started before the criminals were clear. Here then was ample motive for temporarily silencing him.

French next noted the large proportion of the tale which had already been checked, and had proved true. The whole of Raymond's movements up to his going on board the *Nymph* about 3a.m. on the Thursday had been proved to have taken place exactly as he had stated. Again, all his movements from 7a.m. on the Friday up till the present moment had also been checked. The only part of the statement for which there was no independent evidence was for the period during which Raymond said he had been drugged, Thursday and Thursday night. Admittedly this was the crucial period, but it must also be admitted that in the nature of things it was improbable that proof for it would be forthcoming. In fact, the greatest care would naturally be taken to prevent it.

Another point in favour of the story was that it really did adequately account for Raymond's attitude and actions. His fears and his decision to hide were foolish to the last degree, but they were very human. Panic always clouded the mind. Considering the probabilities only, there was no reason to doubt this part of the story.

But the principal point in the young man's favour was, French thought, that he had left such obvious gaps in his narrative. Deeping's arrival on the yacht had not been explained, though Raymond had known — from the papers, if in no other way — that he was on board. His own departure from the *Nymph* he had left a mystery, declaring that he himself did not understand it. Still more striking was his failure to account for his own absence during Thursday, as well as for the means by which he had reached the French coast.

French did not believe that a man inventing a story would have left these gaps. Even if Raymond himself, being supposed to be under the influence of a drug, could not have known what was taking place, he would have hinted at the explanation. He would not have left the tale with an apparent impossibility in its most vital part.

On the other hand the whole statement might be an ingenious tissue of lies, or rather the middle portion of it, the vital portion. On that fatal Thursday Raymond might well have murdered his friends Moxon and Deeping, taken the diamonds, and somehow got ashore, perhaps by the agency of the lugger. He would have had ample opportunity to hide the diamonds in France, intending to get them later when the affair had blown over.

As French sat balancing the probabilities, he began slowly to incline to the view that the story was the truth. His thoughts went back to M. le Capitaine Martin and the lugger F711. There was a certain parallel between Martin's story and Raymond's in that both had been unaccountably missing during the whole of that eventful Thursday. Was this more than a coincidence?

If Moxon & Co. wanted to get rid of Raymond, had they made use of Martin? If Raymond were really drugged, would it not have been easy to set him aboard the smack, Martin for a consideration undertaking to put him ashore?

This certainly seemed likely. If it were true, and if he could get an admission from Martin, it would prove Raymond's statement.

He put his ideas in writing and then went in and discussed them with Sir Mortimer. It was decided that the matter must be tested immediately. French therefore telephoned to Fiquet at Dieppe, and left by the night service for France.

He was received with ceremony. Cigarettes were exchanged, bocks drunk, and his report considered. Certainly, a further examination of Captain Martin and his men should be made forthwith. If it was agreeable to French, Fiquet would accompany him to Fécamp immediately? It was agreeable. But excellent! They would start at once.

In due course they reached the police station at Fécamp and the three mariners were produced. Frightened, they were this time, French noted; much more frightened than before. And the reason was not far to seek. A re-examination evidently suggested to them that incriminating discoveries had been made. French thought the phenomenon hopeful.

"Now, Martin," Fiquet began, glaring at his victims with his usual ferocity, "this has become a very much more serious matter so far as you are concerned. Don't you make any mistake as to what it's about. Two men have been murdered aboard the yacht *Nymph* in the English Channel. That's one thing. The other is that about a hundred and eighty millions of francs have been stolen at the same time. You knew that?"

Martin admitted that he had read about it in the papers.

"Now in connection with those crimes a certain man was put ashore at Senneville on that Thursday night or

Friday morning. He was a man," and Fiquet described Raymond. "Now, Martin, that young man was put ashore by some one." Fiquet suddenly started forward and pointed an accusing finger straight into the captain's face. "Who was it?"

Martin, taken aback, stammered that he did not know.

Fiquet shook his head sceptically.

"Now listen carefully, Martin," he went on, fixing the unhappy skipper with his fiercest stare. "Don't you be more of a fool than you can help." He paused, then continued slowly, shaking his finger as he made his points. "If the men who put Raymond ashore deny it and their guilt is afterwards proved, they will take their trial as accessories after the fact. A case of murder, remember. You know what that will mean?" Again he paused to let the suggestion sink in. "If on the other hand these men come forward and confess and help the police, well, the matter will not be treated seriously. As a matter of fact, Martin," he now grew friendly and confidential, "we don't want you, we want your information. We want proof of how this Raymond got ashore. You were guilty of taking a drugged man aboard your ship, keeping him there all Thursday and putting him ashore on Thursday night. If that was abduction, we'll close our eyes to it. If it was taking a passenger without a licence, we'll not raise the question. If you persist in denying it, it'll mean that you've got some deeper interest in it, that you really are mixed up in the murder or the theft. Come on now; don't be a fool.

Answer my questions. When did you first fall in with the *Nymph*? You see, we know all about it."

Martin presented a piteous spectacle of fear and indecision. Evidently he had done what Fiquet suggested, and equally evidently he doubted the official closing of the eye.

"I'm giving you your chance," Fiquet went on solemnly, "to confess while you can." Again he waited, then added suddenly: "I suppose it didn't occur to you that there was a witness on the shore at Senneville that Thursday night?"

This, French thought, was not quite cricket, but he had to admit its efficacy. Martin started, beads of sweat glistening on his forehead.

"There was not, monsieur," he declared earnestly. "I swear no one was there." Then as he saw what he had said he halted, blank consternation written on his face. With a groan he made a gesture more eloquent of despair than any words French had ever heard, then sank down, his head buried in his hands.

But only for a moment. A moment later he sprang eagerly to his feet, while a torrent of words poured from his mouth.

"Is it a promise you have made me, monsieur?" he cried wildly. "Is it your word that if I tell all you don't arrest me?"

Fiquet gesticulated in his turn.

"But certainly not!" he returned. "I said we would not proceed against you for abduction or carrying a passenger without a licence. But you've admitted it now in any case. Go on and tell the whole story. You can't help yourself."

Martin saw this for himself. Fearful of what the detectives already knew, he decided discretion was the better part of valour and told his story. Separate examination of his men amply confirmed its truth.

It appeared that on the Thursday morning, when they thought it time to make for Fécamp after their night's catch, the motor really did fail. There was no wind and they could do nothing but drift. One of the crew knew something about motors and with the help of the other man he took it to pieces. He found what was wrong, and reassembled it, with the result that it ran satisfactorily. The work, however, had lost some five hours, so that by eleven o'clock they were still far out in the Channel. Just before they were ready to get under way the *Nymph* had appeared. She had evidently been about to pass at some distance, but when she saw the lugger lying to, she ported her helm and came close up. Two men got into the dinghy and rowed across.

These men Martin at once identified as Moxon and Deeping, selecting unhesitatingly their portraits from French's batch of photographs, and thereby setting the seal of absolute truth to his story. The two men came alongside and asked for the skipper. When Martin went forward Moxon came aboard, Deeping remaining in the dinghy.

Moxon asked if the fishermen were out to make a little money. Martin left him in no doubt on the point, and Moxon went on to explain that he had a man on his yacht whom he wanted put ashore and that he would pay well to have it done. The man, he said, was a private detective. It was in connection with a divorce case. A certain man and woman, friends of his own, had left with them on the yacht, and when they had got to sea they had found that this detective had stowed away to overhear what was said and so get his evidence. They had then been in a difficulty. They wanted to silence the man and get rid of him, but they didn't want to hurt him. What they had done, therefore, was to drug him with a harmless drug. This would keep him out of mischief for the rest of the day at least. They wanted the skipper to put him ashore. If he would do so, they would give him ten pounds for himself and five for each of his men.

They positively assured Martin that the drug was harmless and that the man would be perfectly well when he awoke. Martin then called the crew and put it to them. The proposal was agreed to and Moxon and Deeping rowed back to the yacht. Presently they returned with the young man whom the skipper had now learned was Raymond. He was heavily asleep. Martin had seen many a drugged man and he was satisfied from Raymond's appearance that he really was merely asleep, and not poisoned. He therefore took him on board, and twenty pounds was paid, and the little ships parted company.

It had been part of the bargain that Raymond should be put ashore secretly, and this obviously coincided with Martin's interests. They could not therefore go into port on the Thursday. They spent the day drifting about, having hurriedly once again dismantled their motor to supply a reason for their inaction. It was not likely that any one would have asked questions, but Captain Martin was taking no risks. In the evening they put the motor right, did some fishing, and about three in the morning put Raymond ashore at Senneville.

They had entirely believed the tale about the private detective looking for divorce evidence, but when they saw in the papers about the murders and robbery they experienced the same panic as had Raymond. They saw at once they had been made party to some part of the crime, and their hearts failed them for fear. Had it not been for this they would at once have told their story on Fiquet's first call. All three swore positively that Raymond had not awakened while on board and therefore that he could have known nothing of what had taken place there.

After telephoning to the Yard that Raymond could not be held for murder, French made his despondent way back to London. Here was another promising line of inquiry gone west. There had been three of them when he had started the case, leading to Nolan, Raymond and Esdale respectively. That to Nolan had early petered out, and now so had that to Raymond. Their man *must*, therefore, be Esdale. If not, his, French's, view of the case was wrong from beginning to end, for he could think of no one else who could have had a finger in the pie.

He arrived in London in the depths of despair. He was dog tired, having travelled two nights running with a wearisome day in between. Moreover during that day he had suffered a bitter disappointment.

240

But after a slow, luxurious bath a faint silver lining became apparent at the edge of the cloud, and by the time he had finished a good breakfast he saw that the sun was really shining behind it after all. In an almost normal frame of mind he reached the Yard.

There he was still further restored to his old optimistic self by the Assistant Commissioner's greeting. Sir Mortimer Ellison did not seem to share French's disappointment when he heard the latter's report. "I'm quite satisfied with that, French," he said. "I think you've done very well. We've got a decision about Raymond, which was what we wanted."

"Thank you, sir, for what you say," French answered. "Of course it's good to get any decision on any point of the case, but I'm afraid this one leaves us in the air. So far as I can see, the only other man who could have had anything to do with it is Esdale. And Esdale seems to have vanished completely."

Sir Mortimer smiled.

"That's where you're wrong, French," he said genially. "I didn't tell you because the affair of Raymond had to be finished up and left tidy. But as a matter of fact Willis has got a line on Esdale at last."

French was keenly interested.

"What's that, sir?" he asked eagerly.

"Go and see Willis and get the particulars from him. I've told Willis that you will take over from him to-day. Hear what he has to say, then come and report to me before you take any step."

Gone was French's weariness. It was a rejuvenated inspector that swung down the corridor to Willis' room;

so does the quality of the thought affect the physical springs of action. Willis was writing at his desk. They were good friends, these two, so they called each other insulting names and explained how little they thought of each other. Presently they got to business.

I have to go to Lincoln after lunch with Emery of the Home Office about that Hulbert poisoning case," Willis explained, "so I was just putting this affair on paper in case you didn't turn up before I left. I'm just done and I may as well finish. Sit down and keep quiet for five minutes."

French kept quiet for twenty, then Willis threw down his pen, stretched himself, and gathered his pages together.

"There you are," he said. "That's a record of the whole thing. But I'll tell you; you needn't read it.

"First I must admit that I've got uncommonly little to show for all these days' work. And I really did put an immense deal into it. But I had no captains of ships to do my work for me. Any that was done I had to do for myself. It makes a bit of difference, that."

"Don't apologise," French said sweetly. "I wasn't expecting much."

"Oh, you weren't, weren't you, you old humbug! Well, the A.C. wanted this Esdale traced, as you know. You were on to Nolan and Tanner was on to Raymond, and this Esdale was the third of the bunch. Well, things went fine at first. I began at Moxon's offices and there I learned that Esdale had gone to Paris by the 2p.m. service on the Wednesday before the crash. He had gone, so I learned, to get some securities which were in the custody of a firm in Paris, and which were required for the settling up on the Friday.

"Inquiring around, I soon found that one of the office boys had been sent to Cook's to get Esdale's tickets. I therefore brought this boy along to Cook's and saw the man who had sold the tickets. There were no place reservations and at first it didn't seem possible to get any further information. But after a good deal of trouble the man was able to place, within narrow limits, the number of the ticket. It was a book, first and return, numbered between 66,342 and 66,349 and, of course, dated 25th June.

"I then inquired from the administrations of the Southern and the Nord as to the collection of these tickets. I found that the outward portions of all of them had come in with one exception. The Boulogne-Paris portion of No. 66,345 had not been collected. This looked as if the passenger who had held it had travelled from Victoria to Boulogne, but no farther. None of the return portions had yet been collected.

"All the same I made inquiries along the entire route. At Victoria I could find no trace. I went on to Folkestone and tried again. Here I had the passport people as well as the police, but here also I could get nothing. I found the steamer which had worked that service and tried the officers, stewards and men, again without result. Same at Boulogne, where the A.C. had arranged for a French police officer to work with me. Same again at Paris. I can tell you that that journey was done pretty thoroughly, but without the very slightest result."

"Rotten," French sympathised comprehensively.

"Wasn't it? Time running away and nothing to show for it. Well, of course, I went to the Paris firm from whom Esdale was to have got the securities, but they could add nothing to the reply I had already got by telephone immediately on taking over. It was quite correct about the securities. They had been expecting Esdale to call for them. But Esdale had not called, nor had anything whatever been heard of him.

"I had, of course, put general inquiries in hand. A description of Esdale had been circulated in France as elsewhere, and I went round to the other Paris stations on spec. Blank silence everywhere. I got in touch with the police at the other French ports, then the Belgian and Dutch ports; no good.

"At last I went back to Boulogne. The evidence of the tickets was not conclusive, but it suggested that Esdale had doubled off at that point, and I determined to have another try for him there.

"I had done the Gare Maritime as well as I knew how, but it occurred to me that I might have been more thorough about the town station. You know that these boat trains stop at Boulogne Ville, or this one does at all events. Of course no one in his senses would join the Paris train at Boulogne Maritime and get out at Boulogne Ville, because it would be much quicker simply to walk up from the boat. But I reminded myself I was not after a normal passenger and I decided to try the town station again. I did, and to my immense surprise I got something that looked promising."

"Good," French interjected.

"A bit of luck, it was, I can tell you. Well, for the second time I saw the ticket collector who had been on duty at the platform at which the train had stopped. As usual there were a number of people from the town to join it: that's why it stops. On my first inquiry this man said no one had come off the train, but now he told me he had been thinking over it and he believed there had been one passenger. Once he'd remembered that, he'd remembered a lot of details. The man was an Englishman and he held a return ticket from London to Paris. He explained that he had to pay a call in the town and would go on to Paris that evening by a later train. The man was like the description of Esdale, and when I showed him Esdale's photograph he said he thought it was the same. I asked him how he now came to remember the details so well, and he said it was because he had wondered at the time why the traveller had got into the train at all at the Gare Maritime. He reminded me of the considerable wait there was there, and that it would have been much quicker for the man to have gone directly up the town from the *quais*."

"Did he leave luggage at the town station to pick up by the later train?" French inquired.

"No, he had no luggage with him except a despatch case, a small thing, which he carried in his hand. There was no record of such a thing having been put into the cloak-room at either the town or harbour stations that day.

"Well, this seemed news at last. If Esdale had left the train at Boulogne, where had he gone? I sat down to think it out."

"Somewhere in the shade where there was a bock?" French suggested.

"I felt that's what you would have done, and as you were the greater Continental traveller, I thought I should copy you. That's what I did, and some very decent places there are in Boulogne for the job. Drinking my bock, I wondered where Esdale could have gone to from Boulogne. For a while I didn't see it when suddenly it occurred to me. Then I could have kicked myself for not tumbling to it sooner. Where do you say?"

"Back to England?"

"Ah, more than that, you old sinner. You're not quite home yet."

French slapped his thigh.

"By Jove, Willis; the *Nymph!*"

"That's what I thought. But don't be too enthusiastic. I've not been able to prove it. I'll tell you."

French was impressed with the idea.

"I'll lay you any odds you like it's the truth," he exclaimed. "Isn't it the very thing we want? Who committed the murders? Who escaped in the dinghy? Who got the swag? Why, some one who sailed in the *Nymph*. Who had the knowledge to commit the murders? Only Esdale. If we can show Esdale came back to England, there's not much doubt where he went."

"That's all very well, but it won't help you with a jury. However, we've not got to juries yet and by my way of thinking it'll be a while before we do. Let me finish my story.

"That 2 o'clock service from Victoria gets into Boulogne about five. The return afternoon service from Paris leaves Boulogne at 7.10. This gets to Folkestone about half-past eight. There would have been nothing easier for Esdale than to travel by this return service, get off at Folkestone, lie doggo for six or seven hours, and then get aboard the *Nymph*.

"I began at once. Within an hour I had found that a first single ticket for Folkestone had been issued at the Gare Maritime for that service on that night. Comparatively few of these tickets are issued, the enormous proportion of travellers using returns or coming through by rail. But I couldn't find any trace of this traveller going aboard. He had probably mingled with the crowd from the train. Nor could I hear of him at Folkestone. The ticket had been collected on the boat in question, showing the man travelled, but no one appears to have seen him. So there you are, French. I give you my theory, and exit. Your act gets the proof."

"Does it?" said French grimly. "I'm glad you think so. But seriously, Willis, I think that's fine. I bet you're on to the truth. There's only one thing that makes me doubt it a bit, but I don't suppose there's anything in it."

"Being?"

"Being the fact that he came back by the same route. A sharp passport man might easily have spotted something about him which he would have noticed on the return journey. Some chance resemblance, say, to one of the officer's own friends. It's a risk I should have thought Esdale would have avoided."

247

"No, that's just the thing. He couldn't. This one boat by Folkestone is the only way it could have been done."

"Then that's it, Willis, as sure as we're alive. Just another point. Would Esdale not have used the ticket he already had instead of buying a new one? He had his return half, and he would certainly have wanted to keep clear of booking offices."

"He had his return half," Willis admitted, "but the book wasn't stamped in Paris. Some question might have arisen."

"You're right, I forgot that. Then that's how the thing stands now?"

"Yes, I only got that yesterday and then the A.C. recalled me, saying I was wanted at Lincoln and that you'd be back and would take over."

"Right. Good work, Willis. There'll be some heart in carrying on now that I'm pretty sure I'm on the right track. Had you thought out any inquiries?"

"None but the obvious ones, which, as a matter of fact, I shouldn't think would lead anywhere: I mean the hotels, theatres, cinemas, pubs, patrols, and so on. And, of course, people at the harbour."

French nodded. His next step was obvious. After putting his ideas in writing he went in to see Sir Mortimer. The latter quickly approved his programme, saying that he should go on to Folkestone that night, so as to be ready to start work first thing in the morning.

So began what French sincerely believed was the final lap of the case.

CHAPTER
EIGHTEEN

The Secret of the Dinghy

Next morning French entered on what proved to be one of the most wearisome and unproductive inquiries he had ever undertaken. He absolutely combed Folkestone for news of the missing man, but without result.

As for the hundredth time he asked himself how he should have acted in Esdale's circumstances, it occurred to him that if he could have got out of the town until it was time to go aboard the yacht, he would have done it. He therefore had a try at the stations and bus stopping places. From the bus employees he got nothing, but at the Central Station he learned something that he thought might be worth following up.

It was not much; merely that a single first-class ticket from Folkestone to Dover had been taken by the train leaving Folkestone at 9.41 on the Wednesday night in question. This would have allowed a passenger by the Boulogne boat plenty of time to get up to the Central Station. Probably there was nothing in it, but it was only a short way to Dover and French thought he might as well go over and follow it up.

At Dover Priory, to which the train in question ran, he could get nothing. Then he went round the garages and the taxis, again fruitlessly.

It was possible, he thought, that if Esdale had really travelled to Dover, he might have walked back to Folkestone. Indeed, this seemed a likely enough proceeding, as it would fill the time inconspicuously. As a last resource, therefore, French determined to concentrate on the Dover-Folkestone road. Or rather roads, for in addition to the modern motor route, the old road remained open as a footpath.

He went to the police station and put his query. No patrol had reported anything unusual, but inquiries would be made. Would French wait?

No, French was going to the coastguard station. But he would be glad if they would make general inquiries from any one who might have been along that road that night: doctors, nurses, those attending dances, those returning from bridge parties; any one the local superintendent could think of.

The superintendent promised that if any information came his way he would advise the inspector and French went on to interview the coastguards.

Here he had a stroke of the most surprising and unexpected luck.

On putting his question, the roster was looked up to find out who was on duty in the district in question on the Wednesday night. Three men had been, of whom it chanced that two were then in the station. These were called in and the report of the second at once aroused French's interest.

This man stated that about three o'clock on the morning of Thursday, 26th June, he was walking along the road in the direction of Dover, a couple of miles out from Folkestone. At this point, some half-mile on the Dover side of the Warren Halt, the road comes close to the edge of the cliff. It is bounded by a mound fence, beyond which is some thirty feet of rough grass. Then comes a sheer drop of perhaps a couple of hundred feet. At the bottom, between the cliff and the sea, is the shelf of ground along which runs the railway. A dangerous place for the unwary.

As the coastguard reached this spot he thought he saw a shadow flit across the mound fence in front of him. He walked over to investigate and found a man crouching behind the mound. He was ostensibly getting shelter to light a cigarette, but as there was little wind, this seemed a trifle unnecessary. The coastguard flashed his torch over him, reminding him that he was in a dangerous position so near the edge of the cliff, and advising him to get back on to the road. The man did so. He generally resembled Esdale's photograph, though the coastguard could not definitely swear to him. He told the coastguard that he was walking back to Folkestone, having stayed with a friend in Dover till nearly two o'clock.

This was promising enough, but it was the next piece of information which so keenly delighted French. The light of the torch had happened to shine on the man's left hand, and the coastguard had noticed that the little finger was crooked!

Here was all the proof French wanted. Esdale had come back from France. He had gone by rail to Dover and walked back to Folkestone during the night, just as French thought he might have done. That he had gone aboard the *Nymph*, murdered Moxon and Deeping, escaped in the dinghy with the swag, and been picked up by some tramp, French was equally convinced. Let him get his hands on Esdale and he would be at the end of the case.

He returned to Folkestone and settled down to a dogged endeavour to find some one who might have seen Esdale going aboard the *Nymph*. Unfortunately all his efforts were in vain.

So once again the case seemed to come to a stand and French to a dead-lock. An intensified search for Esdale was started, not only in France, but practically all over the world. Through Lloyd's an endeavour was made to get in touch with vessels which might have come across the dinghy. But all to no purpose. Not another ray of light was discovered. French grew moody and his temper wore thin. The Assistant Commissioner shook his head. Persons in high places made comments which all concerned thought would have been better left unsaid. And still nothing happened.

Then at last some information came in which turned French off on to another line and transformed his brooding despair into a somewhat tremulous hope. The Maida Vale branch of the London and Northern Bank rang up to say that one of the ten pound notes on the Yard's list had just been paid in.

In the light of his previous experiences French doubted that he would get anything fresh from the discovery. At the same time action of any sort was a welcome relief from the stagnation of the last few days, and he hurried to Maida Vale as quickly as a taxi could take him.

Here history once more repeated itself. He saw the manager, a clerk was sent for, and the facts were related. They were simple. Some half-hour previously the clerk had observed the note. From his memoranda he was able to say that it had been paid in by a messenger who had just left the bank, a porter in the employment of the Plendy Marine Motor Company of 24B Forres Road.

French was not greatly interested. These notes had been back in circulation for some time, and it was more than likely that they had changed hands many times since they lay in the strong-room of Moxon's General Securities. However, he thanked the bank officials and made his way to Forres Road. In ten minutes he was seated with the manager of the Plendy Company.

Mr. Norton shook his head when French stated his business. Money was passing in and out continuously and it was quite impossible to say from whom any given note had been received. Mr. Norton would be glad to do anything he could, but in this case the inspector was asking an impossibility.

French feared the man was right, but he was not going to give in without a struggle. He thought for a moment, then slowly began to ask questions.

The first piece of information he got was that the note might have been lying in the firm's till for quite a long time. The till, the cashier explained, was seldom completely cleared out, a small balance being always left for chance calls. If this note had happened to get to the bottom, it might have remained there almost indefinitely. For all he knew to the contrary, it might have been there on the date of the crime, or even earlier. From this it followed that it *might* have been paid in by the defaulting men. Again, quite as possibly, it might not.

It seemed a pretty hopeless proposition. French felt sure there was nothing to be learned. But striving desperately to make sure, he did at last put a question which bore amazing and unexpected fruit.

"Tell me," he said, "can you remember any transaction during the last two or three months which struck you as being in any way out of the common? Or any purchase which was paid for in notes of small value; singles, fives, tens, or twenties?"

He pestered every one concerned with these questions. At first every one replied "No," but at last the manager remembered a case which complied with both conditions.

"Let me see," he said suddenly, "what was that man's name who sent the notes? You remember, M'Alpine?" He glared at the chief clerk. "The Waterloo cloak-room man. Began with an H. Haire — Harrod — Have — Havelock! That was it. Bring me the file."

Norton took out a paper and glanced over it. Then he turned back to French.

"It's not the custom, as you can probably guess, Inspector, for my firm to give away any information as to its clients. Before I show you this I shall want your assurance that it really is required in the interests of justice."

To this French replied that as he didn't know the nature of the other's communication, he could not state its value. But he assured Norton that unless the information was vital to his case it would be kept entirely confidential.

"Very well," Norton answered, passing over a sheet of paper, "the facts are these. On Friday, June 20th, we received this letter."

The sheet was taken from one of those cheap blocks which can be picked up in any stationer's, a sheet utterly impossible to trace. The letter, including the signature, was typed by a by-no-means new machine. French noted that it was so worn that it could be identified, were he lucky enough to find it. The date also aroused his interest, as it was just six days before that of the crime.

But French's satisfaction over these minor details was as nothing compared to that produced by the communication itself. Before he had even finished reading it, the idea that it might have been written by Esdale leaped into his mind. For if by any chance it had, the affair would clear up that exasperating problem of how escape by the dinghy could have been carried out.

The letter, which bore the date of June 19, but no address, read:

255

DEAR SIRS, — I should be obliged if you would kindly send one of your twenty-five-horse outboard motors, Class A75, to me at the Cloak-room, Waterloo Main Line Station. The ticket to be put in an envelope and addressed to me, c/o. Mr. John Marks, 118 Brook Street, York Road, S.E.I, and to be left by hand at this address at the same time. I shall ring you up at three p.m. to-day and shall be glad if you will then tell me if you can arrange this matter, and what the cost will be. Yours faithfully, — HUBERT HAVELOCK.

French was keenly interested. Fervently he hoped that this "Havelock" might prove to be Esdale! If so, here was the explanation of how a delicate man like the chief accountant could have propelled the heavy dinghy over some twenty-four miles of sea, swept by fierce tidal currents. Why, with a motor like that, given food and fair weather, Esdale might have made the coast of Spain or Holland or even Norway! Well, through this Marks there was a reasonable chance of finding out. He turned back to the manager.

"This interests me quite a lot, Mr. Norton," he declared. "I think it possibly may be connected with my case. Please continue your statement."

"We got this letter," resumed Norton, "on the 20th June, as I said. Mr. Havelock rang up at the hour mentioned and I told him that we could carry out his order and that the cost would be so much; I can give you the figures if you want them. He said he would send on the money and that he wished the package to be left at Waterloo and the ticket with Marks before four o'clock on the following day, that was Saturday. I agreed that this would be done. He then said that it was impossible for him to get down to our shop to inspect the motor, and asked if we gave a guarantee as to its good order. I reassured him on this point and he said that was all right.

"By the first post next morning, Saturday, we received another letter from him containing the money, curiously enough, in notes. However, all was correct. We therefore packed the motor, sent it to the cloak-room, and delivered the ticket. We assume that Mr. Havelock received the motor and found it satisfactory, as we have heard nothing further about the affair."

"Very interesting," French declared. "You weren't yourself suspicious about this rather peculiar arrangement?"

"I thought it strange certainly, else I shouldn't have told you about it. But I did not think it suspicious. What was there for me to suspect?"

French smiled.

"Perhaps nothing," he admitted. "Those notes now. What values had they, can you remember?"

"Tens, mostly. I think, though I'm not quite certain, that there were seven tens, with the rest in singles."

"Your statement has been so complete, Mr. Norton, that I think you have covered everything I want to know, except this. Would the motor you sent be suitable for propelling a twelve-foot-six dinghy?"

"With square stern?"

"Yes."

"And reasonably strongly built?"

"Very heavy. Massive indeed for a dinghy."

Norton hesitated.

"Normally it's rather a high power for so small a boat," he said. "At the same time, with a dinghy built as strongly as you describe, it should be all right."

"Now another thing. Could one man unpack, lift into place and start the motor?"

"Oh, certainly. We make a speciality of designing even our most powerful motors light enough for one man to handle. This one weighed about ninety pounds."

French rose.

"Thank you, Mr. Norton, for your statement. It may help me materially."

Norton rose also.

"I suppose it would be indiscreet to ask for particulars?"

"I think that seeing that I'm dealing only with suspicions, it would be wiser for me not to make any statements," French said after a momentary hesitation. "If my suspicions prove well-founded you'll be required to give evidence and then will know the whole thing."

Norton had a twenty-five-horse motor brought in for French's inspection, handed over "Havelock's" two letters, and saw French to the door.

The next step was obvious. Within half an hour French entered the small tobacconist's shop in Brook Street, York Road, belonging to Mr. John Marks.

"You give an accommodation address, Mr. Marks?" he suggested, after having awed the proprietor by stating his profession.

Marks admitted that sometimes he obliged people in that way.

"That's all right," said French; "I've nothing against it. All I want is a description of one of the people you've obliged. It has nothing whatever to do with you."

Thus reassured, Marks became communicative. Clearly he wanted to keep on the sunny side of the police.

It appeared that about the date in question he had had a call from a man of medium height, dark and rather thin. The man gave his name as Hubert Havelock and asked if he could have a letter left there for him. On payment of a small fee, the matter was arranged. A letter was delivered by a vanman two or three days later, and shortly after Mr. Havelock called for it. That was the one and only transaction which had taken place between them.

Immediately French reached the crucial question.

"Is he among those?" he asked, handing over his sheaf of photographs.

Marks, unfortunately, could not say. It was six weeks since the affair, and then he had only seen the man twice and for a few seconds each time. French was not surprised. There was nothing to impress the man's appearance on the tobacconist, moreover, owing to the exuberance of the window dressing, the light was bad.

But after a series of skilful questions one suggestive fact came to light. During both entire interviews the man had kept his left hand buried in his trousers pocket!

What, French asked himself, could this be for, if it were not to hide a crooked little finger? And if it were, the man was Esdale.

That he should keep his hand in his pocket was an even more convincing proof of his identity than if the crooked finger had actually been seen. Had some other person been masquerading as Esdale, the hand would have been displayed with the finger held crooked. Indeed, some trick would probably have been adopted to ensure its being observed. But that the caller hid his hand meant that it was Esdale himself.

It was now clear that Esdale had bought the outboard motor with "tainted" notes, one of which had lain in the firm's till from the date of the transaction until that morning. He had done so with the obvious purpose of reaching the French or other coast after committing the crime. Doubtless on getting ashore he had stove in a plank, headed the dinghy for the sea, and started the motor. When the little vessel had got out to deep water it would sink, thus destroying at least part of the evidences of the crime.

French, however, realised that though this conclusion was extraordinarily probable, it had not actually been proved. As he slowly returned to the Yard he racked his brains to find some way of putting the matter beyond doubt.

Then he saw that in his hand was an obvious clue. The typewriter! If he could find the machine on which the two letters had been written, and connect this machine with Esdale, it should meet the case.

What typewriters had Esdale access to? Obviously all those in the Securities offices, to which he had a key. To find out if it was one of these would at least be an easy job. French rang up Knowles and asked him to have samples taken from each machine and forwarded to the Yard.

In an hour these arrived, and with eagerness French settled down with his lens to note defects of type or alignment which might establish his point. There were twenty-four samples, all very much alike. Evidently the same company had the order for all the machines in the office. Fortunately the letters to the motor company showed a slight defect in the tail of the g, and this enabled the samples to be dealt with rapidly.

In five minutes French had it. There was a sample with a similar defect, and as French compared the other peculiarities of the two, he saw that no doubt was possible. No. 17 typewriter on Knowles' list had been used to type the letters ordering the motor!

Half an hour later he was seated in Knowles' office.

"I'm interested, Mr. Knowles, in your No. 17 typewriter," he explained. "Could you let me see where it is and introduce me to the typist?"

French went into the matter very thoroughly, but, unfortunately, with but small result. He was able to establish the fact that Esdale, as an officer of the firm, had access after hours to No. 17 typewriter, and therefore could have typed the letters, but he was unable to prove that Esdale had actually done so. Of course he recognised that it was most unlikely that such proof should be forthcoming.

He wondered if he could pick up any links at the other end of the chain. Esdale had called on Marks to get the cloak-room ticket on the Saturday afternoon. Presumably he had then taken the motor out of the cloak-room and conveyed it aboard the *Nymph*. Was proof of this obtainable?

French doubted it. At the same time he sent Sergeant Carter to Waterloo to try to pick up some information at the cloak-room or from a porter.

In the chain of operations involved in getting the motor from the cloak-room to the dinghy, the outstanding step should surely be the transhipment from land to water, the actual taking of the package out of the car and putting it in the boat. He wondered if he could possibly check that up.

First, when could Esdale have done it?

As part of the routine work of the case, French had made statements of the movements of all the suspects about the time of, and for some days previous to, the crime, so far as these could be ascertained. He now looked up Esdale's.

The chief accountant had left his home in his car on the Saturday at three o'clock, saying he was going out with Moxon for a sail. He was away until late on Sunday evening. From Sunday evening until he left for Paris on the Wednesday afternoon all his movements were accounted for. Therefore, if French were correct, the man had taken the motor aboard on the Saturday night or the Sunday.

The establishing of this was so important that French determined to go down again to Folkestone and make further inquiries. Accordingly, he took the first train and soon was once more talking to John Hurley, Moxon's boatman.

Hurley had notes of the occasions on which the *Nymph* had been out. It appeared that on the Saturday in question she had not left the harbour. Moxon, however, had come down in his car about ten o'clock that evening, with a couple of other men, one of whom was Deeping and the other, Hurley believed from the photographs, was Esdale. They had slept on board and had gone out about eight o'clock on Sunday morning. They had returned about five the same afternoon, when they had left in Moxon's car. From Sunday the yacht had lain at her moorings till she left on the fatal trip on Thursday morning. Hurley was sure that no package which could possibly have been an outboard motor had been taken aboard. He admitted, however, that he had not opened the lockers when cleaning the yacht on the Monday, and that it was therefore possible that the motor was then aboard. He did not think the lockers were locked, but as he had not tried them, he could not be sure of this either.

Balancing the probabilities, it seemed to French that the motor must have been embarked in the middle of Saturday night. He, therefore, settled down to another of his interminable inquiries, employing the same methods as Tanner had done when tracing the embarkation of Moxon and Raymond. But though he was very thorough, he could get no information on the point.

At last, dispirited, he sat down on the shore at the Marine Parade, put on a pipe, and gave himself up to thought.

If he were correct in this theory of Esdale, it followed that Moxon and Deeping were privy to the outboard motor affair. Was this likely?

For the best part of an hour he turned the matter over in his mind, and then a new idea struck him which seemed an advance on any he had yet entertained.

Suppose Moxon, Deeping and Esdale were three partners in crime. Owing to the settling on the Friday they decide to make their get-away on the Thursday. Their first step is to eliminate Nolan and Raymond. This is done by the methods already known. But they see that when the plot is discovered they, Moxon, Deeping and Esdale, will remain as the criminals against whom the energies of the police will be directed. It is therefore necessary that these energies shall be annulled. Is there any way in which this can be done? French thought so.

Suppose the three men had steered the *Nymph* to the point at which it had been found, that is, in the track of the Newhaven-Dieppe steamer. Suppose that their intention had been to transfer themselves and their swag to the dinghy, then having swamped the *Nymph* in petrol to set it on fire and escape in the dinghy with the help of the outboard motor. They would plan to reach the French or other coast at night, and after going ashore, to stove in the dinghy and send it out to sea, knowing that it would sink in a mile or so. The *Chichester* would therefore see the burning yacht.

264

The absence of the dinghy would prove that the travellers had taken to it. As the dinghy would never be heard of again, it would be assumed that the three had perished and the police search would die a natural death. So much for the guilty trio's scheme.

But now suppose that Esdale had determined, while giving apparent support to this scheme, to double-cross his partners. Suppose, when they reached the selected spot, he had shot his two friends, with the object of obtaining all the spoils for himself. Suppose his wound delayed him, and when he was about to get the petrol and start the fire he found he was too late. Perhaps even he had seen the *Chichester* approaching in the distance. At all events he has no time to do anything but jump into the dinghy and make off. The dead bodies, and not the flaming remains of the *Nymph*, are therefore found.

The more French thought over this theory, the more probable its truth appeared. So far as he could see, it covered every single fact that he had learned. And then the relentless resultant question arose: Could he prove it?

He did not see how it could be done. All the same, he worked doggedly on, attacking the problem from every point of view, though always without result. Finally it began to look as if Esdale, the dinghy and the diamonds had really been lost, and that the case would therefore prove insoluble. There was grave dissatisfaction at Scotland Yard. The Assistant Commissioner frowned, reacting from interviews with still more exalted persons, and French became like a bear with a sore head. Then finally news came in which materially altered the situation and made French's problem seem even more exasperating and insoluble than ever.

CHAPTER
NINETEEN

The Two Depressions

In most instances in which information is sent to the Yard, its receipt is due to some previous action on the part of the Yard's officers. In this English Channel case, when banks rang up to say that they had made discoveries about notes, it was owing to circulars French had sent out earlier. The news which now arrived was in a different category. Not only was it unexpected, but it was not due to any previous action taken by any one working on the case. While it resulted reasonably enough from the circumstances of the crime, there were yet elements of chance and luck in its coming to light.

Once again the news came by telephone. The chief of police at Calais called up to say that he had obtained grave information which might have a bearing on the Moxon's General Securities affair, and he suggested that the officer dealing with that case should come over at once to see him. This officer, moreover, should be accompanied by some one who intimately knew the officers of the firm.

Four hours later French and Knowles stepped ashore from the *Canterbury* on to the pier at Calais. There with immense courtesy they were greeted by an officer who led the way to the police station. More greetings ensued. M. le Chef had heard of M. French from his colleagues at Dieppe and was ravished to meet him. And this was M. Knowles? He was ravished to meet M. Knowles. He, M. le Chef, had some news for M. French. He did not know whether it would prove of interest to him or not, but he thought it worth while so far to trouble his distinguished *confrère* as to ask him to come over in person to look into the matter. And now, if M. French permitted, his lieutenant, M. Gaspard, would explain what had taken place. For himself, he was desolated, but he had an engagement and could not be of the party. He trusted his guest would pardon him?

To his guest it all seemed a trifle mysterious. The Chief had not said just what the point at issue was, and now Gaspard seemed equally unwilling to get down to brass tacks. He indicated that a short walk was necessary, and then began hurriedly to discuss French's crossing, which had been decidedly rough. Their way led through the poorer quarter of the town to a small desolate-looking building, standing by itself in a secluded corner.

"It is not a pretty place, this to which we go," said Gaspard as he stopped and rang at the door. Then just as French guessed its purpose, he added: "It is the town *morgue*."

The door was opened by a caretaker, who saluted obsequiously on seeing Gaspard. The police officer pushed past him and led the way down a stone corridor

with white-washed walls and a melancholy reverbera-
tion. At a farther door he stopped, threw it open, and
with a polite gesture indicated that the Englishmen
were to enter.

"It is not pretty, this," he warned them once more as
they passed in.

It was a small room, absolutely bare save for a raised
slab in the centre, on the top of which was a sort of
glass box, like an enormous dish-cover. The floor was
stone, the walls white-washed, and the ceiling rose into
a glass lantern with open *louvres* on the sides. The
atmosphere was heavy and the effect of the whole place
was depressing and sinister.

The visitors moved to the table and looked in
through the sides of the glass box. On the slab lay the
body of a man, a terrible figure which made Knowles
cry out in horror and caused even French's hardened
nerves to twitch.

The man had evidently been dead for a considerable
period. The awful ravages of Time were far advanced.
Moreover it was obvious that the remains had been
lying continuously in water. The clothes — the remains
of a lounge suit — were discoloured, sodden and
draggled. Round the ankles was wound a number of
turns of chain, as if to ensure sinking. A hideous,
loathsome object, this shapeless mass which had once
been a man.

The sight revolted French, but even more it puzzled
him. A terrible affair, yes, he could see that, but how
did it interest him? Why had he been brought from
England to see these dreadful remains?

But Gaspard pushed forward, beckoning him to the other side of the table.

"You see, monsieur," he pointed to the disfigured head, "he was not drowned. Look, monsieur, behold the wound of the bullet. The carotid is severed. He has bled to death."

It was true. The man had been shot. There was a sinister hole in the throat in the position indicated by Gaspard. French, utterly puzzled, stared. But once again, why had he been brought over to see this dead Frenchman?

Then suddenly he understood. Those terrible, swollen features, distorted though they were, stirred a chord of memory. He had never seen them, but he had seen photographs of them, he had read descriptions of them, he had written descriptions of them. Could it be? Was it possible that here lay the remains of the man on whose capture the entire force of Scotland Yard was now engaged? *Was this Esdale's body?*

He looked round for Knowles. But Knowles had disappeared and sounds from without showed that the sight had been too much for him. French turned to Gaspard.

"Esdale!" he exclaimed, almost in awe.

The other nodded briskly.

"But yes," he answered quickly. "So we think. Esdale, yes! Monsieur recognises him? Yes?"

"I never saw him," French said heavily, "but this man is like his photographs." He turned to Knowles. "Sorry, Mr. Knowles, but I'm afraid you've got to look at him. Can you identify him?"

Knowles, deadly pale, and with loathing on his face, once more approached the glass box. Then he nodded. "Mr. Esdale," he murmured, and hurriedly made his way out.

"You're quite sure?" French said, following him.

Knowles was quite sure. In spite of the horrible disfiguration, there could be no doubt whatever.

French did not allow himself to think of what this discovery was going to mean to his theories as they walked slowly back to headquarters. There he was shown the contents of the pockets, the gold watch with the monogram "J.E.," the distinctively marked cigarette case, the leather pocket book with its illegible papers and book of railway tickets. Of all these articles French took charge in the hope of having them identified in London.

"Tell me how it was found," he asked.

As to that at least there was but little mystery. A Calais trawler had been working down Channel and the ghastly relic had been brought up in the trawl. On reaching port the police had been advised, and they had removed the remains to the *morgue*. At first they had not suspected any connection with the Securities crime, but, as one fact after another became revealed, this began to grow more and more likely.

In the first place, the body and clothes answered the description of Esdale. Secondly, on plotting the course of the vessel while the trawl had been down, it was found to pass the place at which the *Nymph* had been found by the *Chichester*. Thirdly, the doctor who examined the remains gave it as his opinion that the

271

man had been dead about six weeks; just the time which had elapsed since the tragedy. Lastly, the nature of the wound would account for the traces found on the *Nymph*. Assuming the man had been near the companion when the shot was fired, the pool of blood would have formed while the chain was being fastened round the ankles, while the trail across the deck would have been caused by the dragging of the body to the opening in the rail so that it might be thrown overboard.

The inference from these facts was sufficiently strong to make an appeal to the Yard inevitable. M. le Chef was evidently delighted at the effect his discovery had had on his distinguished *confrère*, as he persisted in calling French, and discreetly hinted that it would be desirable if the body were taken back to England.

In a dream French made the necessary arrangements, wired the Yard to acquaint the family, and after the French equivalent of an inquest, accompanied the remains back to their last resting-place in the cemetery near where the man had lived. Esdale, no longer a suspected murderer, was entitled to and received the respect which death brings. What if he were party to the frauds? This was not proven, and anyhow, the man was dead. He had left a family: their grief was as real as their loss.

With something approaching panic at his heart French at last faced the situation so far as he himself was concerned. What of his theory of the crime now? What about his mental picture of Esdale shooting his companions and escaping in the dinghy? It had seemed so good, this theory, so obvious, so completely to cover the facts. And now! . . . French did not mind admitting he had been wrong. Every one makes mistakes and no one is the worse for it. It was not that. What was worrying him so much was that he now felt himself bankrupt in the case. He had no alternative theory to put forward. He did not know where to turn for one. He was at the end of his tether.

Even Sir Mortimer Ellison, who should have stood in the position of an avenging angel, was sorry for him. "Never mind, French," he said kindly. "These things will happen. Take a couple of days' holiday without letting the thing into your mind. Then come back and try again. We can't give it up, you know."

French was grateful. He did not take his holiday, but he started again from the beginning to go over his facts, weigh them, balance them, retest his deductions, bring for the nth time all that he had of an ordered imagination to bear on them, hoping against hope that he might see something which he had overlooked before. But the heavens remained as brass above him.

Step by step he went afresh over his theory that the murderer was a trusted companion of his victims on the yacht; that he had treacherously murdered them; and that he had escaped in the dinghy. The more he thought over it, the more absolutely sound it seemed. It was obvious that the murderer *must* have been on the yacht. There was nowhere else that he could have come from. And equally he *must* have escaped in the dinghy. There was no other way in which he could have escaped. If he hadn't escaped in that way, why had the dinghy disappeared? French felt that in this theory he had reached the rock bottom of certainty.

Of course he had been wrong in suspecting Esdale. Esdale was a victim like Moxon and Deeping. Therefore *some one else had also sailed on the yacht.* Who was it?

Suddenly the dark saturnine face of Knowles seemed to swing up before his mental vision. Knowles! French sat quite still wondering if it was possible that he could have made so hideous a mistake as to overlook Knowles.

Knowles he had always felt was a mystery man, the unknown quantity in the equation. Could Knowles represent the answer to his question?

It was not, of course, the first time he had considered the possibility of Knowles' guilt. He had done so again and again. But on these occasions his mind had not really been unbiased. Always he has been convinced of the guilt of some other person and he has therefore been too ready to take Knowles' alibi at its face value.

Fortunately, if he had made a mistake, it was not irrevocable. He could at any moment put his hand on Knowles. Whether from innocence or self-confidence, the man had made no attempt to escape.

French did not lose a minute. With a sort of desperate keenness he got out a fresh sheet of paper and began to follow up his new idea.

In the first place there was this feeling of his that Knowles was a dark horse. From the man's appearance and manner and personality, there seemed nothing inconsistent with the idea of his guilt. French noted "Character" as a line for further investigation.

There was obviously motive, or there might have been. The acquisition of a huge sum of money is universally a potential motive for crime. Motive therefore was provisionally covered.

But was there opportunity? Here was the question which must be settled before troubling further about character or motive.

Knowles' alibi must be dealt with immediately. The man said he was ill; down with 'flu and in the doctor's care. Was he?

Of alibis in general French was profoundly sceptical, and as he thought over this one he was struck by an interesting fact. Its validity hinged on the testimony of Mrs. Knowles, and on that alone. Once again he ran over the details in his mind.

Knowles had been off duty for about a week, ostensibly with 'flu. He was, however, convalescent on the date of the crime, as he returned to the office on the Friday, the day following. Now, French asked himself, was Knowles well or ill on the Thursday? Had he recovered, if he had really been ill, or had he never been ill at all?

So far as French had discovered, no one but his wife had seen Knowles between the hour at which the doctor left him on the Wednesday and the Friday morning, when he went to the office. The servant was on leave. But if Knowles were guilty, Mrs. Knowles might well be his accomplice.

Of course, there was the doctor. Dr. Swayne had certified an attack of influenza. French, however, knew that influenza can be very easily faked. It is possible artificially to raise the temperature, and other symptoms can be simulated. The room would be darkened to ease the patient's eyes, so that close observation would be impossible. If there was nothing to raise the doctor's suspicions, no doubts would occur to him.

What was there, French asked himself, to prevent Knowles driving from his house to Folkestone during the Wednesday night, there joining the other three aboard the *Nymph*, committing the murders at the Point M, escaping back to the English coast in the dinghy, sinking the dinghy, and returning to his house during Thursday night?

Nothing, so far as French could see. But this plan involved the moving of a small boat over many miles of sea, and French started as it occurred to him that Knowles, and not Esdale, must have bought the outboard motor. The two men, though unlike in features, were similar in colouring and build, and it would have been the simplest thing for Knowles to keep his little finger crooked or in his pocket, so as to confuse the question of identity.

As French sat turning the matter over in his mind, another point gradually became clear. Why were there only two bodies on the *Nymph*? Obviously to suggest the very theory which actually had been adopted. If it became known — as it must — that Esdale had also sailed, the fact that he and the dinghy had disappeared would suggest his guilt. French began to picture Knowles shooting all three of his associates, leaving the bodies of Moxon and Deeping to be found by the *Chichester*, and weighting that of Esdale and sinking it, so as to suggest that he had made off with the booty in the dinghy.

French felt that he had been seriously to blame in not having gone into these possibilities. The work must be done now and with as little delay as possible. He turned to the question of how certainty could be reached.

If possible, he would rather begin with some line which would not alarm Knowles. Inquiries from Mrs. Knowles and the servant would be better postponed until all else had failed. French sat puzzling his brains over the problem. Then he went down and had a look at the outside of Knowles' house.

He saw at once that its position would have simplified the carrying out of the scheme. It was on a new road, and though houses were being built close by, none within earshot was occupied. The garage was actually part of the building, and the car could have been taken out and returned during the night without any one being a bit the wiser. If Knowles and his wife were alone in the house, as seemed certain, it was difficult to see how the truth could be learned. The servant might have come on some indirect evidence, but this was far from likely.

There were, of course, the local police, of whom a patrol might have seen Knowles start or return. French looked them up, but, unfortunately, they could give him no information.

He continued worrying over the problem. There were several lines of inquiry, and he noted them in the order in which he would follow them up. The most promising was Knowles' car. Had it been seen on the roads at night? Had it been parked during Thursday? Inquiries from the police and from parks and garages along the South Coast might get this information. There was also petrol. It should surely be possible to learn if the man had used five or six gallons unaccounted for by the runs to which he admitted.

Next there was the dinghy. To reach the English coast from Point M would be a totally different proposition from going to France. Instead of crossing a practically deserted stretch of sea, Knowles would have had to pass through one of the densest streams of marine traffic in the world. Unless he had travelled without lights at night, it would have been practically impossible for him to have reached the shore unseen. A list of the vessels in the neighbourhood at the time could be obtained from Lloyd's, and a questionnaire would almost certainly secure the information.

Finally, there was the *Nymph*. French wondered whether he should not re-examine it. He was fully aware of the importance of the point of view. If he looked at things with this theory of Knowles' guilt in his mind, something might occur to him which, because of a conflicting preconception, he had previously missed. Presently he went in and put his views before Sir Mortimer Ellison.

The Assistant Commissioner agreed at once to the inquiries about the car, the petrol and the dinghy. "You suggest also having another look at the *Nymph*?" he went on. "Now that's rather a coincidence, because for quite a different reason I was going to suggest the same thing to you." Sir Mortimer paused and looked at him whimsically. "As a matter of fact, French, I don't believe for a moment there is anything in my idea, but the thing is so important that we must try everything, no matter how unlikely."

French agreed, eager to hear what was coming.

"It's based on the fact, to me a rather strange fact, that so far as we know, none of the diamonds that these folk bought have come on the market. Why, French, do you think?"

"Too risky, sir. Too soon after the robbery."

"Is it? Remember that these people could have no idea that we were on to the diamond stunt. They would think themselves absolutely safe there."

French, diffidently, was not so sure about that.

"No more am I, of course," Sir Mortimer returned. "However, is there not just the faintest possibility that the murderer never got the stones at all? You had at one time a theory that he intended to set the *Nymph* on fire, but had not time. Suppose something of the kind were true. Suppose he was so hurried that he had to leave the diamonds behind. If he miscalculated his time he would have to do so, because he daren't be found aboard. However valuable the diamonds were to him, his life was more so. Now, French, when you examined the *Nymph* you knew nothing about diamonds.

279

Therefore you didn't look for them. They *may* be hidden on board still. So I want you to go and look again. I'll not be disappointed if you don't find them."

"I'll have a thorough search, sir, and I'll keep my eyes open at the same time for a clue pointing to Knowles."

French had little hope that anything would result from his visit, and yet, such are the chances of Fate, it was to prove the most important single inquiry in the whole case.

He commandeered Sergeant Carter and the two of them went down once again to Newhaven.

Then ensued perhaps the most thorough examination of a yacht ever made by officers of Scotland Yard. It was not merely a matter of looking in visible places. Diamonds were not like gold or banknotes; they bulked small. Therefore every piece of timber had to be tested for hollow receptacles, every piece of metal for a sealed chamber. They took the motor to pieces, looking for hollows in castings or holes bored and plugged. They emptied oil from the various tanks, cut them open and investigated the inside. Every link of every chain was separately inspected, every grease cup was emptied, every piece of furniture probed; in fact, their search was such that if diamonds had been hidden aboard, they would have been hidden no longer.

They had not completed the work by nightfall, so they knocked off till next day. Then they got at it again, working systematically through till they had finished. And then a great, though admittedly unreasonable disappointment, which had been gradually growing in French's mind, overwhelmed him altogether. Not only were there no diamonds aboard, but there was no further clue connecting either Knowles or anybody else with the murder. In fact, he had learned absolutely nothing from the search.

French sat down and wiped his forehead. He was hot and tired. For the last two hours a strong sun had been pouring down on their backs as they crawled about the deck, making sure that nothing was hidden in the upper fittings.

"Curse it," he grumbled. "I could do with a bottle of beer."

Carter's face brightened. In his opinion the inspector had hit the nail very accurately on the head. Tentatively he suggested a pilgrimage ashore.

French murmured a non-committal reply. Looking down into Nolan's launch, floating alongside, had brought back to him the long wearisome case he had recently had around the North Channel. He remembered with grim amusement the story he had told to Victor Magill — a neat invention about a friend of his own who owned such a launch and who had invited him to make the very trip up the West Coast of Scotland which Magill had made with his friends Mallace, Teer, and Joss. And Magill had swallowed the whole story. And so also had the others.

As a matter of fact French thought that such a trip would be extraordinarily pleasant. He wondered whimsically whether if this launch were to be sold cheap he could scrape up the wherewithal necessary to make it available for all his future holidays. Idly he gazed down into the well as he lazily indulged his fancy.

281

It was just getting on to four o'clock and the sun was shining powerfully down from the sou'-west. The two boats, moored against the end of the gangway, were lying pointing a little to the west of north. While the centre and bow of the *Nymph* was wholly, and that of the launch partly, sheltered from the sun by the gangway, the sterns of both vessels projected southwards past its end, and so received the full force of the rays. It happened, therefore, that the rays were coming down on the launch almost, though not quite, parallel to the back board of its square stern.

What, French idly wondered, as he continued gazing down into the well of the launch, were those two almost imperceptible marks on the back board? Two small round depressions in the wood; extraordinarily slight, not, he supposed, a fiftieth of an inch deep; but just now indicated by the slightly increased shadow. In the centre of each was a curious little star-shaped indentation, with eight lines radiating from a point like the spokes of a two-inch wheel from which both hub and rim had been removed. The marks were on the port side, about half-way between the rudder and the side of the boat, spaced eight or nine inches apart and two or three below the top of the wood.

What, French idly wondered, could these be? He gazed at them, lazily curious. It was not a matter in which he was really interested, but for the moment he was too tired to get up and do anything else. Little stars on the back board of Nolan's launch.

Then suddenly French's inertia dropped from him like a cloak and he grew rigid, while his heart began to beat more quickly. *What* were those marks? *What* were they? Could it be? With a swiftly rising excitement French sprang to his feet and began to pace the deck. Yes, it must! There could be no other explanation! *Had he got his solution?*

CHAPTER
TWENTY

The Riddle of the Stars

French moved as if in a dream, then Carter's voice broke in on his meditations. The sergeant thought, if Mr. French was agreeable, that if they went ashore now they could get a dr —

"Carter!" French roared in a voice which made that worthy jump as if a bullet had sliced off a piece of his nose. "Carter, look at those!"

Carter stared anxiously.

"Those marks! Look at them, man, not at me! Don't you see what they are?"

Still Carter stared.

"Man alive, will you look at them!" French shouted again, almost dancing in his eagerness. "Use your head for once in a way. Do you know what they'll tell you? They'll tell you the solution in this case. Finish it up; supply the criminal; give you all the proof you want — everything complete. What, do you not see it yet? Damn it all, then I'll not tell you. Just think it out for yourself."

French was more excited than was meet in the presence of a subordinate. Carter, greatly wondering, rubbed his forehead slowly.

284

"Trying to make it work, are you?" said French. "Some job! Never mind; let's get ashore. We've got all we want. We're going back to Town."

All the way up to the Yard Carter was obviously trying to run to earth French's illusive idea, though without success. Two or three times he tentatively suggested that French should enlighten him. But French wasn't giving anything away.

"Do your own work," he said. "You know all I know. You've seen all I've seen. Use your head and you'll get it for yourself."

When they reached the Yard, French had a hurried interview with Inspector Barnes. Then he went to Sir Mortimer Ellison's room. It was late by this time and Sir Mortimer had gone home. But French could not contain himself until the morning. Greatly daring, he rang up the Assistant Commissioner at his private house to tell him the great news. Sir Mortimer, recognising French's frame of mind, and indeed himself interested, told him to come along and make his report then and there. French did not lose much time on the journey.

"You know, sir," he began when he was sitting with his chief in the latter's study, "what I went to Newhaven to look for. Well, I didn't find it, but I found something else." French could scarcely keep the triumph out of his voice. "I found the solution."

"So you said on the phone," Sir Mortimer answered quietly. "Go ahead, French. What did you find?"

"Two little marks, sir, on the stern of the launch; not the yacht *Nymph*, but the launch, Nolan's boat. They were —" and French went on to describe their position and shape.

Sir Mortimer sat very still, staring at his subordinate. French, now utterly triumphant, waited with a pleased smile on his lips. Sir Mortimer began whistling tunelessly under his breath, as he considered the news.

"'Pon my soul, French," he said at last, and there was a trace of excitement in his manner. "The clips of an outboard motor!"

"The clips of an outboard motor, sir. More than that, the clips of *the* outboard motor! At least, that's what I think. The Plendy twenty-five-horse outboard motor."

"And on Nolan's launch?"

"On Nolan's launch, sir."

Sir Mortimer continued to stare.

"'Pon my soul!" he repeated. "Why, French, if you can prove that and all that would seem to follow from it . . ."

French smiled the smile of the supremely happy.

"I don't think there'll be much difficulty in proving it, sir."

Sir Mortimer rose to his feet and began to pace the room.

"Nolan!" he went on. "Nolan! I can scarcely believe it! We were so sure of Nolan." He paused, frowning as he strode backward and forward.

"Look here, don't let's go too fast," he said at length. "Let me see if I've really understood your suggestion. You've found these marks and you argue, first, that they were caused by an outboard motor; second, that this was the motor which has already figured in the case;

third, that as the marks were on Nolan's boat, Nolan must have bought and used the motor; fourth — What's your fourth point?"

"Fourthly, sir, that Nolan used it to jack up the speed of his launch from ten to thirteen knots."

"Quite so, and fifthly, therefore, that Nolan has been faking an alibi, and so is our man. That it?"

"That's it, sir." French spoke with a happy confidence. Trust the A.C. to get quickly on to an idea.

But the A.C. didn't seem so happy about it.

"Five highly interesting and I hope perfectly sound conclusions," he admitted, "but," he glanced sideways at French, "every single one of them a pure guess. Not a scintilla of proof anywhere."

The smile was stricken from French's face as a sponge takes chalk from a slate.

"Perhaps not actually proved, sir," he agreed, "but still so likely as practically to amount to the same thing."

"You think so? How do you know those marks weren't put on six months ago?"

French felt the conversation was not going as it should. This creation of difficulties was stupid and unlike the A.C. He murmured something about coincidences and probabilities, but had to admit that in the last resort he didn't know.

"I thought not," Sir Mortimer continued. "And there's another thing. Even supposing you're right and that you've got your man, you haven't got your money."

French gasped. This was always what happened. If ever he allowed himself pleasurable anticipation, he invariably got disappointment instead. And he had expected the A.C. to have been overwhelmed with admiration and delight!

"I'm afraid, sir, that's the truth," he answered tactfully, "but the man may lead us to the money."

"He may. I sincerely hope he does. Now, as I said, French, don't let's be in too great a hurry, and jump to conclusions we can't stand over. You've put up an extremely interesting theory which you've not yet been able to prove. I hope you'll do so soon." He sat down, took out his case and offered French a cigar. "Let's have a smoke and go over the thing quietly and see just where we stand. Have you got a match?"

French assured him that so far as creature comforts were concerned, he was in paradise.

"Good. Now, to take your first point. There's no doubt, I suppose, that those marks were really caused by an outboard motor?"

"None, sir. The caps at the end of the clamping screws have those eight little ribs projecting, so as to grip the wood. I understand that if they weren't there she might roll the motor off in a sea."

"I happen to know that that's correct. All the same it isn't enough."

"It won't be hard to test, sir. We can get a similar motor from the Plendy Company and see if it fits the marks."

"Yes, that's simple enough, but here's the difficulty. How are you going to connect the motor ordered on the Securities typewriter with these marks?"

"I'll try following up Nolan's movements, sir."

"Right. That's quite satisfactory. All I wanted to point out is that while your theory is hopeful — in fact, I think it's probably correct — you've not yet got your case."

French admitted it readily. Sir Mortimer sat silent, smoking thoughtfully.

"By Jove, French," he went on presently, "if you're right this is a pretty complete reversal of our previous ideas!"

"There were good reasons for our ideas all along, sir," French declared. "I look at it this way. We thought first of all that Nolan might be guilty, because he was one of the very few who had the necessary knowledge and because he was in the vicinity of the tragedy about the time it took place. After further investigation we eliminated Nolan for three reasons: One, we thought the murderer had been wounded, and Nolan was not wounded. Two, we felt he would never commit the crime without getting the cash, and as we thought this bulked large, he had not got it. Three, we found his launch would not run fast enough to get him to the point of the murder at the time it must have been committed."

"Quite sound it seemed, too."

"Yes, sir, but that was because we had insufficient information. We now know that all three of our reasons were false. First, the blood which suggested the murderer's injury we now believe to have come from a third murder, Esdale's. Second, we now know that the money was in the form of diamonds which bulked small. These facts we've known for a considerable time.

But the third fact, the speed of the launch, still cleared Nolan. Now, however, we see that by the use of the outboard motor, he could have speeded up the launch. So there's not a single reason left for believing in his innocence. On the other hand, the use of the outboard motor can only be explained by assuming him guilty."

"Always, if it was used on the date you think. But really, French, that's not at all bad. All the same, I wish I could feel as sure of your theory as you seem to be. For instance, do you actually know that the outboard motor would really drive that ten-knot launch at — what was it? — thirteen knots?"

Again French was somewhat dashed.

"Well, no, sir," he admitted. "I've not had time to see the makers and, of course, it will have to be tested. But I don't think there can be much doubt about it. You see, you're adding a tremendous lot of power for a small increase of speed."

"Adding it? Do you mean he ran both motors?"

"Certainly, sir. I thought Nolan would get going with the boat's own engine at ten knots. Then when he was out of sight of onlookers he would put down the outboard engine and start it too. I had a word with Barnes and he agrees it's possible . . ."

"Oh, you've seen Barnes, have you? What does Barnes say?"

"Barnes says that ordinarily if you have a boat driven by an inboard motor and you add an outboard motor you'll get practically no increase of speed, because the propeller of the outboard motor is working in the wash — the slip stream, he called it — of the boat's own propeller. That is to say, the water the second propeller is revolving in is already running backwards so quickly that there's nothing for this propeller to bite on, no kick in it."

"That's what I should have thought."

"Yes, sir, but that doesn't obtain in this case. This boat is built on the model of a navy launch and the inboard propeller shaft is not taken through the stern post, but to the side of it, in this case the starboard side. Now Nolan put the outboard motor on the port side, and so got it far enough from the inboard propeller to clear its slip stream, that is, the two propellers were side by side, not one in front of the other. They were both working in undisturbed water and their slip streams, though parallel, were quite independent. In other words, he made a single screw boat into a twin screw. You follow me, sir?"

Sir Mortimer moved uneasily.

"Would not that arrangement drive the boat in a circle?"

"No, sir. You can correct it by setting the outboard motor at a compensating angle."

"That may all be as you say, French, but I understood that while it's easy enough to get a boat up to a certain speed, the least increase beyond that speed means an entirely disproportionate increase of power?"

"That's just what Barnes told me, sir. He says you wouldn't get anything like an increase of speed proportionate to the additional power. But he says you would get *some* increase, and he thinks it might be in the proportion of 10 to 13 knots. You see, sir, as I said, the boat's motor is only twenty-horse and you're adding twenty-five, so that the power proportion is much more than doubled."

"It sounds plausible. I hope you're right, French. But all that must be proved up to the hilt before we can take any step. I think you better go and see those motor people in the morning. Get another twenty-five-horse motor and a representative of the firm and go down to Newhaven and make your test. There must be no doubt about that part of it."

"I was going to suggest that I should do that in any case, sir."

"Very good. Now, just let's see if we're agreed as to what probably did happen. Just run quickly over your theory of the crime."

French was nothing loath to air his views.

"What I thought, sir, was that Moxon, Deeping, and Esdale on the *Nymph* and Nolan on the launch met by arrangement at the point of the murders at twelve-thirty. This, of course, was made possible to Nolan by the use of the outboard motor. Nolan makes some excuse for going aboard the *Nymph*, and there in cold blood he shoots the others — all three — Moxon in the cabin and Deeping and Esdale on deck near the companion. Moxon and Deeping he lets lie where they fell, Esdale he drags to the side and drops into the sea, having first weighted the feet. Then I suggest that he scuttles the dinghy. He does this to suggest that Esdale has committed the murders and escaped in the dinghy. In fact, sir, we thought so ourselves until Esdale's body was found."

"And, of course, in buying the outboard motor Nolan makes up to look like Esdale, keeping his finger crooked."

"He does better than that, sir. He makes up to look like Esdale made up, if you follow me. He keeps his hand in his pocket, so as to suggest that he is Esdale hiding his crooked finger. Rather brainy that, I do think."

Sir Mortimer nodded.

"Then," went on French, "I suggest that after Nolan has got hold of the diamonds he turns back towards Dover, runs a few miles, throws the outboard motor overboard, and turns round again towards the *Nymph*. He times his movements to come up with her after she had been passed by the *Chichester*, as well as at an hour which will work in with the launch's unassisted speed from Dover. He feigns surprise at the tragedy and gets ashore without suspicion being aroused. Once in London he puts the diamonds in a safe place."

For some time the Assistant Commissioner sat in silence. Then he roused himself.

"I admit you've not made a bad case. Now the thing is to get it tested. You'll see to that without delay?"

"First thing in the morning, sir."

Sir Mortimer rose.

"Then, that'll do for to-night. Take another cigar before you go. Nothing else, is there?"

French hesitated.

"There was just one thing, sir, but it can wait till to-morrow."

"No, let's have it now."

"I was wondering whether we could get the proof we want by making Nolan give himself away."

"Let's hear it."

French explained his idea. Sir Mortimer listened, then considered.

"No harm to try it," he said at length. "Well, carry on and let me know the result."

Next day French was early at the offices of the Plendy Marine Motor Company, and an hour later he and a mechanic set off for Newhaven with a twenty-five-horse motor of the same type as that sent to the cloak-room at Waterloo. At Newhaven the first test was quickly made. They fitted the motor to the stern of the launch and to French's delight found that the marks exactly registered. Then they took the launch out, and when it was going full-speed with its own engine, they added the outboard motor. The result confirmed Barnes' prophecy. The speed at once increased to just over thirteen and a quarter knots.

So far, so good. But French's second experiment was a failure. Marks, the Brook Street tobacconist, was taken to the Securities building and placed behind a screen so that, himself invisible, he could see Nolan pass. But he was quite unable to identify Nolan with the "Mr. Havelock" who had called at his shop for the letter. In a way, of course, this was not surprising, as Nolan had presumably disguised himself to resemble Esdale. French was not unduly disappointed, but he thought that in this absence of direct proof there was nothing for it but to try his plan of making Nolan give himself away.

The first thing was to obtain an obviously unsought interview with his victim. This was arranged through Honeyford. Honeyford had not completed his investigation into the firm's finances, and was still working with Nolan at the Securities building. French called to see Honeyford, asking Nolan, who made as if to leave them together, to remain, as his business was not private. He discussed some financial point with Honeyford, who, acting on previous instructions, said he would have to get the required information from a clerk, and left the room. French was left alone with Nolan.

For some time French chatted pleasantly on various topics, then he skilfully turned the conversation to the murders. These were discussed until at last Nolan did what was required of him. He asked if any clue to the murderer had been discovered.

This was what French had been angling for. He at once became more interested.

"We've got one, Mr. Nolan," he said, confidentially, "which we think will lead us straight to him. I'll tell you if you'll keep it to yourself. We've come to the conclusion, rightly or wrongly, that he used an outboard motor to get away from the *Nymph*. Probably he escaped in the dinghy, which we've not yet found, but it may have been in some other boat. We think he may even have used the outboard in some launch or yacht, in addition to the boat's own engines, in order to give him what would seem an impossibly high speed. As a matter of fact we don't know how he used it. All we're pretty sure of is that he did so."

Nolan was obviously impressed. But he pulled himself together and replied in natural enough tones: "Surely it would be impossible to increase a boat's speed in that way?"

"Not under certain conditions," French answered. "If, as I said, you'll keep it strictly to yourself, I'll tell you why we're so sure about it." He leaned forward, lowered his voice, and spoke even more confidentially. "We've found that a twenty-five-horse outboard motor was ordered secretly. It was ordered to be sent to the cloak-room at Waterloo, so that the Plendy people, who supplied it, should not learn the identity of their customer. Now, here's the point. The order for that motor was typed on one of the machines in this building! What do you think of that? No doubt about a connection between the motor and the case, eh?"

Nolan was now very much upset, indeed. He struggled manfully to hide it, and so far as French's manner went, with complete success. After an obvious effort, Nolan remarked quietly:

"That's all very interesting and suspicious, Inspector. All the same I don't yet see how it's going to help you."

"No?" said French. "I should have thought it very obvious. We have only to find the boat it was used on. You see, it's impossible to use a large outboard motor without leaving some trace. The clamping studs dent the woodwork of the transom. Now, if we can find the boat we'll get those marks on her."

Nolan's anxiety was now painful, but French fortunately became engaged in cleaning the stem of his pipe, and noticed nothing.

"Of course, to find her would be a perfectly enormous job only for one thing," French went on, getting even more confidential. "As a matter of fact, Mr. Nolan, we've got a bit more than I've mentioned. I shouldn't perhaps tell you, but I've said so much you've probably guessed the rest." He paused meaningly. "Well," he added with a significant look, "influenza can be faked. You get me?"

Nolan gasped.

"Influenza!" he repeated wonderingly. "Holy saints!"

"We've had our eye on the gentleman for some time," French went on, "but we'd like to get our proof before making a move."

Nolan looked as if he didn't know whether he was on his head or his heels; French, of course, did not observe his embarrassment, but continued discussing the point, gradually leading away from it to the more general aspects of the case. When at the end of the prearranged time Honeyford returned, French thought he had made the required impression. It was now only necessary to see if it produced its hoped-for result.

Immediately the watch on Nolan was redoubled. Ceaselessly and skilfully a never-ending stream of French's myrmidons shadowed their victim. Sometimes it was a policeman in helmet and uniform, obviously on patrol; sometimes an elderly society man, strolling from reception to club; again a middle-class young woman on shopping intent, or a business man having a hurried lunch; in various guises they came, careful only of two things; to stick like limpets to their victim during their turn of duty and to hand over to their successors before suspicion should arise to keep the victim out of the trap.

Whether or not Nolan would react to the stimulus French could not forecast, but he felt sure of one thing. If the man moved at all, he would move at once. This was Saturday, and Saturday night would be the most suitable in the week for his purpose. French believed that before he was twelve hours' older he would have both his man and his case.

With not a little eagerness, therefore, he set to work on his own preparations.

CHAPTER
TWENTY-ONE

The Last Lap

French began by tabulating his instructions to his band of watchers. As long as Nolan remained in London he was to be kept under the strictest observation. But if he left in his car in the direction of Newhaven the shadowing might be discontinued. Under no circumstances was he to be allowed to suspect that he was under surveillance. The police station at Newhaven was to be kept informed of developments.

French then sent for Sergeant Carter, and the two men, having armed themselves with revolvers, took the 6.40 p.m. train from Victoria to Newhaven. They arrived shortly after eight and went at once to the police station.

"Here we are," French greeted Sergeant Heath, "come down to bother you again. We're expecting a 'phone from the Yard later on and we want to wait here till it comes."

The sergeant was pleased to see them, put his entire establishment at their disposal, and begged to know if there was anything he could do to help.

French said not, but recognising the man's curiosity, told him what he hoped the night would bring forth.

"There is one thing," he went on. "I wish you'd keep your men away from the London road and the approaches to the harbour. If Nolan turns up, don't let him be discouraged by finding himself observed by constables. Another thing, sergeant, I wish you'd send a man out for some beer and bread and cheese. We've had no dinner and I don't want to go anywhere that I might be known, lest information would get back to our friend."

The sergeant at once arranged the first of these items, but utterly refused to have anything to do with the second. His house was next door and his wife would be proud to make them a bit of supper. French protested without avail and they passed a not unpleasant evening smoking and chatting in Heath's little sitting-room.

As time passed French began to grow more and more anxious. Had his little trap been properly set? Had the victim seen his danger and determined to avoid its jaws? Misgivings rose more insistently in French's mind. What if, ostensibly starting for Newhaven, Nolan would really make a dash for safety elsewhere? French did not think he could get to the Continent; the routes were too closely watched. But there were endless possibilities of a slip between cup and lip which found an unhappy lodgment in French's mind.

Assuming all went well, he thought that Nolan might adopt one of two alternatives. Either he would start early, say immediately after the office closed, do his business at Newhaven and get back to London at but little later than his ordinary bedtime, or he would go to bed at his usual time, slip secretly out of his house in the early morning, make his journey, and return to London before his household was awake. French thought the second of these courses the most probable.

If so, the man could scarcely leave London before one in the morning. It was now eleven. Two more hours! French felt he could not keep Heath up, and, in spite of renewed protests, he insisted on going back to the station next door. There with Carter he settled down to wait.

It had turned out a dirty night. A sou'-westerly wind was blowing gustily round the eaves and the rain was beating in sheets against the windows. A good night for French's purpose. There was a full moon, but the heavy pall of clouds would dull its light. He would just be able to see, while keeping himself hidden. The wind, moreover, would remove all chance of being overheard. A good night indeed, both for himself and his quarry.

Time in the little office dragged interminably. Twelve came and went and still there was no sign. French recognised that if he didn't hear within the next hour it would mean failure, and after all these preparations failure would be a serious matter for him.

And then at last came the tinkle of the telephone. Good news! Nolan had left his garage at a quarter to one and had run quickly out on the road to Purley.

From London to Newhaven French thought was between 55 and 60 miles; say a two-hours' run. They need not, therefore, get into position for some time yet.

At two o'clock he decided to make a move. He and Carter left the police station and picked their way down the deserted west bank of the river, past the coal depot and the series of loading gangways to where the *Nymph* and the launch were lying. In spite of the clouds it was fairly light. Objects could be seen as dark shadows, with position, but no detail. A band of deeper black showed where sky gave place to earth. The lights across the river stretched out long flickering arms across the inky water, the port light of a tramp, just arrived, showing like an evil trail of blood.

For the second week in August, it was extraordinarily cold. A stiff breeze blew in from the sea, stirring up the water into little waves which splashed and gurgled on the sides of the boats and against the piles of the gangways. From the fenders between the *Nymph* and the launch came an occasional creaking groan.

There was a small shed on the bank opposite the gangway at which the boats were lying, and the men, seeking shelter, crouched in its lee. Then once again they experienced how slowly time can pass. The heavy relentless downpour brought back to French the last time he had waited in rain for a suspect. With a thrill he lived again through that terrible evening of rain and storm, when on the Cave Hill above Belfast, he and Superintendent Rainey had first stalked and then taken their infamous quarry. He hoped that if the seed he had sown in this case bore fruit, the reaping might prove less dangerous and exciting.

An hour came slowly to an end. It occurred to French with something of wonder that so many of his cases should have been connected with the sea. There was that Hatton Garden case, in which the final scene was in a Booth liner, rolling down, not to Rio, but to Lisbon. The Maxwell Cheyne business began and ended with the sea. So did that gruesome case in which all those box-office girls were murdered. The Burry Port affair began with the sea, and in the case he had just been thinking of which ended on the Cave Hill, a launch had borne a decisive part. If this went on, he thought, he might soon take over Barnes' job at the Yard.

Fortunately, the hut gave the watchers a fair shelter or they would by this time have been wet to the skin. It was now after three and French began to have uneasy qualms that the whole affair might be going to miss fire. He would have dearly liked a pipe, but this, of course, was out of the question. And still they waited.

Carter made a few spasmodic efforts at conversation, secure in the knowledge that wind and water would effectually drown the sound of his voice to any one at a distance. But French was afraid to talk. If they got interested they might miss the quarry's approach.

Then a somewhat disquieting thought occurred to French. He had so firmly made up his mind as to Nolan's guilt that he had overlooked one possibility — that there was an accomplice. What if two people were guilty? Was it possible that Nolan and Knowles had formed an evil partnership and that he, French, would now have to deal with two men instead of one? A bad mistake, French thought, not to have brought a couple of Heath's men to assist. Of course, he and Carter should be a match for the other two at any time, even without the advantage of surprise. But the suspects would be desperate men, and a lucky shot from their point of view might easily turn the balance. However, the thing was done now and —

Steady! What was that?

A shadow, an inkier black against the blackness beyond, was moving on the river bank. In a flash French's dreams were dispelled and now keenly alert, he gazed tensely. Yes, there was no doubt. Some one was approaching from the town.

His hand closed on Carter's wrist and together the two men crouched motionless against the wall of the shed. The shadow turned to the left. It flitted down the gangway. It reached the edge and slowly vanished over it. On tip-toes the others followed. Reaching the edge, they dropped on their knees and peered over.

How French blessed the cloud-screened moon with its restricted power of vision! There like a dark smudge was the man climbing slowly down on to the *Nymph*. He reached the deck, crossed it, and got into the well of the launch. He fumbled for some moments at the cabin door, then disappeared within.

Stealthily French and Carter followed him down the ladder and across the *Nymph* to the launch. They climbed into the well, reached the cabin door and looked in. The saloon was in darkness, but the door from it to the motor-room was open, and through it there shone a faint glimmer of light.

French advanced slowly. He was not afraid of being heard, for all kinds of noises were passing through the little hull from the wavelets without. But if Nolan were to step back into the saloon he would be seen, and then good-bye to all chance of a successful demonstration. The chance, however, must be taken. He crept across the saloon and peeped through the door.

The sight which met his eyes caused a little shiver of excitement to run down his spine, and he made room for Carter to see also. Bending over the small auxiliary motor which ran the tiny electric light plant, was Nolan, his back turned towards the watchers. In his hand was a spanner and he was taking the nuts off the bolts holding the bedplate down to the deck.

French, almost breathless with excitement, watched eagerly. He had expected a *coup* from this visit to Newhaven which would help him with a jury. Now it was beginning to look as if he would get a hundred, a thousand, times more than he had hoped for! *What* was Nolan doing with that motor?

He soon knew, as with exultation he found his wildest dreams were being realised there before him. The holding down nuts removed, Nolan with a good deal of trouble lifted off the entire combination. Then he put his hand into what was evidently a space left below it and drew out a small bag!

French could scarcely restrain a shout of triumph at the sight. What that bag contained there could be little doubt. There, within ten feet of him, were the diamonds; diamonds worth a million and a half sterling!

Nolan placed the bag carefully in his breast pocket, then picking up the motor-dynamo, with the same difficulty slipped it into place, put on the nuts, and screwed them fast. When this was done the crisis would come and French braced himself to meet it. But Nolan showed no signs of leaving the launch. He replaced the spanner in the rack and turned back to the motors. This time he busied himself with the large one, which drove the launch. For some time he worked, but French could not see what he was doing. Then suddenly he knew. There came a sound of flowing liquid, while a strong smell of petrol arose.

Instantly French realised their danger. A match, a revolver shot, and they were dead men. No one could escape from that cabin if the petrol got alight. It would go off like gunpowder.

But what was Nolan up to now? Ah, there it was! From his pocket he was taking a small canister with a clock fixed to one end. An incendiary bomb, timed to go off probably hours later; at a time no doubt at which Nolan would be able to prove an alibi.

French quietly made a sign to Carter. "Torch!" he whispered, at the same time drawing his own. Then, ready to charge, they waited.

But only for a moment. Having placed his bomb, Nolan picked up his own torch and began flashing it about the motor-room as if to see that all was right. He was holding it in his left hand and French noticed that he had put his right into the side pocket of his jacket. Then suddenly he flashed the beam through the door and straight into French's eyes.

Instantly French sprang. But as he did so Nolan stepped quickly back. His right hand flashed from his

306

pocket and rose in the air. It held an automatic pistol, pointed straight at French's head!

For a moment the two men stood motionless, staring at one another. Then Nolan spoke.

"My trick, I think, Inspector," he said quietly, but there was a hard tenseness in his voice which showed his pent-up emotion. "You'll please keep quite still, because if my pistol should go off we'd both be in kingdom come. You realise that, of course?"

French remained silent and motionless. In the course of his career he had many times faced death, but always with a reasonable hope, at least a fighting chance, of escape. But this was different. He grew slowly cold as he realised his position. An intolerable weight seemed to descend on his heart. He saw now that he had made a mistake; his last mistake. This was the end. Neither of them would ever again see the light of day.

French lived quickly during those terrible moments. Schemes of escape raced through his brain, only to be rejected as hopeless. If he made a move, or if Carter behind him made a move, the man would fire. And if he fired the whole atmosphere of the cabin would instantly become flame. Even if he, French, were able to reach his own revolver and shoot Nolan, the result would be the same. No, there was no way out.

A wild temptation swept over him to betray his trust, to offer Nolan life for life. To stand aside, to let the man escape with his money, if only he could thereby save himself. Why should he forfeit his life for a mere idea? Wouldn't it be better to temporise? French's life was valuable to his country. Besides Nolan couldn't really escape; they would get him again . . .

Then French saw that he couldn't save himself this way even if he would. To attempt it would be to save Nolan, not himself. The man would play him false. He couldn't do anything else. He — But Nolan was speaking.

"I expected this, you know," he went on quietly in that hard, hopeless voice. "It's the price I've to pay for overlooking those cursed marks. But I'm surprised at your thinking that your outboard motor story would take me in. Not very complimentary to me, but just like the intelligence the Yard has shown all through. Well, your story told me the game was up. I thought I'd play up to it on the incredible chance that you really were the fool you pretended to be, but I never thought I'd get away with it." He took the little bag out of his breast pocket and laid it on the motor. "There, as I suppose you know, is the million and a half in diamonds you have wanted for so long. Well, you won't get them. Neither will I, of course. When the charred remains of the launch settle to the bottom they'll be scattered over a hundred yards of ooze. No one will think of looking for them there; no one could find them if he did. A pity, French, isn't it? I'm even sorry in a way about you. You were only doing your job. But if I let you live I should hang, and I'm not going to hang. But I'll do it quickly. I have bullets here for us both and I'm a good shot. We neither of us need be afraid of the fire."

Nolan paused for a moment, then he aimed his pistol more carefully for French's head and went on:

"Well, good-bye, French. Shut your eyes, for I'm —"

"Look here, Nolan," French suddenly heard himself say in a voice which he didn't recognise. An overwhelming desire to live had swept over him. "Don't you be such an almighty fool. We've both got our lives; well, they're worth more to us than anything else. See, can't we compromise on this? There must be a way out. Don't be in such a hurry."

French scarcely knew what he was saying. A blind instinct to gain time at all costs had swept over him.

Nolan smiled bitterly.

"There is a way out," he answered, "the way we're going to take. It's no use, French. I've thought it out hundreds of times. It's no use. Shut your eyes, man, for I'm going to —"

Before he finished his sentence the shot came, and with it a sharp tinkle of broken glass. Stupefied, French stared before him. In the name of goodness, what had happened? There was no fire. French was conscious; he was able to stand; he seemed none the worse. But Nolan! Nolan's pistol had fallen with a clang to the floor and the man was staring stupefied at his right hand, from which the blood was spurting out in a welling stream. So both men stood for the fraction of a second. Then, with a shriek of fury, Nolan flung himself on French, striking out wildly.

Nolan had dropped his torch as he leaped. His blow did not reach French's body, but by a bit of ill-luck it struck his torch. It also fell with a crash, also going out. Instantly the motor-room was smothered in inky blackness.

"Your torch," French screamed to Carter, as he grappled with Nolan.

Immediately a desperate struggle began. The two men went staggering and swaying about in the confined space, banging at one moment into the motor and at the next into the side of the boat. Nolan fought with the fury of a wild beast, striving desperately to get clear of French's clinging arms. Then they engaged in a lock and only their panting breaths could be heard above the noises of the sea. So for æons they swung, till suddenly French tripped over a pipe, and the pair of them came down with a crash which shook the breath out of French's body.

"Quick, Carter," he gasped wildly, as he felt his strength go from him.

But Carter did not come and for what seemed eternity the struggle went on. French, sick and quivering from his fall, was growing rapidly weaker, but he clung on doggedly with all the strength he could muster. He had hurt his side against the motor, and only that his enemy was himself hampered by his injured hand, he knew the end would have already come. As it was he felt a deadly faintness creeping over him. And then in spite of all his efforts Nolan got a grip on his throat with his uninjured hand. French still feebly struggled, but his hold on life was going. With a roaring in his ears thought slipped away. For a time longer he was conscious of pain, then this also vanished and he knew no more.

When he came to he was lying on the locker in the launch's saloon. A strange man was bending over him.

"A nice trick you've been playing on us now, Inspector," he heard a cheery voice say, "but you'll be as right as rain in no time. You got off well. Three broken ribs, but nothing serious."

"Nolan?" French gasped.

"Lost his thumb. Otherwise all right. Don't you worry about anything. We're just going to move you to bed. Then you'll be more comfortable."

It was not until the next day that French heard what had actually occurred. It was to Carter's presence of mind that he owed his life and that of his prisoner.

When Nolan flashed his torch on the cabin door Carter instantly realised that he himself had not been seen. He was, as a matter of fact in French's shadow. He had his revolver, but he knew that he could not use it in that confined space of petrol vapour. Nor by retreating out of the danger zone could he fire, for then Nolan would be out of his sight. A plan, however, flashed into his mind and stealthily he began to retreat. Once he had got out of the cabin he rushed to the engine-room skylight, intending to fire down through it at Nolan. But he found himself foiled. It was glazed with obscure glass. There were portholes to the engine-room, but these were over the side of the launch. One set were screened by the *Nymph*, and when he tried the other he found that he could not reach down to it from the deck. For a moment he had been baffled, then he had seen the way. Climbing quickly over the rail, he lowered himself down the side, hanging on with his left hand. He was in the water up to his middle, which took some of the weight off his arm. In this way he found he could just see in through a porthole. By drawing up his knees he was able to push himself out from the side of the launch far enough to ensure that no flame would pass into the engine-room with the bullet. Then, just in time, he fired. The delay in going to French's further assistance was due to the difficulty he had in climbing back on deck.

Taking Nolan with the diamonds actually in his possession gave the authorities all the proof they wanted with their case. There were, of course, many points still to be cleared up, but with the information they now had, this took them a comparatively short time.

Briefly, the theory French put forward to Sir Mortimer Ellison proved to be the truth. When the affairs of Moxon's General Securities began to grow involved, the partners at first did all they could to bring them straight. But when they found that this was impossible and that a crash was inevitable, they decided to save themselves at the expense of their honour. They realised all the cash they could and made a bolt for it. Moxon, Deeping, Esdale and Nolan were all in it. Raymond they knew wouldn't join in such a scheme and the other partners were negligible.

Nolan early determined to double-cross the others, partly to try to ensure his own safety by destroying dangerous witnesses, but principally from sheer greed. He laid his plans accordingly. When buying his share of the diamonds he made up to resemble Esdale, carefully keeping his finger crooked, as he believed Esdale obtained the diamonds in his own personality. But when he came to negotiate about the outboard motor, Nolan showed the subtle quality of his ingenuity. He reasoned that if Esdale were the purchaser he would try to hide his identity, and Nolan, therefore, kept his hand in his pocket instead of exhibiting a crooked finger.

Meanwhile Nolan had been the moving spirit in fixing up the plan of escape. The scheme agreed between the four was, so he told French after the trial and when no hope of a reprieve remained, for him in his launch to meet the other three in the *Nymph* at the agreed point on the track of the *Chichester*, sink the dinghy, transfer to the launch and set the *Nymph* on fire, so that it would be found burning by the *Chichester*. This was to convey the impression that the fugitives had taken to the dinghy. As the dinghy would never be heard of again, the conspirators believed that the police would assume that they had met their death, and that the hue and cry would cease. In reality all four would go ashore in France, the launch being scuttled as French had suggested. The partners, after disguising themselves, would make their way by devious routes to the Argentine, there gradually turn their diamonds into cash and so live happily ever after.

Nolan had a lot of trouble in inducing the others to agree to his plan. They argued that as the launch would be known to be in the neighbourhood at the time of the fire, and as it also would disappear, the fact that all four had escaped by it would be suspected and the hue and cry would not die down. To this Nolan had replied admitting the objection, and asking the objectors to produce a better scheme. The suggestion that all four should sail in the *Nymph* and really take to the dinghy he ruled out as impossible for the reason that if the dinghy were seen by a steamer, they would be taken for shipwrecked men and picked up. In the launch, of course, they would be safe from this.

The fate of Raymond was a difficult problem. None of the four wished to murder him, yet for their own safety he must be got out of the way during the escape. They had determined to take him aboard the *Nymph*, drug him and take him ashore with themselves in the launch, leaving him on the shore to sleep off the drug while they escaped. This, however, had the objection that it would suggest their own trail. When, therefore, they had seen the smack lying broken down, the idea of putting him aboard it had at once arisen. They had hurriedly talked it over and unhesitatingly adopted this modification of the original scheme.

The meeting, the burning of the *Nymph*, the sinking of the dinghy, and the escape in the launch was then the arrangement between the four. What actually happened was very different. First Nolan provided himself with the outboard motor, carrying the negotiations through so that if suspicion were aroused, it would fall on Esdale. Nolan himself picked up the motor at the cloak-room at Waterloo. He considered it too dangerous, however, to take it openly aboard the launch. On that Saturday night, therefore, he had run it in his car to a deserted point on the shore near Hastings, and at low tide, about 4 a.m. on Sunday, he carried it down to the water's edge, buoyed it, and watched till it was covered.

Then he had driven to Dover, got out his launch and returned to the place. By this time there was plenty of water to float the launch over the package, and he simply picked up the buoy and drew the motor aboard. Then he fitted the motor, tested it and stored it in the locked cupboard.

The murder was carried out exactly as French had imagined. Nolan had bought the pistol in France and thrown it overboard when its work was done. The outboard motor was got rid of in the same way. Fear of suspicion and a consequent personal search led Nolan to hide the diamonds beneath the small motor. He had intended to go down to Newhaven on the first possible night to retrieve them, having duplicates of the keys, but he had become aware that he was being shadowed and he had been afraid to do so. However, on hearing French's tale about the outboard motor, he felt that, whatever the result, the risk must be taken.

After landing with Mackintosh at Newhaven, Nolan assumed the rôle of the honest man who had been careless and too trusting of his fellow partners. He expected a short term of imprisonment, looking upon his return to face it in the light of a safeguard from suspicion of the major crime.

One of Nolan's most difficult problems was to induce Moxon to ask him in the presence of a witness to go to see Pasteur. Moxon didn't see the need for this refinement, his own idea being simply not to turn up at Fécamp. But Nolan recognised that the story he proposed to tell would, without corroboration, be the weak spot in his case. He, therefore, brought all his powers of persuasion to bear. He argued that it would never do for Moxon, Deeping, Raymond and himself all to give out that they would be absent from the office on the day before the settlement. Some one, he said, would be sure to raise the question of the office being left without a responsible head, and if that had once been raised, their absence would immediately become suspicious. It should, therefore, be given out that he, Nolan, would be in charge on the Thursday. To account for his absence, some accident at the last minute would, therefore, be necessary. This accident, Nolan insisted, would be less suspicious if it didn't *directly* cause his change of plans. Something requiring Moxon to alter his, which would react indirectly in himself, would be more like real life. Though not convinced, Moxon at last agreed to the proposal, because he didn't see that it mattered.

The recovered diamonds realised very nearly the million and a half which was missing. This did not avert the final failure of Moxon's General Securities, but it enabled nearly twelve shillings in the pound to be paid and thus in many cases reduced utter ruin to serious loss.

For French himself there remained the consciousness of work well done, and he hoped, another step taken towards that chief inspectorship for which his soul longed. All the Assistant Commissioner said, however, was: "Ah, French, I wish you'd get that job squared up in time to catch the 11.40 for Maidstone. I want you to look into that Aylesford burglary."

Other titles published by Ulverscroft:

MURDER UNDERGROUND

Mavis Doriel Hay

When Miss Euphemia Pongleton is found murdered on the stairs of Belsize Park station — strangled by her own dog's leash — her fellow-boarders in the Frampton Hotel are not overwhelmed with grief at the death of a tiresome old woman. But they all have their theories about the identity of the murderer, and help to unravel the mystery of who killed the wealthy "Pongle". Several of her fellow residents — even Tuppy the terrier — have a part to play in the events that lead to a dramatic arrest.

SIDNEY CHAMBERS AND THE DANGERS OF TEMPTION

James Runcie

Archdeacon Sidney Chambers is beginning to think that the life of a full-time priest (and part-time detective) is not easy. So when a bewitching divorcee in a mink coat interrupts Sidney's family lunch, asking him to help locate her missing son, he hopes it will be an open and shut case. The last thing he expects is to be dragged into the mysterious workings of a sinister cult, or to find himself tangled up in another murder investigation. But, as always, the village of Grantchester is not as peaceful as it seems. From the theft of an heirloom to an ominous case of blackmail, Sidney is once again rushed off his feet!